Christmas in Sweet Meadow Park

LIZ DAVIES

CHAPTER 1

Frankie Fox hitched the strap of her leather bag higher on her shoulder as she stepped into *The Sweet Meadow Observer*'s office.

The battered, green-painted door squeaked as it swung shut behind her, setting her teeth on edge. One of these days she would remember to bring in a can of WD 40 and give the hinges a squirt. That should do the trick. Unfortunately, it would take a hell of a lot more than WD 40 to sort out the rest of the office. It consisted of a largish room with four desks, only two of which had computers on them because only two reporters worked there now, a separate office for Neil, who owned the newspaper, a small kitchen and a tiny toilet. Everything was run down and frayed around the edges.

Wondering what the day had in store for her (please, no more leaves-clogging-the-drains stories, she prayed), Frankie made her way to her desk, passing by the editor's office where she could see Neil furiously bashing away at his keyboard. Sweet Meadow Rangers had lost their match on Saturday, so he was most likely writing a piece about useless referees or something similar. There was one thing to be said about Neil, and that was he loved his rugby. Frankie could take it or leave it – preferably leave it. Thankfully she was never required to report on it and neither was her colleague Vince, because Neil always did that himself.

She tossed her bag onto her desk and slumped into her chair, wishing she'd bought a coffee on the way. She would have a quick look at her emails and at the yellow sticky notes that were stuck to the monitor, their edges curling as they threatened to peel off, then she'd go make one – assuming there were some granules left in the jar and that the milk she'd brought in on Friday was still drinkable.

Neither the emails nor the notes revealed anything exciting. Mind you, she hadn't expected them to: several photos of last night's super moon, all of which were nondescript, a new knitting circle meeting, a coffee morning in the community centre…

Frankie gave up. Caffeine was what she needed if she was to have any hope of staying awake to read the rest.

'Frankie!' Neil's voice boomed across the room, making her jump, and she turned to see him standing at his office door, waving a piece of paper. 'Got an assignment for you.'

Frankie groaned. 'Can't it wait until I've had a coffee? I'll make you one as well,' she wheedled, although she knew he wouldn't object. He was a pussycat, really. Somewhere north of sixty, he'd been in the newspaper business since he was a boy, and he knew it inside out. Frankie had a lot of respect for him. She liked him, too. He was fair, undemanding and a good man to work for.

He grinned at her. 'Ta. Although I shouldn't. Health kick.' He patted his generous stomach.

'*Another* one?'

'It's the same one.'

'It can't be! You had pie and chips from the chippy for lunch on Friday and a chocolate éclair afterwards,' she pointed out, wondering how he could possibly be on a health kick if he packed away stuff like that.

'I fell off the waggon,' he explained. 'I'm back on it now.'

'Who blabbed?' Neil's wife, Karen, had been trying to get him to lose weight and eat healthier for years, and since his heart scare at Easter she'd developed a network of spies all over town.

'Your friend Harper was in the bakers,' he said glumly. 'I tried telling her that the éclair was for you, but she didn't believe me.'

'Do you know why?'

Neil shook his head, pushing his glasses back up his nose. They had a habit of sliding down until he invariably ended up peering over the top of them like a stern secretary.

'Because she knew I had a date on Friday night and that I was hoping to squeeze into my new dress, so no way was I going to be eating a chocolate éclair.'

'Remind me to co-ordinate our stories next time,' he groaned.

'Don't drag me into it. Karen will kill me if she thinks I've been aiding and abetting you.'

Changing the subject, he said, 'Do you want this assignment or not?'

'Not.'

'I don't know why I don't sack you. You're more trouble than you're worth.'

'Because I write a great human interest story,' she replied, walking over to him and plucking the sheet of paper out of his hand.

Stuffing it into her trouser pocket, she wandered into the tiny kitchen (sink, cupboard, kettle, battered fridge, and temperamental toaster) and ran the tap. The pipe rattled, spurting out murky water, then settled down. She filled the kettle, plugged it in, and sniffed the milk. It would do.

As she waited for the water to boil, she thought back to her date on Friday. It hadn't gone well. They rarely did, and she honestly didn't know why she bothered. It was as though she felt she *had* to date, that it was expected of her because everyone she knew, apart from her friend Harper, was in a relationship and some had even found Mr Right.

Frankie had no interest in commitment. She wasn't ready. Twenty-eight was too young to settle down, especially since she had her career to focus on. Such as it was.

'Coffee,' she announced, setting a chipped mug on Neil's desk.

'Ta.' He took a gulp and pulled a face. 'Milk's off.'

'It's all we've got.'

'You can pick some up on the way back.'

'Back from where?'

'Sweet Meadow Park.'

'Why would I be going to the park?'

'You didn't read your brief, did you?'

'Do you mean this?' She pulled the piece of paper from her pocket and sighed. 'Why can't you use email like a normal person? What is it this time? Another lost dog?'

'Read it.'

'*Festive Fayre. Molly Brown. 11 a.m. Sweet Meadow Park.* Is this supposed to mean something?'

'It means there's going to be a Christmas event at the park and I want you to cover it.'

Frankie shrugged. 'OK, I'll put it in my diary. You've written eleven a.m. so I'm assuming you mean the eleventh of December?'

Neil took another swig of his coffee. 'Nope. Eleven o'clock today.'

'You're not making any sense. It's only just November – a bit early for a Festive Fayre, isn't it? I mean, no one is a bigger Christmas fan than me, but people are still letting off fireworks and putting out bonfires.'

'I thought you could follow the preparations from start to finish, since you're so good at human interest stories.' He emphasised the words *human interest*.

Hoisted by her own petard! 'Ha bloody ha,' she said, looking at the crumpled paper again. 'Molly Brown… What's she done now?'

'Done?'

'If I remember rightly – and I do, because I wrote the copy – back in the spring, a kid nearly drowned in the pond because she had a bee in her bonnet about making the park nice again, and the man she's shacked up with was involved.'

'*Shacked up?* For a journalist, you've got a nice turn of phrase.'

'Thanks.'

'I was being sarcastic,' Neil said.

Frankie was trying to be earthier, more hard-nosed, like an old-fashioned reporter. Maybe she should knock it on the head. She was finding it hard work. 'Wasn't there some kind of vandalism to the cafe before it opened?' she asked, digging around for the memory.

Neil said, 'As I understand it, that had nothing to do with Molly. But you should know, you covered that, too.'

'Oh, yes, so I did. It was the most excitement I've had since a wheelie bin was set alight behind the library,' she said dryly.

'Be careful what you wish for,' Neil replied, his tone ominous. 'Excitement isn't all it's cracked up to be. We're lucky that Sweet Meadow isn't in the middle of a war zone, or in the path of a hurricane.'

Frankie agreed wholeheartedly with that, but she would have liked a little more action, something to sink her teeth into. All she needed was a break, a story meaty enough to get her noticed. One article, that was all it would take to get her foot in the door of one of the national publications.

'Don't forget to take some decent photos,' Neil reminded her, before he barricaded himself in his office.

Frankie scowled at his door. Why couldn't Vince cover this story? Why did it have to be *her?* It wasn't fair that she got all the crappy jobs simply because she was younger than him and more junior. On a cold day like today, Frankie would much prefer to be in the warm if rather stuffy (in more ways than one) council offices, covering one of their interminable meetings, rather than freezing to death in the middle of Sweet Meadow Park.

She brightened. At least she could pop into the cafe after she met with Molly. It sold decent coffee and the cake was to die for, so maybe it *would* be a better gig than the council one. She could always live in hope.

***

Julian Blade peered out of his bedroom window and grimaced. It was a bright, crisp, autumn morning, golden-leafed and misty-breathed, with a glittering frost on the grass. It looked lovely, but that wasn't why he was gurning. Julian was pulling a face because he didn't want to go out in it.

He would be quite happy to stay indoors and mope about. There was the ironing to be done, a documentary on the solar system to be watched, and he had today's online word game to tackle. Then there was also the lure of bed. He'd only just got out of it, but he could feel it calling.

Julian gave himself a shake. Going back to bed wasn't an option – not if he wanted to slay this beast of his – because he was scared that if he *did* crawl under the covers, he mightn't want to get out of them ever again.

So, breakfast first, then a walk.

Morag, his therapist, hadn't been able to stress enough the benefit of a daily walk when it came to mental health, especially if that walk took place in nature. Therefore, Julian forced himself to take a walk in the park every day. He had been doing this since he'd moved to Sweet Meadow four months ago, and in the beginning he'd felt better for it, but lately it had become something of a chore.

He could guess what his problem was. All the days had become the same: bland, boring, predictable. However, the opposite was worse. Exciting, frenzied and volatile had been his downfall. Burnout, they called it.

Julian called it failure.

***

Frankie drew in a lungful of chilly autumn air and blew it out in a cloud of mist around her head. She inhaled again, this time letting out the air in little bursts, so her breath looked like the steam from an old locomotive, and resisted the urge to cry, 'Woo-woo, chuff, chuff, chuff.'

Despite her reluctance to do yet another lighthearted piece for the paper, she was enjoying her walk. It was such a nice morning it had seemed a shame to drive the short distance from the office to the park, even if it was cold. Besides, the exercise would do her good: she'd be able to get her steps in without having to try too hard, and therefore earn the snack she intended to treat herself to at the cafe.

The park was on the outskirts of Sweet Meadow, but outskirts was a relative term because the town was a small one. *Everywhere* was in walking distance as long as you didn't mind hills. Being in one of the valleys in South Wales, Sweet Meadow had an abundance of them.

It was a brisk ten-minute walk uphill, and Frankie soon felt the pull in her leg muscles. Before long, she was panting, feeling warm in her long woollen coat and boots, and was thankful when the park's main gates came into view. They were tall, wrought-iron affairs, that were currently padlocked to prevent random vehicles from driving in and out, although there was a smaller side gate for pedestrians, which was open.

Because she lived on the other side of Sweet Meadow, Frankie didn't frequent the park often, and until recently it hadn't been the nicest of places to visit. Run-down and unloved, its flower beds had been full of weeds, the paths litter-strewn, and the pond a dumping ground for supermarket trolleys.

All that changed when Molly Brown bought the derelict former park keeper's cottage and made it her mission to restore the park to its former glory. She'd renovated the cottage, resurrected the boarded-up cafe, tidied up the flowerbeds and cleared the pond of rubbish. She hadn't done it all herself – she'd had a lot of help from her boyfriend Jack, and several volunteers – and now the park was a pleasant place to be. There was still some work to be done (the children's playground was an eyesore and the bandstand was a wreck, for instance) but she was getting there. Frankie admired the woman's dedication and vision.

She paused inside the gates, her gaze drawn to the mature trees and their vibrant autumn colours of orange, russet and gold. Fallen leaves crunched underfoot, a squirrel darted between the tree trunks with quick jerky movements, then froze, his little paws clutching a nut, and a robin perched on a bush and watched her with bright black eyes.

For a Monday morning, the park was busier than she'd expected. A toddler wearing bright red wellies kicked through the leaves, his mum watching indulgently, two dog-walkers were having a natter, their dogs scampering on the grass, and a tall man, hunched into his coat with his hands in his pockets scuffed along the path. His head was bowed, and he seemed more intent on studying the ground than on enjoying the scenery.

Frankie, the ultimate journalist, wondered what his story might be. At a guess, he was maybe four or five years older than her, not bad looking as far as she could tell, but he seemed to have the weight of the world on his shoulders.

As though sensing her scrutiny, he glanced up, catching her eye, and she managed a semblance of a smile before hastily looking away.

The dog walkers finished their chat, one going one way and the other heading in her direction.

'Morning,' the pug's owner said to the guy as he passed by.

The tall man nodded, his expression unchanging.

'Morning,' the dog walker said to her.

'Good morning,' Frankie replied chirpily, because it *was* a good morning. She wasn't thrilled with this assignment, but it was better than some she'd been given recently, and the fresh air wasn't as fresh as she'd anticipated. It was a perfectly pleasant day for a stroll.

The dog came up for a sniff and she ruffled its ears. She rather liked dogs, which was a good thing since Molly and her boyfriend Jack, had a large black crossbreed.

Molly's house was situated a short distance from the park's main gates and Frankie walked towards it. Who would have thought that the old park keeper's cottage with its boarded-up windows and overgrown garden could scrub up so well? Set back from the path, it was separated from the rest of the park by a cute picket fence and a long garden. The cottage was chocolate-box pretty, a far cry from the semi-derelict boarded-up house Frankie remembered from when she was a child.

It had lain empty for years, and she'd assumed that the only thing it was good for was demolition, but Molly, who was an estate agent and had seen its potential, had worked magic on the place. Frankie felt rather envious. She lived in a one-bed flat above a hairdresser – handy for getting a cut and blow dry but cramped and with no outside space. Molly had the whole park for a garden, or so it seemed.

She opened the door before Frankie had a chance to knock, the dog at her heels. She was a couple of years older than her, with a slim figure and a pretty face, and greeted her with a wide smile.

'Jet heard you coming,' Molly said. 'It's weird, but he doesn't bother with anyone in the park, but the second he hears the garden gate open, he comes to fetch me. Shall we go to the cafe for a coffee? My treat?'

'That would be lovely.' Frankie noticed that Molly was wearing a coat. She hadn't intended to invite Frankie into the house, which was a shame because she would have loved to see inside. Another time, perhaps? If she was to be covering the preparations for this festive festival, she expected she would be seeing more of Molly over the following weeks – unless something else landed in her lap, something more exciting than a little Christmas fayre in a small park in a quiet Welsh town.

Unfortunately, she highly doubted *that* would happen.

CHAPTER 2

Three circuits of the park were Julian's limit. He supposed he could walk somewhere else – on the hillside above the town, for instance – but recent rain had made the grassy tracks incredibly muddy underfoot, as he'd found to his cost the other day, when he'd returned home with enough dirt stuck to his boots to fill a large plant pot.

Miserably, he scuffed through the leaves, unable to decide whether to go home or go to the cafe. He didn't particularly want to do either. To be honest, he didn't know *what* he wanted. All he knew was that he was sick of feeling so damned miserable.

Moving to Sweet Meadow hadn't been as beneficial as he'd hoped. Removing himself from the rat race that his life had become was one thing, but seeking solace in a small Welsh town probably hadn't been the best idea he'd ever had. He should have gone on an extended holiday or taken a year out and gone back-packing in Asia instead; but even as he thought it, he knew that wasn't the answer. His money would have run out at some point, and he would have been forced to return. Instead, he'd looked for a more permanent solution, and a complete change of lifestyle had seemed the only option.

Unfortunately he didn't feel any better for it, and walks in the sodding park weren't helping. The fresh air might be better for his lungs than the polluted London stuff he'd been breathing in for years, but he didn't think his mental health had improved significantly. He'd merely swapped one set of problems for another. Admittedly it was a relief not to feel so panicked and for his heart to no longer race so fast that he feared he was having a heart attack. Instead he now felt sad and worthless. He'd merely swapped burnout for depression and right now he had trouble persuading himself to get out of bed in the morning.

Thankfully, he still had some money left over from the sale of his riverside apartment (even after the purchase of the small, terraced house he now lived in) which would keep him afloat for a while, so at least he didn't have to worry about where his next meal was coming from.

However, he *did* worry, because his savings wouldn't last forever and sooner or later he would have to get a job.

The thought filled him with dread.

Despite not wanting to talk to anyone, Julian contrarily felt the need to be near people this morning, so he decided he would go to the cafe in the park after all. He'd have a coffee and pretend he was still part of the human race. He needn't interact with anyone, but being in the same space as normal people might help him believe he was normal too – whatever "normal" was. He would keep himself to himself and read *The Financial Times* on his phone, even though his therapist had advised him not to. Morag, that was her name, and although he hadn't spoken to her since he'd fled the city, he could still hear her calm voice in his head.

Julian glanced up, feeling someone's gaze upon him. A woman was staring at him, and he caught her eye before quickly looking away.

The brief glance was enough to tell him she was in her mid to late twenties and rather pretty: long blond hair falling in waves over her shoulders, blue eyes, full pouty lips, a smart coat, a large shoulder bag, and a curious gaze.

She gave him a brief smile. Or was it aimed at the man walking the little, tan-coloured dog?

The man said 'Morning' to him, and Julian nodded in response. However, the woman's reply to the dog owner's greeting was a breezy 'Good morning,' and unlike himself, she wasn't wandering aimlessly. She walked with purpose, straight through a gate set into a picket fence, and marched up a path to the front door of the cottage which was set in the grounds of the park.

He guessed she must be a friend of the couple who lived there. He'd seen them in the garden when he'd been out on his walks.

He saw a lot of the same faces on his walks.

But knew the names of none of them.

***

If I'm ever asked to describe my perfect cafe, this would be it, Frankie decided, as she stepped onto the terraced area with its outside seating to the front of the cute little building. The terrace was currently unoccupied (which wasn't surprising considering the chill in the air), but in the warmer months it was a lovely place to sit and enjoy a coffee. Flower beds had been planted on either side. Even now cyclamens bloomed, their pink and red flowers bright and cheerful.

Inside was even nicer. Painted a light blue with cream, pink and aqua accents, the cafe was a light and airy mix of shabby chic and American diner, with its pastel shades, chrome coffee machine, and ornate wrought-iron tables and chairs. The eight tables had marble tops, as did the counter that ran along the rear wall.

It was small but quaint, quirky and very homely.

Molly greeted the woman behind the counter warmly as she reached over to give her a hug.

'Madeleine, what delights have you got for us today?' Molly asked.

'How about white chocolate and coconut cake?' The woman plucked a dog treat out of a jar and gave it to Molly's dog, who had accompanied them to the cafe. He accepted it gently, with a wag of his tail.

'It sounds yummy. I'll have a slice of that and a latte. What would you like, Frankie?'

'The same, please.'

Madeleine said, 'Take a seat, I'll bring it over. Fiona and Bill should be here any minute.'

Frankie arched an eyebrow. She thought her meeting was with Molly, but it looked like there might be a few more, and this was confirmed when Molly pushed two tables together.

'I've had an idea about holding a festive fayre in the park,' Molly explained, seeing her curiosity. 'So I've asked a few people to join us.'

Sitting down, Frankie shrugged off her coat, then withdrew a pad and a pen from her bag. She'd found that people reacted better to old-fashioned scribbling rather than if she tapped away on her laptop. Anyway, her unique brand of shorthand was much faster than her typing speed, so it was a win-win situation.

When an elderly couple accompanied by a tan and white Jack Russel terrier entered the cafe, Frankie recognised them immediately. Bill had been the driving force behind assembling a group of volunteers to help Molly tidy up the park when she'd first moved into her cottage, and Fiona used to own the cafe in town but sold it a couple of years back when she'd retired. Recently she'd been involved with renovating the cafe in the park, and Frankie was aware she helped out here now and again. Bill and Fiona were an item.

Next, two lads around fifteen or sixteen years of age who she'd also met before, trooped in and sat down, and when the door opened again and the tall man she'd seen earlier entered, she wondered whether he would also be joining them. However, when he hovered uncertainly by the counter, she realised he wasn't part of the committee.

Pity, she would have liked to know more about him. She sensed a story behind his nervous eyes – but then, didn't everyone have a story? What was it about him that made her think that his story might be worth listening to? Or did she want to get to know him purely because he was good-looking?

She couldn't help being a red-blooded female and, despite not having room in her life for a relationship, a bit of harmless fun wouldn't go amiss, because she was seriously lacking in fun at the moment.

She watched as Madeleine served him, noticing that his lanky frame was topped with wide shoulders. He had dirty blonde hair, short at the back, slightly longer on the top, a few locks falling over his forehead. Clean-shaven with a strong jaw, defined cheekbones and nice lips, he was quite attractive, and when she caught his brooding gaze, she amended *quite* to *extremely.*

Realising she was staring, Frankie looked away as Molly said to her, 'I believe you've already met Bill and Fiona, and Madeleine, as you know, manages the cafe.'

Frankie nodded and smiled a greeting.

'I think you also know Liam and Connor.' Molly glared at them. 'I hope you've got permission to be out of school this morning?'

'Yeah, we're good.'

'Hmm, I didn't ask if you were good,' she said, 'but I'm going to trust you. Everyone, if you don't already know her, this is Frankie Fox and she's a journalist with *The Sweet Meadow Observer.* She's going to be writing about every step, so hopefully we'll drum up some interest right from the start.'

'Drum up interest for *what,* exactly?' Bill asked.

'I'll tell you in a minute,' she said, and as soon as everyone had a drink and a slice of something sweet and gooey in front of them, Molly began. 'More and more people are using the park, but it still needs a lot of work, so I've had an idea. I think we should hold a festive fayre to raise more funds.'

As Molly went on to explain what she meant by a festive fayre, Frankie studied the people around the table, noting the range of ages. Bill was in his seventies, as was Fiona, Madeleine was in her late thirties, and finally there were the teenagers.

Then her gaze strayed to the tall, good-looking guy on the table next to them, and as he studied his phone, she studied him. Damn, he was hot. Not her usual type (she preferred more muscly men) but there was something about him…

He caught her looking at him again, and she blushed.

Turning her attention back to Molly, Frankie discovered she'd missed a chunk of what had been said. Hoping to fill in the gaps, she paid close attention to Bill as he asked, 'Who's going to build them, that's what I want to know?'

Build what, Frankie wondered.

Molly said, 'I was hoping to speak to Gavin about that.'

'He can't build ten, twenty, or however many stalls we need, all by himself,' Bill said.

'We're doing woodwork in school,' Liam piped up. 'We'll help. We could say it's for our coursework.' Nudging his friend, he said, 'It'll get us out of class for a bit.'

Bill frowned at the boy. 'If you say you're going to help, then you're going to help. This isn't so you can skive off school.'

'Course not.' Liam looked affronted.

'Where will we get the materials?' Madeleine asked. 'The cafe is doing well I think, but not *that* well. Can we afford to buy the wood?'

'Pallets,' Molly said. 'Jack reckons he can get his hands on as many as we want and they won't cost a penny. These stalls aren't going to be permanent structures, we only need them to last a couple of days.'

'What if it rains and the fayre is a washout?' Fiona wanted to know.

Molly sighed. 'Unfortunately, we can't control the weather, but I'm hoping that the ice rink will be enough of a draw on its own.'

'The *ice rink?*' Fiona exclaimed.

'What ice rink?' That was from Bill.

Liam cried, 'There's going to be an ice rink? *Effin hell!*'

'Language,' Fiona scolded.

'Effin ain't swearing,' he objected.

'It's close enough.'

'I could have said fu—'

'Liam!' The adults all seemed to tell him off at once, and Frankie tried not to smile as he rolled his eyes.

Molly said, 'It was Jack's idea. I've already made enquiries, and due to a cancellation, there's a pop-up rink available. I hope you don't mind, but I went ahead and booked it.'

Fiona reached out a hand and clasped Molly's. 'Why would we mind? It's *your* park.'

'Hardly,' Molly replied. 'It belongs to the council.'

Bill cried, 'Pah! If it wasn't for *you*, it would still be an eyesore. I know Jack tried his best, but his department didn't have the funds to knock it into shape.'

Frankie was aware that Jack worked for the council in the Parks and Highways Department.

Bill carried on, 'And what with the likes of Liam and his mates treating the place like a rubbish bin…'

Liam pulled a face. 'We don't do that anymore!'

'I know you don't,' Molly soothed. 'You and Connor have been a massive help.'

Frankie was bewildered. 'Um…' she began, her gaze darting from one face to the next. As far as she remembered, the boys had been somewhat of a problem when one of them (who shouldn't have been in the park in the first place), had almost drowned in the pond and had to be rescued by Jack.

'Sorry, let me explain,' Molly said. 'Not only were the boys fundamental in helping Bill round up volunteers to clean up the park last spring, they also helped renovate the cafe, didn't you, boys?' They nodded vigorously. 'I couldn't have done it without their help, and the help of everyone here. And I'm asking for your help again.'

Deciding it was time to stop observing and start interviewing, Frankie said, 'Why is this fayre so important?'

A frown flitted across Molly's face. 'To raise funds for the play area, of course.'

Ah, so *that* was what Frankie had missed while she'd been drooling over the handsome man with the troubled face. Confidently she said, 'I wanted to make sure I had it right. How much do you think it will cost? Will the council be making a contribution? Have you raised any funds so far?'

'No idea, probably not, and a bit,' Molly replied.

'Wouldn't it be an idea to know beforehand how much you need to raise?' Frankie asked. 'We could print it in the paper, and then see if you've achieved it after the fayre has taken place. Readers like that sort of thing.'

'Good idea,' Molly said. 'I'll get around to it as soon as I can.' She looked apologetic. 'I'm so busy at work at the moment, the property market is booming, that I don't have the time. And neither does Jack. He's still trying to get to grips with his new job.' She said to Frankie, 'He's recently had a promotion,' then to the others, 'And for another thing, I don't think it's a good idea for me and Jack to be in sole charge of the finances. We're too close to the fundraising, too involved. It would help if someone unconnected, someone with no vested interest, took over the accounting. I want to ensure that everything is above board, and that neither Jack, I, nor anyone else, can be accused of doing anything we shouldn't. Do you know of anyone suitable? Anyone who might be willing to take the job on?' Molly looked at around the table.

They all shook their heads.

'*I'll* do it.'

Frankie glanced up from her pad to see who had spoken, and her mouth dropped open.

'Julian Blade,' the tall, good-looking man said, getting to his feet. 'I'm, er, I *was* a financier. If you want, I can help.'

And when Frankie gazed into his face, she prayed Molly would take him up on his offer, because Frankie would dearly like to get to know him better and interviewing him as part of her coverage of the Festive Fayre would be the perfect way to do it.

***

If Julian lived to be a hundred, he wouldn't be able to explain why he'd offered his services (such as they were) to a bunch of people he didn't know, for an event he had no interest in. Not even the pretty blonde woman was a good enough reason.

What a motley crew they were: two pensioners, a cafe manager, the woman who lived in the cottage in the park, a couple of teenagers and a reporter – and they were all staring at him as though he had two heads.

The ringleader, Molly, had a wary expression on her face and he didn't blame her; he could be anyone.

Feeling idiotic, he quickly backtracked. 'Never mind,' he said, 'stupid idea,' and reached for his coat which was hanging on the back of his chair.

'Wait a second,' the reporter said. 'Why don't you tell me – *them* – more about yourself? Like where you work and whether you're local?'

The dreaded question, *where do you work*, was one of the reasons he tended to shy away from people. In the four months since he'd moved to Sweet Meadow, he'd made sure not to put himself in a position where he could be asked that question. Nevertheless, he had an answer prepared.

'I'm on a sabbatical,' he said. It was as good an explanation as any, even if it wasn't strictly true. The truthful answer was that he was between jobs. The even more truthful answer was that he was unemployed and probably unemploy*able*, burnt out and over-the-hill at thirty-three.

Shame made his cheeks burn.

'Financier, you say?' This was from the old guy.

'That's right.'

'Banking or corporate?'

Julian blinked. 'Banking. Stocks and shares.'

'What's a sabbatical?' one of the lads wanted to know.

The journalist, who hadn't taken her eyes off him, explained absently, 'An extended amount of time off from your normal job to pursue other things.'

'Like what? Can we have another piece of cake?'

Bill said, 'Isn't it time you went back to school? What lesson should you be in?'

'Maths.' The boys glanced at each other and the one who'd asked for more cake subsided into his seat.

'Your face is familiar,' Molly said. 'Where do you live?'

Julian pointed vaguely in the direction of the other side of the park. 'Elm Road.'

'What number?' Bill asked sharply.

'Seventeen.'

Bill slapped a palm on the table. 'I *thought* I'd seen you before. You live two doors down from me.'

He *did?* That was news to him. He'd been too busy keeping himself to himself to notice his neighbours. The reality was, Julian didn't *want* to notice them. He hadn't been very good company of late.

Molly said, 'OK, everyone, I think that's a wrap for today. Shall we meet again on Saturday? Is that all right for you, Frankie?'

Frankie nodded. Julian caught her eye again, unable to understand why he felt so relieved that she was going to be there.

Molly said, 'Do you have to rush off, Julian?'

'Not right now.' Not ever, if he was honest.

She waited until the others had left, then said, 'Thanks for your offer of help. I'll need your email address to share some documents with you. I take it you know your way around a spreadsheet?'

'I'm familiar with them, yes.'

'I thought you might be. I've got to warn you, the one I've created is rather basic.'

'I don't mind basic.' He could tart it up as much as she wanted. He loved a good spreadsheet.

She wrote his email address into her phone, then gave him her phone number, and he was touched by her trust in him, especially since she didn't know the first thing about him.

When he said as much to her, she grinned. 'I work for Watkin and Wright Estate Agents. We handled the sale of the property you bought. I'm sure if there was anything dodgy it would have shown up when we ran our AML checks.'

'Anti-money laundering,' he said, nodding to himself. The estate agent was also required by law to check his identity.

'I didn't handle the sale myself,' she said, 'but all the necessary checks would have been done, so I'm pretty sure you're above board.'

'Apart from looking over the spreadsheets, is there anything else I can help with?' he found himself asking.

Molly studied him. 'How good are you at designing leaflets?'

'I can't say I've ever tried, but I'll give it a go.'

'Brilliant! See you on Saturday, and you've got my number if you need me.'

He certainly did. But it wasn't Molly's number he would have liked to have, it was Frankie's.

As Julian strolled along the path on his way home, the park suddenly seemed a much nicer place.

CHAPTER 3

Frankie didn't have any plans for Saturday, and even if she had she would have altered them. There was something quite intriguing about Julian Blade. She did, however, have plans for Friday evening, and as she was getting ready to meet her friend Harper for a drink, she couldn't wait to tell her about him.

They were going to the Farmer's Arms, one of Sweet Meadow's three pubs, and she was looking forward to a catch-up. Frankie had already written her first Festive Fayre piece, which had been little more than an announcement, along with a photo of Molly and another of the park gates.

It was hardly her finest work, but Neil had seemed pleased and had run it in this week's edition. She should have another Fayre instalment for him after tomorrow morning's meeting. There was the risk that it could be rather dry if she wasn't careful, so she'd decided to focus on the people behind the event, as much as the event itself, and she was hoping to interview everyone involved and tell their stories. It would make for more interesting reading than simply reporting on the facts. She would start with Molly, obviously, and her partner Jack, then see where she went from there.

She and Harper met outside the pub and went in together.

'How has your week been?' Frankie asked, as they waited at the bar to be served.

'Electric,' Harper replied, deadpan.

Frankie rolled her eyes. That joke had got old years ago. Harper was an electrician in her dad's three-man firm. Or one man and two women to be exact, as both her dad and her sister were also sparkies.

'One rewire, a cooker installation, three new sockets fitted, two smoke alarms and a partridge in a pear tree.' The last bit was delivered in an off-key warble to the tune of *The Twelve Days of Christmas*. 'How about you?'

'If you read *The Sweet Meadow Observer* you'd know.'

'I get all my news online.'

Frankie sighed. 'And that's the problem, right there. I keep telling Neil that we need to go digital, but he's having none of it.'

Diminishing sales was a real concern, which was another reason why Frankie wanted to break into big-time reporting. People didn't want to read about Ralph Curtis's prize tomatoes, or who won the bowls tournament. They wanted to read about weightier and more meaty issues. And she wanted to write about them.

After they'd bought their drinks and sat down, Frankie said, 'There's going to be a Christmas fayre in the park.'

'I know, my mum told me, and I've had a call from Molly Brown asking if I could help out with the lighting.'

Cross, Frankie said, 'You know as much as I do, and I'm supposed to be reporting on it.' She needed to get her act into gear. 'Are you going to help?'

'I suppose so. It's for a good cause. All monies raised will go towards re-opening the children's play area, plus we get free advertising.'

'Have you come across a guy by the name of Julian Blade?' Frankie asked.

'It doesn't ring a bell. Why?'

'He was in the cafe when Molly was holding a meeting the other day, and he volunteered to do the finances.'

'Young or old?'

'Early thirties, I'd guess.'

'Good-looking?'

'What makes you ask that?'

'You've got a look in your eye.'

'What kind of look?'

'The kind I haven't seen for a while. You look... animated.'

'Animated?' Frankie screeched. 'What am I – a cartoon? Anyway, I always look animated.'

'You usually look bored when you talk about work and you don't look bored now, so I can only surmise that this Julian Blade is the reason. I can't see you getting excited by a Christmas fayre.'

'I *love* Christmas.'

Harper raised an eyebrow.

'OK,' Frankie conceded. 'He *is* good-looking, in a whipped puppy kind of way.'

'He sounds delightful.'

'Seriously, he's got a story.'

'Don't we all?'

'You know what I mean.'

'Any idea what it might be?'

Frankie shrugged. 'He says he's on a sabbatical, but that could be for any number of reasons.'

'A sabbatical from where?'

'A bank. He works in stocks and shares, or so he says.'

'Don't you believe him?'

'I've got no reason not to.'

'So why the interest?'

'I'm not sure.'

'You fancy him. Go on, admit it.'

'A bit.'

'I can't wait to meet him. There aren't many men who tickle your fancy. Talking of which, how was your date last week?'

'Ugh. Not good.'

Harper said, 'I'll get another round in, and you can tell me all about it.'

Frankie pulled a face after she'd taken a sip of her fresh drink, and explained, 'He talked about fish. A lot. All the flipping time. Catching them, cooking them, eating them.' She shuddered. 'I know more about filleting fish than I ever wanted to know, and I'm pretty sure he's put me off cod and chips for life. I don't think I can even face a fish finger. Fishing has got to be the most boring pastime in the world. Who wants to sit on a muddy damp riverbank and stare at the water for hours on end?'

'You didn't hit it off, then?' Harper chortled, and Frankie gave her an evil glare.

'I made an excuse that I had to work in the morning so I could get away early.'

'How early was early?'

'Ten o'clock. I think I deserve a medal for lasting that long. I ended up buying a kebab and eating it on the way home to cheer myself up.'

'Look on the bright side,' Harper said. 'It's not as though you're looking for your soul mate. You only want a bit of fun, so there was no harm done.'

'God help me if I was looking for The One. I wouldn't find him in Sweet Meadow.'

'Maybe this new fella will be up for a date or two?'

'He's a banker,' Frankie replied glumly.

'Stocks and shares,' Harper reminded her. 'That's got to be more exciting than approving people for mortgages or dealing with loan applications. Does he look anything like Leonardo di Caprio?'

'Eh?'

'*The Wolf of Wall Street*. Or is he more of an Alexander Skarsgård type?'

'Who?'

'He was in *The Hummingbird Project* and *True Blood*. Surely you must have seen *True Blood*? Vampires?'

Frankie had no idea what Harper was on about. 'You watch too much TV,' she said.

'Better than going on crap dates,' Harper shot back with a laugh.

'True.' Frankie thought for a minute. 'No, he's nothing like Leonardo di Caprio. Anyway he's, like, in his fifties. Who's the other bloke, Alex…?'

'Alexander Skarsgård.'

Frankie Googled him. 'He's no spring chicken either.'

'Try him in *True Blood*.'

Frankie did and her eyes widened. 'Ooh, *nice*.' She zoomed in on the image. 'Do you know, Julian Blade *does* look a bit like him. He's tall and moody-looking, and his hair's similar.'

Harper whooped, 'I definitely can't wait to meet him!'

'Molly has arranged for everyone to meet up tomorrow morning at the cafe in the park. I'm going, so if you fancy keeping me company…?'

'Meh, I'm not *that* keen.'

Frankie supposed she shouldn't be all that keen either. However, she *was*, and she was already planning what to wear.

With a sigh (she was sighing a lot lately) she sipped her drink and tried to figure out how she'd got to the point where the highlight of her week was hoping that a miserable-looking guy would turn up to a meeting where the main topic of discussion might well be about how to make pallets look festive.

***

Julian couldn't decide whether he was apprehensive or pleased to be making his way through the park on Saturday morning.

37

A bit of both, probably. After trawling through the spreadsheet and tidying it up, then introducing a few snazzy special effects (pivot tables were a firm favourite of his), he'd quickly taught himself the ins and outs of Microsoft Publisher and had managed to produce some half-decent leaflets.

Molly had seemed pleased when he'd emailed them to her for approval, and she'd told him she was going to print some out and bring them along today. She'd also asked (rather apologetically) if he wouldn't mind posting the event on a couple of social media sites and collating the responses from anyone interested in renting a stall.

This had been another steep learning curve for him, and if he was honest he hadn't particularly wanted anything to do with social media. Once he'd got his head around it though, he could see the benefits – for the Festive Fayre that is, not for him personally. He didn't think he'd ever be a convert.

Julian felt a bit of a poser walking through the park with a laptop case under his arm, but he wanted to be able to refer to his spreadsheet if needed. He snorted – *his* indeed. It surprised him how quickly he'd taken ownership of it, and he'd also realised there'd been several occasions over the past few days where he'd been so absorbed in what he was doing that he hadn't thought about his own miserable self once.

Miserable was the perfect description: he *was* miserable. He felt a total failure. How the hell could he be washed up at his age? But burnout was a real thing. It was a pity he hadn't understood that until it was too late.

Not for the first time, he wondered whether it was a genetic thing. His mother, when she was alive, had been laid low with bouts of depression, sometimes for months at a time. It was one of the reasons he was so good with money – he'd had to be, since weeks used to go by when he'd been in sole charge of the household's finances, and he'd only been eight years old at the time.

As the cafe came into view, Julian was jolted out of his reverie by the sight of Frankie Fox pushing the door open, and his spirits unaccountably lifted. When he stepped inside, she was at the counter and he stood next to her, waiting his turn to order.

She turned to him and smiled. 'Hi, I'm not sure if you remember me, I was in the cafe the other day with Molly? I'm Frankie and I'm a reporter for *The Sweet Meadow Observer*. Molly has asked the newspaper to cover the Festive Fayre.'

'I remember. I'm Julian.'

'Do you fancy grabbing a coffee after the meeting?'

Julian took a mental step back. He might be attracted to her, but he didn't want to date anyone.

However, when she carried on talking and he realised that she wasn't asking him out on a date at all, he was rather dismayed.

'I'm hoping to do a quick interview with all the volunteers,' she continued.

Feeling an idiot, he replied, 'I'm not a volunteer; I'm just helping out for a bit.'

'Latte please, Madeleine, and a scone,' Frankie said, then she asked him, 'What's your poison?'

'Tea please, and I'll have a scone as well.' Eating would give him something to focus on, rather than the people sitting around the table.

Julian was disgusted with himself for feeling this way. What the hell had happened to the guy who had confidently given presentations, who had made split-second decisions involving hundreds of thousands of pounds, who—?

'So, what do you say?' Frankie asked.

'To what?' He stared down into her earnest face and his tummy did a slow roll as she gazed back at him. Her pupils were large, and he had the odd sensation of being sucked into them.

'To a coffee and a chat? And by the way, helping out *is* volunteering.'

'I'm not sure,' he hedged. 'What would you want to chat about?'

'How you're helping with the Fayre, of course. What your contribution is.' She took out her purse.

'Let me,' he said, wrestling his wallet out of his pocket and almost dropping his laptop. He thrust his bank card at the card reader and hoped Frankie didn't notice the company's name emblazoned on it. It wasn't your typical high street bank.

She said, 'You should have let me. I could claim it on expenses. Not that I do, but I *could*.'

'You can pay next time,' he said.

She was quick to pounce. 'So, there *will* be a next time?'

'Um…'

Madeleine said, 'Thanks love, it's all gone through. Grab a seat and I'll bring it over. You're the first to arrive, but I've shoved a couple of tables together.'

No sooner had Julian sat down, Frankie beside him, than Molly walked through the door with two guys around his own age, neither of whom had been there on Monday.

Molly said, 'I can't stay long, I've got a viewing in an hour, but Jack can take over if necessary.' She said to Julian, 'He's my boyfriend, the one in the red fleece. The other guy, in case you don't know him, is Gavin. He's a builder, and he helped renovate the cafe.'

Julian gave each man a nod and an awkward smile. He was starting to wish he hadn't come; he found more new people disconcerting.

Realising part of his problem was that he'd had hardly any real interaction with anyone for several months (the staff on the checkout in the supermarket didn't count), Julian decided to stick it out. What had his therapist said? *'You need to nurture relationships outside of work.'* Easy for her to say. Work relationships were the only ones he'd had; and now that he no longer had a job and he no longer lived in the city, how on earth was he supposed to make friends?

It reminded him of when he was little and his mother used to take him to Ballyhoo's (a local soft-play centre) and push him towards a pit of plastic balls filled with children, telling him to 'go find someone to play with'. It was one of his better memories of her…

'Hello, again.' This was from Fiona, and she placed a friendly hand on his shoulder as she pulled out the chair next to him.

'Hi,' he replied.

Bill asked, 'Had a good week?'

'Not bad.' He was being truthful, of sorts. It hadn't been bad compared to some other weeks he could mention. 'How about you?'

Before Bill could answer, Molly said, 'Can I do my bit first, because I need to get off? I'll start by saying what a great job Julian has done in designing the leaflets and posters.' She held them aloft. 'What do you think?'

Julian's cheeks grew warm at the murmurs of approval.

'And he's sorted out my spreadsheet for me,' she continued. 'Plus, he's posted news of the Fayre all over social media and on the county's *What's On* website. We've already had a few enquiries from interested stall holders, haven't we, Julian?'

All he could do was nod, as every pair of eyes zeroed in on him.

Thankfully, they turned back to Molly when she carried on outlining the progress made so far, followed by a swift update on what needed to be done and who might be able to do it, then she was making her apologies and heading out the door.

'She's a whirlwind, that one,' Bill said. 'I wish I had half her energy.'

'So do I,' Jack laughed. 'You ought to try living with her. Is there anything anyone wants to add or ask before we call it a day?'

'Pallets,' Gavin, the builder said. 'How many can you get hold of?'

'As many as you need. I've got a yard full of the damned things.'

'Fab. I'll give you a bell when I've got room in the van to pick them up, then I can start thinking about how best to put the stalls together. They'll be a bit rough and ready, mind. Julian, can you keep me in the loop as to how many you think we'll need?'

'Um, sure, yeah.'

'I'll give you my mobile number. How good are you with an electric screwdriver? I could do with a hand, if you've got some free time.'

Julian blinked. He didn't think he'd ever used one.

Gavin gazed around the table. 'That goes for the rest of you.' He turned to Jack. 'How about it, Jack? You're handy with a saw.'

Jack rolled his eyes. 'Go on then, but only if you let me have a go with the nail gun.'

'You drive a hard bargain, and I bet you expect me to supply the nails as well?'

Julian listened to the banter, feeling envious. It was friendly and lighthearted, and the two men obviously respected each other. There was none of the backstabbing or undercurrent of competitiveness that he'd been used to at the bank.

'What are you doing this evening?' Gavin asked.

'I'm *not* messing about with pallets on a Saturday evening,' Jack retorted.

'I was thinking about the pub.'

'Ah, that's different. No can do, I'm afraid. Molly wants to go to the cinema.'

Gavin said, 'How about you, Julian? Do you fancy coming to the pub?'

'Um…'

'Or would you prefer to nail some pallets together?'

'No! Definitely not.' Julian shuddered.

'No to the pallets, or no to the pub?'

'Um…' God, was that all he could say?

'I'll be in the Farmer's Arms at about half seven, if you fancy a pint. No worries if you don't. A few of us meet up most Saturdays, but there's always one or two who can't make it so don't worry of you can't. See you.'

Julian watched him leave, then thought he'd better make a move himself. Not that he had anywhere to go or anything to do: he just didn't want to be the last to leave.

Bill disappeared out the door with his little dog, and Fiona donned an apron and began helping Madeleine clear the tables.

Which left just him and Frankie.

She was studying him, and he squirmed uncomfortably.

'Another coffee?' she asked. 'It's my turn, I believe. Would you like a toastie or a panini to go with it? I'm having one. That scone didn't touch the sides.'

Julian was about to refuse, but what else did he have to do? Nothing, that's what. There was only so much social media checking to be done.

'OK, a panini, I think.' He took a quick look at the chalk board on the wall. 'Ham and cheese, please.'

His gaze followed her as she strolled up to the counter, fascinated by the swell of her hips and the way they swayed as she walked.

Her long hair tumbled down her back and he wondered if it was as silky as it looked. The thought of running his hands through the golden strands made his pulse race.

Julian didn't know whether to celebrate this as an indication that he might be returning to pre-burnout days, or whether to view it as another weird manifestation of how topsy-turvy his life had become since he'd been sent home from work a blubbering mess.

Shoving the unwelcome memories to the back of his mind, he made a pledge to try not to think about anything negative for the rest of the day, and instead focus on the things he was grateful for (another tip from his therapist), such as having lunch with a gorgeous woman.

And one never knew, he might even pluck up the courage to go to the pub later.

Feeling better about life and less anxious in general, Julian settled down to enjoy his lunch and hopefully find out more about the woman he would be eating it with.

CHAPTER 4

'So, what is it that you do, exactly?' Frankie asked when she returned from ordering their food. Julian was rather unreadable: reserved, cautious, self- contained. For someone who used words for a living, she wasn't sure how to describe him.

'Banking. Finance.'

'You're on a sabbatical, you said?'

'Yes.'

'Doing what? Work stuff or personal?'

'Personal.'

'Like a gap year?'

'Mmm.'

'What brings you to Sweet Meadow?'

'It's a nice place.'

'It's hardly what you would call a *destination*,' she said.

'Why not?'

'It's a backwater.'

'*I* don't think so.'

Frankie narrowed her eyes. Julian definitely had a story, and she wanted to know what it was. Some people might say that it was none of her business, but she was a journalist: other people's business *was* her business. She could feel her investigative nose twitching. His reluctance to engage might be due to a distrust of reporters, but it also might be because he was hiding something. And she was determined to find out what. A small town in the heart of the South Wales Valleys wouldn't be her choice. Why was it his? Was he in hiding?

Nah, she didn't think so, otherwise why would he have drawn attention to himself by volunteering at the park's Christmas fayre? Julian could be running away though – from a bad relationship, maybe?

'Sweet Meadow is an odd choice, that's all,' she said. 'Why not Cardiff or the coast?' Wales's capital city was less than an hour away, and the coast of West Wales was particularly stunning.

'I like it here,' he replied.

That didn't answer her question.

She tried a different tack. 'What does a typical day look like for you?'

'How long have you been a reporter?'

'Checking my credentials?'

'Something like that.'

'Seven years.'

'All of them with *The Sweet Meadow Observer?*'

'That's right.'

'I bought a copy on Thursday.'

At least someone had, she thought dryly. The paper's circulation had shrunk alarmingly over the past couple of years.

'Nice article on blood donors,' he said.

'Thanks. Ah, here's our food.' She smiled as Fiona bustled over with a laden tray.

Julian couldn't see the older woman's face from where he was sitting, and thankfully he missed her knowing smile and wink. Frankie gave her a look. Julian might be attractive, but that wasn't what this was about. She was trying to interview him, not date him, but he wasn't making it easy.

Frankie didn't say anything for a couple of minutes as they tucked into their paninis, thinking that she might lull him into a false sense of security if he thought that she'd given up on the personal questions.

After a while, she asked again, 'Typical day?'

'Is it relevant?'

'To what?'

'To the Festive Fayre?'

'Readers are always interested in the person behind the job.'

'I would hardly call it a job. I'm merely a volunteer, remember? And a very recent one, at that.'

'You clearly have valuable skills.'

'I know my way around a spreadsheet. It's hardly that valuable a skill.'

'I'm more of a wordy person,' she said, trying to break through his frostiness. 'Would you say you're more at home with numbers?'

He raised an eyebrow. 'I'm a financier, so yes.' His tone was faintly sarcastic.

Fair point: she *had* asked an inane question. She wasn't getting anywhere, was she? He was as adept at avoiding answering a question as a politician. He could probably give them pointers.

She tried yet another tack. 'Are you married?'

His lips twitched. 'Not relevant.'

'In a relationship?'

'Again, not relevant.'

'Maybe I'm not asking for my readers. Maybe I'm asking for *me?*'

When his eyebrows shot up, she almost fist-pumped the air. Gotcha! That had rattled his cage.

'Why would you want to know?' he replied. 'Are you going to ask me out on a date?'

Frankie batted her eyelashes. *Now* she was getting somewhere. 'Would you say yes if I did?'

'Probably not.'

'Oh.' She blinked and bit her lip. Damn it, she hadn't expected that. She could have sworn there was a spark between them. How wrong could she be? Mind you, knowing her track record with men, she shouldn't be surprised.

He went on to explain, 'The reason I wouldn't go on a date with you is that I wouldn't know whether you were asking a question because you genuinely wanted to know, or because you had your reporter's hat on.'

'I don't mix business with pleasure,' she informed him.

'So, are you asking me on a date?'

'No, I'm an old-fashioned girl. I like the man to do the asking.' She wasn't old-fashioned at all, but was playing hard to get.

Unfortunately, she played a bit too hard, because he popped the last bite of panini in his mouth, dabbed his lips with a serviette, and pushed his chair back.

'That hit the spot,' he said, 'but you must excuse me, I've got things to do.'

'Typical-day stuff?'

'Exactly. See you around.' Then he was gone, leaving Frankie even more determined to find out what he was hiding.

***

Frankie slumped back in her chair, defeated. Social media was supposed to be her friend; or, if not a friend, an accomplice. But it had failed to reveal anything about Julian Blade. Aside from a very recently constructed avatar, used (as far as she could tell) solely for Festive Fayre purposes, he had no online presence.

A careful search of the internet hadn't told her anything she didn't already know, except for how much he'd paid for his house in Sweet Meadow – then she manged to lose herself down a rabbit hole of house prices for a while, until she remembered what it was that she'd been doing.

It was now going on for six-thirty and aside from her hastily written article which, if she was honest, had little fresh information to impart when it came to the Fayre, she was no further forward.

Feeling hungry, she trotted to her minuscule kitchen area in search of something to eat and was defeated when nothing in the fridge or the cupboard tickled her tastebuds. What she fancied was a takeaway; Chinese or Indian, she wasn't bothered.

She'd nip out and get one in a minute—

Frankie froze in the middle of closing the cupboard door. Hadn't Gavin invited Julian to the pub this evening? If she remembered rightly, Gavin had said he'd be there from about seven-thirty. Maybe she could be walking along the high street at that time? But what was to say that Julian wouldn't be early? Or late? Or he mightn't go at all. She could hardly dawdle up and down the street for the next couple of hours; she'd likely end up being arrested for loitering with intent.

She could always kill two birds with one stone and have a meal in the pub, instead of having a takeaway, but did she want to sit in a busy bar on a Saturday evening and eat dinner all on her lonesome? She would be like Jilly-no-mates. On the other hand, journalism – the pursuit of a story – *was* a solitary game and she was used to working on her own. If she thought of this evening as work and not as a social occasion, eating a meal on her own in her local was a perfectly OK thing to do.

Frankie decided that the comfy joggers and sweatshirt she was currently wearing wasn't her best look and she needed to change into something less scruffy if she was off to the pub, then she spent longer than necessary debating what to wear. She didn't want to look as though she was on a night out, but neither did she want to look like she was going for a job interview. Finally satisfied with her appearance, she grabbed her trusty bag and headed out the door.

The main street was at that intermediate stage where the Christmas decorations had been attached to lamp posts and strung overhead, but not yet lit, and not all the shops sported Christmas windows. So despite sitting in on the Festive Fayre planning meeting this morning, Frankie didn't feel in the least bit festive. Hopefully that would change in the coming weeks, because she really did love Christmas.

Warmth hit her as she opened the pub's door, accompanied by a wall of noise, and she flinched. Almost changing her mind, she hesitated, then she spotted Gavin.

A tall man with dirty blond hair was standing next to him.

She inhaled sharply and walked towards him.

'Hiya, fancy seeing you here,' she said, and was gratified by the flare of interest in Julian's eyes when he saw her, although he masked it quickly.

'Hi.' His tone was neutral, and now that she was here, she didn't know what to say to him.

Feeling foolish and faintly ridiculous, she turned away. She would have a quick drink then beat a hasty retreat. A couple of excuses to explain why she was leaving almost as soon as she'd arrived, flitted through her mind: she had only popped in on the way to somewhere else, she was needed urgently at home, the friend she was supposed to be meeting hadn't been able to make it...

Then she sensed Julian behind her as she stood at the bar waiting for her drink. She didn't know how she knew it was him, but she did.

'Are you on your own?' he asked, trying to catch the attention of one of the bar staff.

'I'm meeting my friend, Harper, but she's not arrived yet,' Frankie said. 'Excuse me… I've got a message.' She looked at her phone and sighed dramatically. 'Damn, she can't make it – something's come up. Never mind, I'll have this, then I'll go home. Cheers.' Lifting her glass, she pretended to take a large mouthful of gin, when in fact, she barely tasted it. She wanted to make this drink last. Putting a sad expression on her face, she allowed her shoulders to slump.

'A pint of lager, please,' Julian said to the barman, oblivious to her acting skills.

'I haven't seen you in here before,' she said.

'That's because I've never been here before.'

'How long have you lived in Sweet Meadow?'

'Four months.'

'And you've never had a drink in the Farmer's Arms?'

'Never. Cheers, mate, keep the change.' He lifted the glass to his lips.

Frankie's eyes settled on his mouth, then she flushed when she realised he'd noticed the direction of her gaze.

Julian smiled, a polite, dismissive smile, and Frankie's shoulders slumped for real.

Oh, well, she'd given it her best shot.

It was a shame he didn't want to talk to her, because she genuinely wanted to get to know him better. But maybe this was for the best. She was only in the market for a bit of fun, and she sensed Julian wasn't a fun-loving guy. Then there was also the question of his relationship status. She was acutely aware that he hadn't answered her.

He returned to Gavin, and she swallowed half of her drink, the gin making her eyes water. Curiosity still burned though, a heat not to be denied, and she turned her attention to her phone. There was one way to find out if there was a Mrs Blade in the picture – Molly would know. Then she remembered that Molly was in the cinema, probably cuddled up next to Jack and sharing a large carton of popcorn. Maybe it would be better to wait until Monday to ask her. It would look less like a personal query and more of a professional one, if she left it until then.

Julian turned to look at her and Frankie lifted her glass, a regretful smile on her lips. Tossing the contents down her throat, she placed the glass on the bar and made for the door.

Julian stopped her. 'It seems a waste to leave after one drink.'

'A waste?'

'You look nice.'

Frankie was taken aback. 'I'm not sure whether that's a compliment.'

'It is. All dressed up and nowhere to go.'

'I do have somewhere to go – home.'

'Where's that?'

'I've got a flat above the hairdresser in State Street.'

'Would you like me to walk you back?'

'I think I can manage.' Bloody hell, he couldn't wait to get rid of her!

'How about if you stay and have another drink, and I'll walk you home after?'

'Just the one?'

'You can have as many as you like, but I warn you now, if you get pie-eyed I'm not carrying you.'

'I never get drunk.' She wouldn't mind him scooping her into his arms and striding off down the high street, though. She bit her lip and looked up at him from under her lashes. 'OK, thanks. But will walking me home get you into trouble with your other half?'

'I don't have one. What are you drinking?'

Frankie smiled with satisfaction. Now she knew something else about him.

She noticed that he hadn't drunk more than a third of his pint, so when she asked for another gin, she stressed the tonic and vowed to make it last. Alcohol on an empty stomach was rarely a good idea.

He carried the drinks to a free table, and they sat down, then once again Frankie discovered that she had no idea what to say to him. Numerous questions swirled around her head, but she didn't think it prudent to ask any of them. He clearly didn't want to talk about himself, so she went with the banal and the faintly absurd.

'What's your favourite colour?' she asked.

'Pardon?' His expression was bemused and slightly wary.

'Your favourite colour. What is it?'

'Why?'

'I'm curious.'

'Blue.'

'Predictable.'

'I take it yours is pink?'

'Nuh-uh, silver.'

'Do I get a turn?'

'Go for it.'

'Favourite karaoke song?'

'Do you like karaoke?'

'No.' His face was deadpan.

'But you think *I* do?' Frankie wrinkled her nose.

'A lot of people love karaoke.'

'I don't.'

'OK, then, favourite food?'

'Pizza.'

'Favourite topping?'

She shook her head. 'It's my turn. Dog or cat?'

'I thought we were doing favourites, not either-or.'

Frankie said nothing. Her stare should say it all.

He relented. 'Dog. You?'

'Hamster.'

'That wasn't the question. Do you always change the rules whenever you feel like it?'

'Not always. Favourite holiday?'

'We're back to favourites, are we? Skiing.'

'Where?'

'Andorra.'

'Do you go often?' Frankie had never been skiing. She'd ice skated once and had quite enjoyed it, but she'd been about six years old at the time. Whether she would enjoy it as much now that she was older, was debatable. Maybe she'd have a go on Molly's pop-up ice rink. Or maybe not.

He said, 'Not as often as I'd like. Do you have a favourite holiday destination?'

'Bali. Sun, sea, cocktails, white sand.'

'I can see the appeal. Favourite sport?'

'None.' Her reply was instant.

'Not any?'

She shook her head.

'You don't watch the Olympics?'

'Nope.'

'Or the Five Nations?'

'Only if Wales is playing England, and even then I'm not keen. Footballs are bad enough, but those rugby balls are a weird shape.' Some of the men who played the game were rather hunky though, so maybe she should start watching it.

'Favourite kids' programme?' he asked.

'I believe it was my turn, but I'll answer your question. SpongeBob SquarePants.'

Julian barked out a laugh. 'I loved that programme, too.'

Finally, she thought, *we've got something in common.* 'Squidward or Patrick?'

'Squidward,' they chorused together.

He caught her eye and laughed, and she was delighted to see him relax in her company. He was even sexier when his eyes crinkled at the corners.

'Ice cream?' she asked.

'Pistachio.'

'That figures; you look like a pistachio man.'

He made a quirky face. 'What does a pistachio man look like?'

'You.'

'I'm going to let that slide because I'm not sure I'll like the answer. OK, what's *your* favourite, vanilla girl?'

She hesitated and looked deep into his eyes. '*Definitely* not vanilla,' then she licked her lips slowly, teasing her tongue across her top lip.

His eyes widened and he swallowed.

Unable to keep it in, she burst out laughing. 'Gotcha!'

'You minx!'

'Minx?' She was laughing hard now. The expression on his face had been priceless.

'No more gin for you,' he joked, finishing his lager.

'Butterscotch. My favourite ice cream is butterscotch, although I prefer sorbets to ice cream, and my favourite pizza topping is chorizo.'

'All this talk of food is making me hungry,' he said. 'I haven't eaten since the panini and that was hours ago.'

'Neither have I.'

'Were you going to have a meal here with your friend?'

It took Frankie a second to remember that she'd told him she was supposed to have been meeting Harper this evening.

'Yes, a meal.' She waited for him to suggest they order some food, but he didn't.

Instead, he said, 'I think I'll get some noodles on the way home.'

'Good idea.'

He nodded at her empty glass. 'Do you want another?'

'Not unless you do?'

He shook his head. 'I think I'm going to head off. Would you like me to walk you back?' he offered again.

What she wanted was to stay in the pub and chat some more, but it looked like that wasn't going to happen. Damn. 'There's no need, but I'll walk to the Chinese with you and get some food. If I don't eat soon, I'll keel over.'

Stepping outside she zipped up her coat and shivered, her breath clouding above her head in the chilly night air.

As they fell into step, Julian asked, 'Do you think Molly can pull this fayre off? She's cutting it fine, time-wise.'

'Absolutely she can. When she first moved into her cottage, both the house and the park were a mess and the cafe didn't exist. If anyone can do it, she and Jack can.'

'I'm worried she won't have enough stalls.'

'What has the response been like so far?'

'Only three bookings.'

'It's early days. It's not been a week yet,' Frankie pointed out.

'But the Festive Fayre is only six weeks away. I wish I could help drum up interest.'

Frankie stopped walking, an idea beginning to form, one that would benefit the Fayre, give her something to write about and promote local craftspeople at the same time.

That it would also mean she'd get to spend more time with Julian, was neither here nor there.

'What are you doing tomorrow?' she asked

CHAPTER 5

This is the smallest car in the world, Julian thought, as he tried without success to stretch out his cramped legs. He was currently squashed into Frankie's tiny mint-green hatchback as it hurtled down the M4 motorway.

'Are you *sure* you've never been to St Fagans?' Frankie asked, glancing in her rear-view mirror before indicating to move into the outside lane.

'I can't say that I have.' When she'd suggested going there yesterday and he'd asked her what St Fagans was, she'd been incredulous that he'd never heard of it. She still was, so it seemed.

'Every kid within a fifty-mile radius goes there for an obligatory school trip at least once,' she said.

She was fishing for info again, so he decided to give her some. 'I'm not from around here.'

She snorted. 'I never would have guessed. You're accent – or should I say, lack of one – gives you away. Are you from London?'

'No.'

Her eyes narrowed and she pressed her lips together, and he guessed she wasn't happy with the brevity of his answer. 'I'm from Northants, originally,' he went on to explain. 'But I've lived in London for years.'

'Why Sweet Meadow?'

'Someone I used to work with grew up in South Wales. Merthyr Tydfil, I believe. He was always going on about how much he missed it.'

'Why didn't you go there?'

'I stuck a pin in a map.' He hadn't, but he may as well have done. He'd picked Sweet Meadow for no other reason than he liked the name, and he'd liked the outlook of the house he'd bought. It was ironic to think that he was now in the process of helping that very same outlook organise its first ever Christmas fayre. Which was why he was on his way to somewhere called St Fagans this morning.

Obviously, he'd looked it up. After he and Frankie had parted ways last night (him with a noodle dish, her with chicken Foo Yung), he'd eaten his solitary supper whilst trawling the internet to check out where, exactly, he would be going.

St Fagans (or to give it its full title, St Fagans National Museum of History) was a mostly outdoor museum of old, and some quite ancient buildings, which had been moved from various locations in Wales and re-constructed in the grounds of an Elizabethan manor house. The historic buildings included a farm, a tannery, a mill, a chapel and dwellings that had once been lived in by ordinary people.

It promised to be fascinating, and he couldn't wait to look around, although what they were primarily going there for was the craft market, as he was hoping to persuade one or two crafters to have a stall at Sweet Meadow's Festive Fayre.

When they arrived, they parked the car and walked up a small slope to the entrance. He'd been expecting an old, possibly Victorian building, and was surprised how modern and airy it was. He was pleased to see there was a huge cafe, because he had a feeling they might need some sustenance before the journey back. It also had a gift shop, which Frankie was excited about (him, not so much) and a large gallery on the upper floor that housed some incredibly interesting artefacts, such as an impressive and very ornate trophy called "Caradog's Cup" as well as other, much older exhibits. Julian was particularly interested in the Bronze Age gold on display.

'Wow, look at these!' Frankie cried, and he followed her over to a display of Welsh national costumes. 'Aren't they fab? When I was a child, we used to dress up in costumes like these on St. David's Day. Do you know what that is?'

'I'm not a complete ignoramus. St David is the patron Saint of Wales. First of March, I believe.'

'I'm glad to hear you've learnt something about your adopted country,' she teased, then flitted off to look at something else. Her energy and enthusiasm were rather endearing, and he found himself smiling as she scampered from one exhibit to another.

There was such an eclectic mix of items and Julian was so utterly fascinated that he could have stayed there all day, but eventually Frankie dragged him outside to explore the rest of it.

They hurried past the children's play area and made their way to the old buildings. The first one they came to was a farmhouse, and he was delighted to be able to go inside. The fixtures, furnishings and decorations were the same as they would have been back in the day, and there was even an old outhouse, whitewashed and grim.

Frankie shuddered as she peered into the circular hole in a wooden board that was the toilet. 'Thank the lord for indoor plumbing!'

Julian wholeheartedly agreed. 'Can you imagine having to trek outside on a dark wet night to do the necessary?'

'I can,' she replied, 'and it gives me the shivers.'

'Not as many as if you really *did* have to come out here.'

'Can we move on?'

'I think we should. What's next?'

'Iron Age round houses,' she announced, consulting a map.

Then there was a magnificent old church, with the most incredible medieval wall paintings which had once been painted over with lime wash during the Reformation, when the Catholic faith was outlawed. Julian was awed, and so was Frankie. Her eyes were wide with wonder.

Further along and several buildings later, his nose was assaulted by the most delicious smell – beer-battered fish and chips!

He looked at Frankie, and Frankie looked at him. No words were necessary.

As one, they made a beeline for it and were soon clutching a portion of heavenly fish and fluffy chips. Even though the temperature was cold enough to see their breath, they ate their food while sitting at a table on the covered seating area outside.

'The best Sunday lunch ever,' Frankie announced, licking her fingers.

Julian watched her pink tongue flick out, and lust hit him in the gut.

She caught him staring and wiped her mouth self-consciously as he averted his gaze.

She was lovely – cute and sexy – but until he sorted his life out, he wasn't in the right headspace to get involved with anyone. He didn't need to add additional pressure to his already fragile mental health. Although he had to admit, that so far this weekend he was feeling more like his pre-burnout self.

Hope flared in his chest: could he be on the road to recovery? He prayed that he was. Finally.

With their meals finished, they headed off to see what else was there.

A row of eighteen-century cottages made Julian pause. There were six houses in all, the interior of each one decorated in a different period in history, from 1805 to 1985, and he was enthralled to see the gradual modernisation that had taken place over the years.

Next was a general store, then a tailor's shop, and a sweet shop where Frankie coveted a small chocolate hedgehog.

Against his better judgement, he bought one when she wasn't looking.

'Here you go,' he said, handing her the paper bag when they were outside.

Frankie took it, her expression quizzical. 'What's this?' she asked, peeping inside. *'Oh!'*

The smile that lit up her face made his heart constrict. Did she know how gorgeous she was? He didn't think she did. And when she stood on tiptoe and kissed his cheek, he had to hold himself rigid in order not to respond.

'Thank you so much,' she gushed. 'That's so thoughtful.'

'It's only a little something to say thanks for bringing me here. I've had a lovely time.'

'It isn't over yet; there are the formal gardens to look around and the manor house itself. But before that, hadn't we better go check out the craft fair?'

Oh, yes, that *was* why he was here. But why was *she?* She could have simply told him about St Fagans. She needn't to have offered to bring him.

'You ought to write an article about this place,' he suggested, wondering whether that might be the reason.

'I think St Fagans has been written about enough. I wouldn't be able to add anything meaningful that people don't already know. Besides, I'm not into reporting about this kind of thing. I prefer harder-hitting stories.' She must have sensed his surprise because she added, 'I don't intend writing about fayres in parks for the rest of my life.'

'What *will* you be writing about?'

'I like more investigative stuff.'

'Such as, who put a traffic cone on top of the flagpole outside the school?'

She rolled her eyes. 'Finding out who did, was my finest hour – *not*. No, I want to write about things that matter, important things like crime, or the state of the NHS, or corruption: that kind of thing.'

'Is there a lot of that in Sweet Meadow?'

'Not much, although the residents are affected by such things, obviously. Just a couple of months ago I reported on the difficulties one lady had in getting a routine appointment at the GP's surgery. And recently, the cafe in the park was subjected to a spate of vandalism. But those kinds of things are hardly likely to get me noticed.'

'Who do you want to get noticed by?'

'A national publication. I want to be a feature writer for the likes of *Vanity Fair*. A feature writer is a journalist who writes detailed articles. It's not as dry as pure factual reporting; it's more long-form articles or narrative journalism. I suppose you could describe it as halfway between reporting the facts and telling a story.'

'Does that mean you'll have to leave Sweet Meadow?'

'That's the aim. Nothing exciting ever happens there. You've got to be where the action is.'

Julian remembered feeling that way, once upon a time. But being where the action was, had almost been the end of him. God, he sounded ancient, but he was only a few years older than her. Four or five tops. It felt like fifty.

She was saying, 'I'm always on the lookout for the story that'll open that door, one which will be taken up by one of the big players, to give me a foot in the door.'

'What kind of story?'

'I don't know until I see it, and until that happens, I'm stuck writing about traffic cones and Christmas fayres.'

'Is that so bad?'

She didn't answer, and he saw they'd arrived back at the main building and that her attention was now elsewhere. The craft fair was being held in the atrium, a large double-height space, and there must be about forty stalls selling a whole range of hand-crafted products such as pens, love spoons, metal work, soaps, candles, and jewellery.

'How are we going to play this?' she asked, her eyes shining.

Julian produced a wad of leaflets from his coat pocket. 'We're going to give each stallholder one of these, along with some patter if they show any interest.'

'And if they don't?'

'We'll just have to hope they'll go away and think about it. There's not much else we can do.'

Frankie was grinning. 'I think there is! Who doesn't love free publicity? Leave it to me.'

So that's what Julian did, happily taking a back seat as Frankie charmed the craftspeople, and when she was done and she announced that she had seven sign-ups, Julian was overjoyed, and he knew Molly would be too.

***

Frankie stared at the face peering back at her from the computer screen. 'Is it OK if I record this?' she asked, 'purely so I don't have to take notes?'

'That's fine,' the woman said. She made the most delicious chocolates, and Frankie knew this because she'd had a taste of them yesterday at St Fagans. And now she was interviewing her very first stall holder, plus she had two more to interview today after this.

'First things first, could you email me some publicity photos?' Frankie asked. 'Yourself, your products, a link to your website if you've got one, and your socials?'

'Of course. I'll do that now, before I forget.'

While she waited for the info to come through, Frankie quickly scanned the list of questions she had prepared yesterday after they'd returned from St Fagans. But even as her gaze roamed over them, her thoughts were on Julian and the lovely day they'd spent together. She'd been sorry to see it end and had half-hoped he would ask her in when she'd dropped him off at his house. He hadn't, and her disappointment had been out of all proportion, especially since she was no further forward in finding out more about him.

Lying awake last night, the day running through her head, she wondered why she was so determined. She should let it go. Whatever his secret, it was unlikely to be earth-shattering, although from a human interest perspective, it might be interesting to *The Observer's* readers.

Frankie was jolted out of her thoughts by a voice coming from her computer. 'Has my email arrived yet?'

She checked. 'Yes, it has. Thanks for that. Lovely photos, by the way. Your chocolates will go down a storm.'

And she was off, in full-on professional mode as she made sure she had all the information she needed. The readers would love to learn how the woman came to run her own artisan confectionery business and how the chocolates were made.

After half an hour, Frankie had more than enough material, and by the end of the day the article was written and emailed to Neil for his approval.

Finally closing the lid of her laptop, Frankie got stiffly to her feet. She should think about food since she hadn't eaten much today, but she was itching to speak to Julian.

Deciding that a phone call was too full-on, she messaged him instead. *Any more sign-ups?*

She'd only managed to walk into the kitchen when he replied a few seconds later.

3. That's eleven altogether. Molly says 20 minimum.

Yay! Frankie was impressed. When Neil had given her this assignment, she hadn't for one minute imagined she could be so invested.

Another message from Julian. *Going to post again this evening.*

Good idea. I've just sent the first of the interviews to my boss for approval.

She peered into the fridge. There was an unopened pack of minced beef, and she knew she had a jar of bolognese sauce somewhere. *Let's hope I have some spaghetti*, she thought.

How did they go? he asked.

Got some good copy. I think Molly will be pleased. Any more news? She opened a cupboard and rooted around inside.

Going to help Neil make stalls on the weekend.
Nice. Yes! Spaghetti.

It won't be for him. I'm no good at DIY.

I bet you are.

You'd lose. I've never even put up a shelf.

Honestly??? As she picked up the frying pan, the handle slipped through her fingers and she dropped it, swearing loudly when it almost landed on her slipper-clad toes.

Honestly.

Neither have I she admitted, but that was due to her flat being rented, so she wasn't allowed to drill the walls without permission. And there was also the small detail of not owning a drill. *I'm an ace at assembling that pack furniture, tho* she added.

She dumped the mince in the pan and turned on the gas, then filled a saucepan with water and put it on to boil. Did she have any garlic bread, she wondered.

Never done that either he messaged.

You haven't lived. Next you'll tell me that you've never been to IKEA

I haven't

You don't know what you're missing. They do a full cooked breakfast for next to nothing. No garlic bread. Bugger.

You go there for the food?

It's the whole experience - all those little rooms

The water had come to a boil, so she lowered the strands of spaghetti into it, coiling them around the bottom of the pan as they softened, then she turned her attention to the mince.

What little rooms?

Your education is sadly lacking. IKEA have room mock-ups so you can see everything in situ.

Stirring the mince with one hand, she used the other to find an image on the internet to send to him, with the caption I LOVE IKEA.

For some reason, it felt perfectly normal to be cooking a meal while chatting online to Julian, though why she was waxing lyrical about IKEA was a mystery.

I can tell.

Next time I go, would you like to come with me?

I think I'll give it a miss, but I wouldn't mind company when I go to the garden centre tomorrow. Molly asked if I could collect some Xmas lights for her

If Frankie didn't know that Molly was head over heels in love with Jack, she might be starting to think there was something going on between them, the number of times Julian had mentioned her.

I've got to go into the office in the morning. Neil was holding a team meeting – all three of them.

Afternoon?

Cool.

Time?

2pm? I can pick you up from work.
Great.
See you tomorrow.

As Frankie plated up her food, it occurred to her that she would be seeing Julian for the fourth day in a row. If these had been actual dates, she would be starting to worry that it was getting too serious too soon!

CHAPTER 6

Neil was already in the office when Frankie threw her bag on her desk and dropped into her chair. Why were mornings so hard? She'd never been a morning person, but the time of year didn't help. It should be against the law to have to get up when it was still dark.

'Got a minute?' Neil asked.

'Coffee, first?'

'Go on, then. Two sugars.'

This time the milk was fresh, and she dumped two heaped spoonfuls of granules into hers, hoping the extra caffeine would kick start her brain.

'There you go,' she said, placing a steaming mug on his desk. She slumped into the chair opposite, cradling her drink, waving to Vince who had just strolled in. 'Kettle's just boiled,' she told him, watching him go to the kitchen.

In his mid-thirties and having worked at *The Observer* for twelve years, Vince was more experienced than her – but not by much. Frankie had often wondered why he hadn't moved on, but he seemed comfortable in his role, so maybe he wasn't as ambitious as her.

Neil took a sip of his coffee. 'Nice work on the Festive Fayre article. What have you got planned for the next one?'

'Three more plugs for vendors, and Gavin, the builder who worked on the cafe, is making stalls out of pallets, so I thought I'd put that in it as well. I'm wary about it being too much of an advert.'

'But that's what it is, essentially – one long advert for the Festive Fayre.'

'I know, but I want readers to get more than "buy this and buy that" out of it, so I'm thinking of the human interest side.'

'Such as?' Neil's gaze was steady over the rim of his mug.

'Remember that kid who almost drowned in the pond earlier this year? The one Jack Feathers jumped in to save?'

'I do.'

'He and his mate are supposed to be helping Gavin make the stalls, so I thought I'd do a piece about bad lads turned good. A redemption story, if you like.'

'I like. You'll need parental permission.'

'I'll see if I can speak to the boys' parents today, or if not, tomorrow.'

'Anything else?'

'Not sure yet.' She was still convinced that Julian had a story, but whether it would be one worth telling was a different matter.

'OK, keep me posted,' Neil said. 'I've got a couple of assignments for you, as well as the usual.' He pushed two pieces of paper across the desk.

The "usual" involved contacting the local funeral directors for the death notices, trawling the council's website for anything relevant to Sweet Meadow, such as a change to the bin collection day (a hot topic), notifications about forthcoming road closures (an even hotter topic), and their *What's On* page, in case there was an event she hadn't heard about. The library usually had something going on, so if news was light, she could always big-up the mother and toddler sing-along.

Frankie gave the assignments a quick glance and sighed: fly-tipping on the mountain above the town, and the local rambling group's monthly stomp. Neither were riveting. She'd tackle the fly-tipping first. A local farmer had called it in, so she'd pay him a visit this morning. The ramblers weren't rambling until tomorrow, so she'd phone the guy in charge (the head rambler?) and arrange to be there at their starting point.

A couple of quotes, a photo or two, and a map of the route were all that was needed. She'd follow up with a quick phone call afterwards to make sure nothing untoward had happened.

'It's nice to see you getting involved in the community,' Neil said.

Frankie was confused. 'What do you mean?'

'Helping out with the Festive Fayre.'

'When have I helped out?'

'Going to St Fagans to drum up vendors. It was your suggestion, I believe.'

'Who told you that?'

'A good reporter has his ear to the ground, and I never reveal my sources.'

'*Bill* told you.'

'Yup.'

'I resent that. I'm *always* involved in community stuff.'

'Writing about it, isn't the same as being involved. You report on it, but you don't get stuck in.'

'That's my job!' she protested. 'I'm *supposed* to report on it.'

'Yes, you are. All I'm saying is that it's nice to see you getting involved as well.'

Frankie didn't like to tell him that the only reason she'd "got involved" was because she'd been hoping to get to know Julian better. And because she wasn't entirely sure of her reason for that, she didn't want to answer any questions Neil might have.

'That's the joy and burden of living in a small town like Sweet Meadow,' he said. 'You can't live in a place like this and not get involved.'

Yes, you can, she thought. She'd not been getting involved all her life. Well, not since she'd left Brownies. You kind of had to get involved if you were in the Brownies and you wanted to earn all the badges.

He continued, 'It's your civic duty. That's the reason I own and run this newspaper. It's the *only* reason, because I certainly don't do it for the money.'

His face clouded and Frankie beat a hasty retreat before he started on about falling readership and the need to cram its pages with adverts to keep it afloat. It was Neil's favourite topic of conversation and something he'd moaned about since her very first day on *The Observer*, seven years ago.

Going back to her desk, she gave the farmer a call and arranged to meet him in the lane where the rubbish had been dumped. With enough time to check her emails, she'd just opened the first of far too many when her mobile rang.

'You're still alive, then,' the voice on the other end said.

'Hi, Mum.'

'I was about to call the police. I haven't seen or heard from you in over a week.'

'I've been busy.'

'Too busy to phone your poor old mother?'

'You're not old. You're fifty-three. Anyway, *you* could have phoned *me*.'

'What do you think I'm doing? I'm phoning you now.'

'Have you called to moan? Because if you have, I'm—'

'Busy,' her mum interrupted. 'Yes, so you said. I'm busy too, you know. You don't have a monopoly on busy.'

'You can be so annoying!'

'So can you.'

'Yeah, but I'm cute and you love me,' Frankie chuckled.

'You got me there,' her mum said. 'I rang to check you're all right.'

'I'm fine. How are you and Dad?'

'We're fine too. Got any news?'

'Ha, ha.' It was one of her mum's favourite jokes and was seriously unfunny. Frankie said, 'I'm going to the garden centre this afternoon. Do you need anything while I'm there?'

'Ooh, I love a garden centre at Christmas. If you leave it until the weekend, I'll come with you.'

'Sorry, this is to do with work.'

'Never mind, we can go another time.' Her mother sounded disappointed.

Now Frankie felt bad. 'I don't mind going again on Sunday, but I can't do Saturday.' She was hoping to see Gavin and the boys putting together a stall or two, and maybe catch Julian having a go. She refused to believe that he'd never put up a shelf.

'Tell you what,' her mother said, 'why don't we leave off visiting the garden centre, and you come to lunch instead?'

'Lovely!' Frankie adored her mum's roast dinners. 'Chicken?'

'If you want.'

'Stuffing and cranberry sauce?'

'Of course.'

'Afters?'

'Naturally. I'm doing apple pie and custard.'

Although it was nowhere near lunch time, Frankie's mouth watered. She would eat her mother's roast chicken dinner every day of the week, if she could.

Suddenly realising the time, she leapt out of her chair. She'd better get a move on if she didn't want to be late for her interview with the farmer.

***

Julian's little black sports car wasn't new by any stretch, so he was taken aback by Frankie's surprise when she saw it.

'Wow!' she cried, getting in. 'Nice car.'

Feeling somewhat defensive, he said, 'It's sixteen years old.'

If someone didn't know a lot about cars, they probably wouldn't realise its age because the personalised number plate masked the year of production. It did look a bit flash sitting outside his little terraced house, he conceded, but he'd parted with so much when he fled London that he hadn't wanted to part with this as well.

As he drove down the bypass, Julian was tempted to put the pedal to the floor and show her what the car could do, but that would be stupid and dangerous, and he was no boy-racer. So why did he feel the need to show off? To impress her?

To counteract the urge, he drove like a pensioner towing a caravan instead, but the beauty of being so low to the ground was that the car appeared to be going faster than it was.

'Had a good morning?' he asked.

'Interviewed a farmer about fly-tipping, spoke to the funeral director about funeral notices and been told off by my mother – a normal day. You?'

His had been equally riveting: he'd read the financial news, gone for a walk, smooth-talked a guy who made stained glass ornaments into taking a stall at the Fayre and who had been on the fence about it, then had twiddled his thumbs until it was time to collect Frankie.

'Nothing much. Pottered around a bit,' he replied.

'You can tell me to mind my own business, but what does your sabbatical involve?'

He sensed her frustration and debated whether to tell her. The problem was, how much was he prepared to divulge? He was starting to think of her as a friend, and if he told her the truth would he lose that?

His therapist had tried to impress upon him that mental health was nothing to be ashamed of. Morag had asked him whether he would have felt the same way if it had been his body that wasn't well and not his mind, but he couldn't help how he felt. If he'd been able to control his feelings, he wouldn't have been in a position where he'd needed a damn therapist in the first place. He would have been able to cope with the pressure, the responsibility, the pace…

The shame, the utter helplessness he'd felt when he'd realised that he hadn't been coping, the sideways looks, the whispers, the awful day when he'd been advised (*ordered*) to take a leave of absence – he'd coped with none of it. He was a highflyer who'd been burnt by the sun of his ambition.

'Julian, are you OK?' The concern in Frankie's voice touched him.

'I will be,' he replied. He had to believe that. He *did* believe it, because otherwise what was the point? And these past couple of weeks, he *was* beginning to feel more like his old self.

She said, 'Forgive me for asking, but are you ill?' There was that concern again.

'Not in the way you think. I'll explain another time.' Telling his deepest, darkest secret whilst hurtling down a dual carriageway at sixty miles an hour, wouldn't be wise.

Frankie's brief touch on his forearm was light, yet he felt the weight of it throughout his whole body. 'I'm here if you need to talk,' she said.

'Off the record?' he joked weakly.

'I can't guarantee that – if you're a spy or you're on the run from the police, people have a right to know.'

Was she joking? He couldn't tell. 'I don't think I'm cut out to be a spy,' he said.

'Oh, I don't know... you're mysterious enough.'

'Me, mysterious? Ha! Anyway, isn't that the exact opposite of what a spy should be? A spy should blend in, surely?'

'You've got a point.'

'Ditto when it comes to being a criminal on the run.'

'Witness protection?'

'Same rules. I can assure you, I'm not that exciting. I'm taking some time out, that's all.'

'The offer stands. I'm here if you want to talk.'

'Thanks. I appreciate it.' He pretended to concentrate on navigating the slip road and the subsequent roundabout, and was relieved to see the turnoff for the garden centre up ahead.

Frankie's attention was diverted away from him and his possible spy status, by the number of retail units on the site. As well as the garden centre, there was a food hall, a couple of clothes shops, and a pet shop, amongst others.

'Why haven't I been here before?' she cried, and became even more excited when they walked into the garden centre and she saw all the colourful Christmas decorations on display.

Julian trailed behind bemused, as she darted from bauble to candle, and from cushion to mug, and she was fairly hopping up and down with excitement when she spotted numerous Christmas trees all lined up: dark-green, light green, frosted, silver, gold, white, and even pink. Julian, not a fan of Christmas at the best of times, drew the line at pink.

'Look at all the lights!' she squealed. 'They're so pretty. And the garlands and wreaths, and— Ooh, a reindeer!' It wasn't a real one. It was metal and covered in tiny lights. 'I want it!' she exclaimed, 'but I don't have anywhere to put it.'

Then, like a butterfly flitting from bloom to bloom, she was onto the next thing to catch her eye, this time a pretty snow globe.

'I'm going to get this, and tonight I'm going to put up my tree. I don't care if it isn't December yet. When will you put yours up?'

'I don't usually bother.' He didn't bother at all.

'What! You must!'

'Must I?'

'Yes.' She nodded emphatically.

'There doesn't seem much point just for me.'

'There's even more point if you're on your own. I'll help you put it up, if you like. We can have Christmas tunes on in the background, hot chocolates and mince pies on the go…'

Julian pulled a face, which Frankie interpreted incorrectly.

'Or,' she said, 'you could have gingerbread, or a slice of Christmas cake?'

'It's not that, it's—' he began, but didn't get to finish because Frankie leapt in with, 'It's no problem if you don't want any help. I can get quite possessive over my tree. I like it decorated just so.'

'No, it's—' he started again and stopped, then told her, 'You can't help me decorate my tree, because I don't have one.'

'Ah, admittedly it is a little too soon to buy a real one. They don't like being indoors for too long. I love the smell of a real tree, but I put my deckers up so early the poor thing would be on its last legs by Christmas Eve. Do you buy one, or rent one? I love the idea of renting one, and then after a couple of years it's retired and planted in a forest.'

'Neither,' he admitted apprehensively.

She whirled around, the movement making the snowflakes in the globe she was clutching swirl. 'No artificial tree, no real tree, no rented tree? You don't put a tree up at all, do you?' she accused.

'That's what I've been trying to tell you. I don't bother.'

'We'll see about that,' she muttered. Tucking the snow globe into the crook of her arm, she grabbed his hand and began to pull him along. 'Come on.'

'Where are we going?'

'To find you a tree.'

'A real tree?'

'No, I don't trust you to take care of a real one.'

'Why not? Do I look like the type of person who neglects trees?'

She stopped, and he almost bumped into her. She didn't let go of his hand and he hoped she didn't intend to. It felt incredibly nice.

Looking him in the eye, she said, 'You look like the type of person who neglects *himself*.'

Julian blinked, but before he could formulate a reply, she was off again, pulling him behind her like a small, determined tug towing a tanker. This woman wasn't going to take no for an answer.

Coming to a halt in front of the display of trees, she let go of his hand and commanded, 'Pick one.'

Feeling as though he'd been set adrift, Julian stared at them helplessly. He'd never bought a Christmas tree in his life, and didn't know where to start.

His confusion must have shown, because she said, 'Let's take this one step at a time. Do you prefer green or not green?'

'Green.' That was easy; he preferred Christmas trees to look like trees. Though he suspected Frankie didn't feel the same, because she was eyeing the pink one with the kind of avarice that a cat eyed a mouse.

With a visible shake and a toss of her head, she dragged her gaze away from it and focused on the green ones, of which there were many. 'Dark green, light green, or the one that looks like it's got a dusting of snow?'

'The snowy one looks nice.'

'Pre-lit, or do you want to buy your own lights?'

'What do you suggest?'

'It depends how much you enjoy untangling them. Because no matter how carefully you pack them away in January, by the time you get them out next Christmas, they'll be a ball of wire that will take you all evening and a bottle of wine to unravel.'

'I sense you've been there.'

'Haven't I just!'

'Pre-lit, then.'

'Multi-coloured, gold or white?'

'Can I bow to your greater knowledge of all things festive?'

'Gold.'

'Gold it is.' He was rather enjoying himself. Who knew choosing a Christmas tree could be this much fun?

'How tall?' she asked. 'This one comes in three sizes.'

He peered at the one on display. It was about the same height as him, but as it was standing on a plinth, he guessed it was about a head shorter. 'The next size up?'

'Perfect! Grab a ticket. When we pay for it, they'll bring out a boxed one. OK, now for the best bit – the decorations. We're going to need a trolley.'

Julian was alarmed: how many decorations did she think he'd need?

'Same questions again,' she said. 'Multi-coloured, or colour coordinated?'

'Um…'

'I like multi-coloured myself, because I've got baubles going back years and none of them match, and I buy a few new ones every year.'

'Can you choose for me?'

Frankie giggled, 'I can, but you mightn't like my taste.' She picked up a ballerina and raised her eyebrows.

'What does a ballerina have to do with Christmas?' he asked with a frown.

'Nothing, but isn't it pretty?'

'I think I prefer more traditional decorations.'

'Like snowflakes and reindeer?'

'Maybe, but something like that.' He pointed to a round glass bauble painted with a village scene, and a small length of ribbon with which to hang it.

Now that she knew roughly what he wanted, Frankie was off, holding up bauble after bauble for him to either nod or shake his head at. Before long, he had quite a few in his trolley and was wondering how much this little lot was going to cost.

He soon found out when he got to the till and the cashier rang up his purchases. Trying not to wince, he paid, then hassled Frankie out of there before she talked him into buying anything else he didn't need.

It was only when they reached the car, did he realise three things. The first was that he'd forgotten the very thing he was here to collect – namely the outside lights that the garden centre was very kindly donating, so he had to go back. The second was that the tree was too big to fit in his car with the roof up, so he had to take the top down. And the third was that, despite the eye-watering amount he'd spent, he would happily spend it all over again for another afternoon like this. So when Frankie offered a second time to help him put the tree up, he accepted.

And he was looking forward to it so much, that he felt like a kid on Christmas Eve.

CHAPTER 7

Frankie parked her little hatchback behind Julian's car, smiling as she remembered the journey home from the garden centre this afternoon. It had been cold, windy and uncomfortable, but she hadn't laughed so much in ages. Two-seater sporty models like Julian's weren't designed to carry seven-foot Christmas trees, even if the tree was folded into a box. She'd had to sit with her legs twisted awkwardly to the side, with the bottom of the box in the footwell. Although she hadn't been able to see a great deal because it obstructed her view, what she had seen were the curious and amused looks from both fellow road users and pedestrians alike.

By the time Julian had pulled up outside her flat, her hair was all over the place, her nose was frozen, and her sides ached from laughing every time Julian cursed or apologised – which he'd done frequently and in equal measure.

With her hair now tamed and hanging down her back in a silky wave, and with her nose powdered, she hoped she looked more respectable.

Julian's house was in the middle of a terraced street, backing onto the park, and as she got out of her car, she glanced up the road, wondering whether Bill was peering through his curtains, watching her arrival. If he was, Neil would be the first to hear of it.

Each house had a small front garden with a short path from the pavement to the front door. Julian's looked neat enough, with a gravelled area directly in front of a bay window and a porch with original Victorian tiles.

He opened the door seconds after she rang the bell, and she suspected he'd been hovering behind it. When he stepped aside for her to enter, she shoved a carrier bag at him. 'Put the cream and milk in the fridge,' she instructed.

'Cream?' He peered into the bag.

'For hot chocolate. You can't make proper hot chocolate without cream.'

'Can't you?'

'No.'

'You were serious about Christmas tunes, hot chocolate and mince pies, weren't you?'

'I was. I don't joke about festive fun. It's important business decorating a tree. You've got to get the mood right.'

He gestured for her to go into the living room, and she glanced around, noting the black leather L-shaped sofa, a tan-coloured leather chair, a desk with a computer sitting on it, along with an angle poise lamp, and a huge TV on the wall. It was blokey, but not *too* blokey, and she was relieved to see it was clean and tidy. White walls, a cream carpet and soft lighting completed the picture. Compared to her tiny flat, it was sleek and minimalist, without any hint of female presence, and although it needed a cushion or two and a couple of candles to make it feel more cosy, she liked it.

The box with the Christmas tree in it lay on the floor in front of the bay window, the bags of decorations next to it.

'You've decided on a home for it, I see,' she observed.

'It's the obvious place. Can I get you a drink? Gin, wine?'

'I'd better not, I'm driving.'

'You could leave the car here and pick it up in the morning. I'll walk you home.'

Frankie nearly agreed, but being alone with Julian with alcohol inside her might prove to be too much of a temptation, and she didn't want to make a fool of herself. She was enjoying getting to know him, without the pressure of dating him.

It concerned her that she liked him as much as she did. She wanted fun, not commitment, and although she wasn't averse to having a boyfriend, she didn't want to have a serious relationship – and she had a feeling she could get far too involved with Julian if she wasn't careful.

'A soft drink would be nice,' she said.

'Black cherry?'

'Lovely.'

He went off to fetch it and Frankie tackled the box. By the time he returned she'd selected her favourite festive playlist on her phone (yes, she had more than one Christmas playlist – *don't judge me*, she thought), had removed the tree from its cardboard prison and had put it together, and was now in the middle of tweaking the individual branches into place.

'I haven't plugged it in yet. I thought I'd let you do the honours, since it's your tree.' She felt rather guilty for railroading him into buying it, especially when she'd seen how much it had all cost.

No wonder he'd flinched. Frankie would have cried.

Consoling herself with the knowledge that the tree and its decorations would last for many Christmases to come, she handed him the plug and stood back.

Julian put it into the wall socket, pressed the switch and—

'Bloody hell, it's like a nightclub in here!' he exclaimed, as the lights flashed on and off in a frenzy.

Frankie hastily crouched down and scrabbled around for the remote control that had come with it. 'Try this,' she said, shoving it into his hand.

After going through the light sequences a couple of times, he settled for a gentle fade in and fade out, before switching them off again.

'Now for the fun bit,' she announced, picking up one of the bags and carefully emptying the contents onto the sofa.

When Julian grabbed a large angel and hooked the ribbon over a branch at approximately shoulder height, Frankie let out a shriek.

'Not there!' she cried, then giggled at the alarm on his face.

'Why not?' He looked at the bauble in his hand, then looked at the tree.

'Bigger ones at the bottom, smaller on the top. It's all about the balance.'

'You've put a lot of thought into this, haven't you? Here?' He chose a lower branch.

Frankie frowned. 'Do you mind if we sort them all into size order first?'

'Good grief,' he muttered. 'I think I'm going to need something stronger than cordial!'

'Don't abstain on my account.'

'I bought the gin for you.'

'For *me?*'

'I didn't know whether you liked wine, so I picked up a bottle of gin after I dropped you off earlier.'

Frankie was touched. As she emptied another bag, she said, 'That's very thoughtful. Save it for another time though? As I said in the pub, I don't drink an awful lot and I've got work tomorrow. But there's nothing stopping you from having a glass.'

Julian shuddered. 'I can't stand the stuff.'

'Maybe it's the tonic you don't like? It can be rather bitter. Try adding it to the cordial.'

'Interesting combo,' he said, 'but I think I'll pass.'

Yeah, she didn't blame him: that wasn't her best idea. She said, 'If I sort the decorations by size, would you like to start hanging them?'

'Do you trust me to do it properly?'

She laughed. 'I'll have to – it's *your* tree.'

'But you'll rearrange them if I don't do it right?'

'It's a possibility.'

Julian grinned. 'It's more than a possibility. It's a certainty.'

'I can't help it if I'm a perfectionist,' she shot back. 'Put this one there.'

'I thought *I* was going to decide where to hang them?'

'I didn't say that.'

'You implied it.'

'You must have misunderstood.' She flashed him a cheeky grin.

For the next half an hour they worked steadily (with some considerable rearranging) until Frankie declared herself satisfied.

'Thank God for that!' Julian exclaimed. 'If I'd known that putting up a tree was so exacting, I'm not sure I would have bought it.'

Frankie studied him. There was something about his statement that bothered her. 'Have you never decorated a tree?'

'Never.'

'Always got someone else to do your dirty work for you, eh?'

'Something like that.'

His response was guarded, and she had the feeling there was something he wasn't telling her. Then she gave a mental huff: there were *a lot* of things Julian wasn't telling her, but his reluctance to talk about himself only served to fuel her curiosity, and even if she wasn't a journalist she would have been itching to find out more about him.

Hoping to prise it out of him eventually, she backed off for now. His expression had become guarded, and she guessed she wouldn't get any further this evening.

'Are you ready?' she asked.

'For what?'

'The best bit – switching on the lights.'

'We've already switched them on. They work fine.'

Frankie gave him a withering look. The man was hopeless. 'That's not the point. It has to be done properly, with reverence. And hot chocolate.'

'I wondered when you were going to suggest that. Do you want me to make it?'

Frankie pulled a face

He sighed. 'You want to do it yourself, don't you?'

'Do you mind?'

'Not at all.' He showed her into the kitchen. 'What do you need?'

'Just a saucepan. I brought everything else with me.' She removed crushed chocolate pieces, cocoa powder, marshmallows, a tiny bottle of vanilla essence and a whisk from the bag, and giggled as his eyebrows shot up. She'd even remembered a measuring jug for the milk and a plastic bowl for the cream. She'd also brought two mugs: Christmas ones, naturally.

Frankie held up the tub of chocolate pieces. 'Half dark chocolate, half milk. I crushed a couple of bars earlier because the smaller the pieces, the quicker they melt. Could you get the milk and cream out of the fridge, please?'

Julian placed them on the worktop, along with a heavy-based saucepan, then stood back as Frankie got to work. She loved making hot chocolate almost as much as she loved drinking it. First, she poured half the cream into a bowl and whisked it, then she put the remaining cream, along with a precisely measured amount of milk, a teaspoon of cocoa powder and a couple of drops of vanilla essence into the pan and heated it gently until it began to simmer.

Taking the pan off the heat, she added the crushed chocolate and whisked it into the mixture until it was frothy.

After dividing the hot chocolate equally between the two mugs, she added some dollops of the whipped cream and a handful of tiny marshmallows.

'Voila! Frankie's deluxe hottie choccie.'

'Oh, wow. It looks amazing. And the *smell…*'

'I know.' She picked up one of the mugs and gave it to him, but when he went to take a sip, she said, 'Not here. In the sitting room.'

'This whole tree decorating business is a real thing for you, isn't it?'

'Putting up the tree marks the start of the festive season. It's magical and should be treated with the reverence it deserves,' she announced emphatically.

Taking her mug with her, Frankie walked back into the sitting room. After telling her phone to pay *Silent Night,* she said to Julian, 'When I switch off the lamp, you turn on the tree lights, then we can drink our hot chocolate.'

As the first moving notes of the carol filled the air, Frankie turned off the lamp, plunging the room into momentary darkness, then the tree lit up and Julian let out a gasp.

Frankie sighed with pleasure. Her work here was done. Even if she did say so herself, she'd brought the magic of Christmas to Julian's sitting room.

He came to stand by her side, the music rising and falling around them, as they drank their hot chocolate, mesmerised by the twinkle and sparkle of hundreds of lights.

'Thank you.' His voice was soft.

'You're welcome.'

'This is…' He trailed off, and she didn't think he was going to say anything further, but then he said, 'One of the nicest things anyone has done for me.'

'Surely not.' The music died away. The silence it left behind was full of words unsaid, emotions unexpressed, pregnant with a meaning she was unable to decipher.

Frankie glanced up at him.

He was gazing at the tree, the glow of the lights shimmering in his eyes. 'I was in foster care for half my childhood,' he explained quietly.

'Ahh…' Frankie uttered a long, drawn-out sigh of understanding.

'Christmases could be…' He trailed off again, leaving the rest of it to her imagination. And what she imagined, made her heart ache for him.

She didn't like to ask about his family, whether he had one and if so whether they were still in touch. But what she did want to know was who he would be spending Christmas with, because she hated the thought that he might be spending it on his own.

Frankie would be spending hers with her parents.

The idea, when it came, filled her with pleasure – if she had her way (and assuming he didn't have plans) she was determined he would spend Christmas Day with her and her parents. They wouldn't mind, and she knew they would welcome him with open arms if they thought he'd be all alone at Christmas.

Vowing to make it her mission to give Julian a Christmas to remember, Frankie knew she would have to be subtle. She hadn't quite worked out how to do that, but she was sure something would come to her.

Abruptly, he turned the lamp back on and the mood was broken.

As he finished the last of his hot chocolate (Frankie had drank all of hers during *Silent Night*), she thought his eyes looked unnaturally bright and she hoped she hadn't upset him.

It hadn't been her intention, and she felt bad about bulldozing him into buying a tree and then inviting herself to his place to decorate it.

'Right then,' she said. 'If there's nothing else I can help you decorate, I'd better be going.'

Julian pressed his lips together and nodded, not meeting her eye.

'See you Saturday,' she said.

That got his attention. 'Saturday?'

'Aren't you helping Gavin?'

'As I've said, I'm no good at DIY.'

'You can lift a pallet,' she pointed out.

'I suppose.'

'I'll see you there. I want to do a couple of interviews and take a photo or two.' And when he looked alarmed, she added, 'Not of you – unless you want me to?'

'No thanks.'

'I thought not. The last thing a spy wants is to have his face in the papers.' She smiled to show she was joking. 'And if you get bored before Saturday, give me a ring.'

'Why?' His tone was cautious.

'Because you've got a front door in sore need of a wreath, and I'm sure we can find a few more festive bits and pieces to adorn your house. A light-up metal reindeer, perhaps?'

'God no! You like spending other people's money, don't you?'

'It beats spending my own!'

'I bet.'

She shrugged on her coat, and he said, 'If you give me a minute, I'll wash up your whisk and bowl.'

'No rush. You can give them to me on Saturday, if I don't see you before.'

A tentative expression stole across his face. 'I haven't put you off, then?'

Frankie frowned. 'What do you mean?'

'Nothing. Forget it. I'll see you out.'

It was only when she was driving away did it occur to her that he was worried that telling her he'd spent his childhood in care might make her not want to see him again.

Frankie had intended to go home, but she suddenly had a change of plan. She needed to talk to her mum.

***

'What are you doing here at this time of night?' Yvonne demanded when she saw her daughter on the doorstep. 'What's wrong?'

'Nothing's wrong, and what do you mean "this time of night"? It's only nine-thirty.'

'When you get to our age, nine-thirty is practically the middle of the night. To what do we owe the pleasure?'

Frankie trooped into the sitting room and threw herself into a chair as her mum continued, 'I know I was saying that we hadn't heard from you lately, but I didn't expect you to turn up as were about to go to bed.'

'Mum, it's nine-thirty!' Frankie repeated.

'So? Couldn't you have come earlier?'

'No. I've been helping a friend decorate his Christmas tree.'

'*His?* A male friend? A guyfriend? Or a boyfriend?'

'*Guyfriend?* Ugh! Please don't say that word again.'

'Why not? Isn't that what you youngsters call your male friends: *guyfriends*?'

'No, we don't. Mates, that's what we call them.'

'So, what is he? Who is he? Do I know him?'

'He's a *friend*, Mum. His name is Julian, and I'd like to bring him to lunch on Sunday, if that's OK?'

'For lunch? I suppose.'

Frankie could tell that her mother was dying to know more, but all Frankie said was, 'I've got a favour to ask. Can you pretend that it's yours and dad's idea that he comes to lunch because you want to pick his brains?'

'About what?'

'Stocks or shares. Or stocks *and* shares.'

'We don't own any, and I don't think we want to. It's a risky business. Your father prefers poker.'

'Poker? Look, never mind, it was a stupid idea.' Frankie heaved herself out of the chair.

'I don't mind this Julian coming to lunch, but I'm going to need more than *pretend you want to buy stocks and shares*.'

Frankie subsided. It was a reasonable request. 'I don't think he's got anywhere to go for Christmas lunch, and I hate to think of him on his own.'

'I thought you said you want him to come to lunch on *Sunday*.'

'I do. Let me explain. I suspect he's not got much in the way of family, but if I invite him to spend Christmas Day here, he'll refuse. *However,* if he gets to know you and Dad first, then maybe he'll accept the invitation. But to get to know you, he needs to meet you, so I thought about inviting him to lunch on Sunday, but if I ask him outright, he'll think I'm taking

111

pity on him and he'll refuse that too.' She finally stopped for breath.

'Why stocks and shares?'

'He works – *worked* – in finance. So if I say you want to pick his brains, then he's more likely to agree to come.'

'But we don't know anything about stocks and shares.'

'That's the point. You can say you're thinking about investing in them.'

'It's not a scam, is it? He's not a conman, and this is his angle?'

'No, Mum. He's not. And anyway, it isn't as though he could talk you into buying any.'

'Good lord, no! ISAs are tricky enough. OK, I'll prime your father, but if he gets his head turned and thinks that if he buys shares in Tottenham Hotspur he'll be a millionaire by Monday, you and I will have words.'

'You'll keep Dad in check – you always do.' Frankie clambered out of the chair, its squashy grip holding her prisoner for a moment, and kissed her. 'Thanks, Mum. I'm seeing him on Saturday, so I'll let you know for definite then.'

'Seeing him?'

'Not like that. As I said, we're just friends.'

'Are you sure I don't know him? Where does he live?'

'Elm Road.'

'What's his name?'

'Julian Blade.'

Her mother wrinkled her nose. 'Doesn't ring a bell.'

'He's not lived in Sweet Meadow long – about four months.'

'Where was he before?'

'London. Please don't ask him too many personal questions on Sunday. You'll embarrass him, and me,' she fibbed.

'Are you sure he isn't shady?'

'I'm sure.'

Julian being so reluctant to talk about himself might worry her, but Frankie was convinced he wasn't into anything illegal.

However, he *was* hiding something, and sooner or later she would find out what.

CHAPTER 8

A pallet wasn't something Julian thought he'd ever get excited about, yet here he was, on a glorious winter morning, standing in Molly's back garden, gazing at a pile of them and itching to get stuck in. The only problem was, he had no idea what he was doing.

Thankfully, Gavin did, and so did the two teenage boys. Bill had some idea too, as did Jack, and all of them were busily discussing the best way to construct a basic market stall. Julian couldn't tell whether it was going to be super hard or really easy. Or what part he was going to play. At present he was standing there feeling both useless and quietly excited.

Someone give me a job to do, he begged silently.

'What do you think, Julian?'

Julian realised Gavin was speaking to him. 'About what?' he asked.

'Tarpaulin.'

'Excuse me?'

'We've got to protect the sellers' merchandise from the weather, and I reckon tarpaulin will do it.'

Julian didn't know anything about tarpaulin, so he remained silent.

Gavin continued, 'And we're going to need a few lengths of four-by-four timber.'

'Oh, OK.'

'For the uprights, you see – one at each corner. Those are the only bits we'll have to buy, plus the nails and screws of course. We can use pallets for everything else.'

'Won't we have to buy the tarpaulin?' Bill asked, and Gavin shook his head.

'I know a bloke who is building his own house – daft sod – and he only got the roof on last week. Up to that point, it was covered with tarp. He won't say no to me taking it off his hands. Saves him having to get rid of it.'

Bill said, 'Shall I crack on and order the wood? Have we got enough money in the kitty?'

Everyone turned to look at Julian. *Finally* he could contribute something useful. Despite not having access to the funds themselves (and it was right and proper that he didn't), he knew what was in the account. 'How much will it cost?'

Gavin tapped his chin. 'About four quid a length, and we'll need four lengths per stall.'

'OK, that's sixteen pounds per stall and we've got fourteen stalls to date. Yes, there's enough in the kitty,' he confirmed.

'I'll order it,' Gavin said, and wandered away with his phone pressed to his ear.

'Tea? Coffee?' Fiona called, picking her way down the path. She was holding a tray containing two insulated jugs of hot water, Molly following behind with another tray bearing the milk, sugar and mugs.

Julian had been hoping to see Frankie since she'd promised she would be here, and was disappointed she wasn't. Maybe she'd turn up later?

Then there she was, and his heart squeezed with pleasure at the sight of her.

The plates she carried in each hand were laden with biscuits and cupcakes, and she walked carefully so as not to drop any. When she glanced up and met his eyes, his heart did that funny thing again.

Gavin said, 'I've ordered the wood from the builder's merchants. They'll put it on the lorry for Monday. I told them to drop it around the back of your house, if that's OK, Molly?'

'Let me know how much I owe you,' she said, looking to Julian who nodded.

As he nibbled on a cupcake and drank the hot coffee, he studied the people around him and felt a warm glow spread through him. Among this diverse group of strangers, he felt part of something and accepted, despite them knowing next to nothing about him.

But the warm glow was quickly followed by a cold blast of worry that if they *did* know they mightn't be quite as welcoming and non-judgemental.

His therapist had made him aware that these thoughts were harmful and self-defeating, and he knew he shouldn't listen to the voice in his head, but it was hard not to.

'Bugger off,' he muttered.

'I will if you want me to,' Frankie whispered in his ear.

Julian jumped. 'Oh God! Sorry, Frankie, I wasn't talking to you.' Feeling a right dork, he wished the ground would open up and swallow him.

Frankie's eyebrows rose as she surveyed the others, before her attention came to rest on him once more.

He quickly added, 'I wasn't talking to them, either. I was talking to myself.'

'Does that happen a lot?'

'More than it should.' Now she was going to think he had issues. Which he did, but not of the talking-to-imaginary-friends kind.

She said, 'I talk to myself, too. Or to the computer, or the car. The kettle has been known to get an earful, as well.'

Julian wasn't sure whether she was making fun of him or empathising with him. Either way, he couldn't take his eyes off the curve of her full lips.

'Have I got...?' She touched a finger to her mouth.

'No.'

'If not crumbs, then what? I can't have lipstick on my teeth because I'm not wearing any.'

'You don't need to.'

'I don't believe you, but thanks anyway.' She pointed to the stack of pallets. 'Am I going to get any shots of you doing woodwork stuff?'

Gavin had already made a start, looking perfectly at home with a pencil behind his ear and a tape measure in his hand. The teenagers were also hard at it, and Julian felt guilty that he'd been stuffing his face with cake whilst the others had been getting on with it.

'I'd better see what I can do to help,' he said reluctantly. He could have stayed there all day talking to Frankie.

She put a hand on his arm. 'Before you do, can I pick your brains?'

'You'll be disappointed,' he quipped. 'I haven't got many.' It was an old and rather pathetic joke, but she smiled.

'I'm sure I won't. Or should I say, my *parents* won't be. It's my mum and dad who want to do the picking. I happened to mention that we'd gone to the garden centre the other day and that you knew about stocks and shares, and they wondered whether you'd be able to give them any advice. Frankly, I think they're off their trollies for even thinking about buying shares, but what do I know about it? Not as much as you, hopefully!'

Julian was taken aback. That was the last thing he'd expected, and he wasn't sure what to say. 'I wouldn't want to give them the wrong advice,' he replied cautiously. He didn't want to advise anyone about anything. Not anymore. What if he got it wrong?

'You won't—' she sounded confident '—as long as you talk them out of it. They won't listen to me, but they'll listen to *you*.'

Ah, that's different, he thought. He could give them plenty of reasons *not* to buy shares. However, purchasing shares might actually be *right* for them and—

'Please,' Frankie pleaded. 'My dad doesn't have a clue what he's doing.'

She was putting him in a difficult position and his instinct was to refuse, but he didn't want to come across as a git. He could at least hear them out, and if necessary give a reason as to why he couldn't offer advice. He was sure he'd be able to come up with something plausible that wasn't the actual truth — which was that he'd lost his nerve and his confidence.

'OK, when?' he asked.

'How about tomorrow? They'll be around in the morning. I tell you what, why don't you come to lunch? My mother does a mean roast chicken with all the trimmings.'

'I couldn't possibly—'

'Yes, you could! She'd love to have you.'

When Julian had agreed to speak to Frankie's parents, he'd been anticipating a five-minute chat, not a *meal*.

Frankie continued, 'Not only can you talk them out of this silly idea, but you can also tell them we're not dating.'

'Not *what?*'

'Dating. My mum thinks you're my boyfriend.'

'Why would she think that?' What on earth had Frankie told her?

'Because people in Sweet Meadow can't mind their own business. We've been seen together in the cafe and the pub. I've told her we're just friends, but she doesn't believe me.'

'You want me to have lunch with your parents so I can persuade them not to buy shares and tell them I'm not dating their daughter?'

'Pretty much.'

How odd. It would liven up his Sunday though, and he'd also be fed. 'What time and where?'

'Penyfan Place, number three. Be there for one o'clock?' When he nodded, she said, 'Thanks Julian, I owe you. You're a star.'

Bemused, he watched her dart away to hassle Gavin, and he was left to wonder what he'd just agreed to.

***

Frankie was nervous; there was potential for things to go wrong and for her to make a total fool of herself if one or the other of her parents slipped up. For the life of her, she couldn't understand why she'd concocted such a ridiculous story.

Correction – she *knew* why. Because Julian would probably have refused if she'd simply asked him to lunch without giving him a reason. But it had still been a silly thing to do.

'For pity's sake, make yourself useful and lay the table,' her mother said, fed up with Frankie's pacing.

She'd been on tenter hooks ever since she'd arrived at her parents' house half an hour ago. She'd offered to help in the kitchen, but her mum had shooed her out because all she was doing was getting in the way. So she'd paced around the living room instead, occasionally poking her head into the kitchen to check on progress.

'What the Dickens is up with you?' her mum demanded when she dropped a handful of forks as she was trying to take them out of the cutlery drawer. 'Are you sure he's not your boyfriend?'

'I'm sure.'

'You do like him though.' It wasn't a question.

'He interests me.'

'As a journalist or as a woman?'

'Mum!'

'It's a legitimate question.'

'I feel sorry for him. He's… I don't know, insular I guess.' Should she tell her mother about Julian having been in foster care for a big part of his childhood?

Frankie considered it for a moment before deciding against it. It wasn't anyone else's business, and she was under the impression that he wouldn't like it to be general knowledge. Silly of him to mention it to a journalist, she mused, but perhaps he didn't consider it to be newsworthy.

'Here he is,' she declared, spotting him walking along the street. 'Dad, stick to the story – you're only *thinking* about investing, and you don't know anything about the stock market.'

'I *don't.*'

'And try to wrangle Christmas into the conversation, Mum, but without asking him what he's doing for it.'

'You don't want much, do you?' her mother grumbled.

Frankie waited for Julian to ring the bell before casually strolling to the door. 'Hi, thanks for coming. I hope you're hungry. Mum's cooked enough to feed the whole street!'

Her mother called, 'I have to. You eat enough for six.'

Frankie flushed. *'Mum!'* Mortified, she said to Julian, 'She's joking.'

Her mum appeared in the hall, a tea towel in her hand. 'I'm not. You ought to see the way she hoovers up Yorkshire puds. I'm Yvonne, by the way. Nice to meet you. Are you going to invite him in Francesca, or do you expect the poor man to eat his lunch on the doorstep?'

Frankie did a slow blink. This wasn't going to end well, was it? Was it too late to cancel? They could go to the pub instead.

Wishing she'd thought this through, she stepped aside and gestured for him to come in, ignoring the smirk on his face, saying, 'My mother thinks she's funny, but she really isn't.'

He said, 'Nice to meet you, Mrs Fox.'

'Call me Yvonne. I hope you like chicken?'

'I do. Thank you for inviting me.'

'Technically, it was Frankie who did the inviting, but you're more than welcome. Frankie, take Julian into the living room to meet your father. They can talk balls while I finish seeing to lunch.'

Frankie blew out her cheeks. 'She doesn't mean that the way it sounds. My dad loves sport, especially when it involves balls: football, rugby, tennis, golf, snooker…' She led him into the living room where her father was watching darts.

'And sharp pointy things?' Julian whispered. 'I hope it's not symbolic.'

'I doubt it. Dad, say hi to Julian Blade. Julian, this is my father, Arnold.'

Her dad got to his feet. 'Arnie, the name's *Arnie.*' He held out a hand. 'Nice to meet you.'

'Your daughter and I are friends,' Julian said, shaking it.

'I'm glad to hear it. I wouldn't like to think of her asking total strangers to lunch.'

'No, I—' Julian shot her a helpless look, and Frankie glared at him. Subtle – *not.* Did he have to blurt it out like that?

She said, 'What Julian means, is we're *just* friends. He doesn't want you to get the wrong idea.'

Her dad looked confused for a moment, then his face cleared, 'Oh, right.'

'We're not dating,' she added, for good measure.

Arnie repeated, 'Right. Good. Glad that's cleared up.' He pointed to an armchair. 'Take a pew, Julian. Do you like darts?'

'Can't say I know much about it.'

'Never played?'

'Never.'

'Bowls?'

'Only tenpin.'

'Not the same as lawn.' Her father looked disappointed.

'I like tenpin bowling,' Frankie said. 'I'm not any good at it, though.'

Julian perched on the edge of his seat and sat forward, with his elbows on his knees and his hands clasped. He looked as awkward as she felt.

Her dad said to him, 'Are *you* any good?'

'Not really.' Julian's smile looked forced.

'Do you watch much sport?' Fair play, her dad was trying his best.

'Now and again. I don't mind athletics, or a bit of Formula One.'

Arnie scrutinised him. 'I can see you as a golfer.'

'I've never fancied golf, but I do ski occasionally.'

'I've always wanted to go skiing, but Yvonne is having none of it. She doesn't like the cold. Says she gets enough of it in this country, so doesn't want it when she's on holiday.'

'I don't want what?' Yvonne asked, bringing a pot of cranberry sauce from the kitchen and placing it on the table.

'Cold, when you're on holiday. Julian here says he likes skiing.'

Yvonne shuddered. 'No thanks. I want to lie in the sun and drink something with an umbrella in it. You follow me for that, don't you, Frankie? She prefers tropical to snowy.'

'Only because I've never been anywhere snowy,' Frankie said to him. 'Sweet Meadow gets a bit most winters, but not snow like the Alps.'

'Skiing is great fun,' Julian said.

'I'd like to have a go—' her dad began, but her mum cut him off.

'You'll be going on your own. I'm not wasting a holiday. Or if you're that desperate to break a leg, try that new Snow Globe place near Cardiff.'

Frankie's eyes widened. 'I'd forgotten about that. They've got real snow.'

'You ought to go there,' Julian told her. 'You'll have great fun.'

'You could take her, couldn't you Julian?' Yvonne piped up. 'I'm sure Frankie would appreciate going with someone who knows what they're doing.'

'*Mum.*' Frankie rolled her eyes. 'Julian does *not* want to take me skiing. Sorry, Julian.'

'I don't mind. I'll happily go with you, if you want.'

Frankie was surprised but before she could react, her mother said, 'Frankie, can you help me dish up, please?'

She followed her mum into the kitchen, and once they were safely inside, she hissed, 'What are you playing at?'

Her mum said, 'He's very good-looking, isn't he?'

'Yes, but that's beside the point.'

'Is it?' Her mother's stare was penetrating.

'Please stop trying to matchmake.' Frankie changed the subject. 'What do need me to do?'

'Take the plates out of the oven. Careful, they're hot. And ask your dad to see to the chicken.'

Frankie carried the hot plates into the living room and put one on each place setting. 'Dad, you're needed for chicken carving duty.'

As soon as he was out of earshot, she let out a huff and said to Julian, 'See what I mean? They think we're an item!' Her mother had unwittingly played right into Frankie's hands. 'Please don't feel obliged about the skiing thing.'

'I don't. It'll be good fun. Shall I see if I can book a session?'

Taken aback, she said, 'OK, that would be great.'

Yvonne bustled in with a tureen of vegetables. 'Take your seats – lunch is served,' she announced grandly.

Frankie and Julian obediently sat.

'It looks lovely,' Julian said, when his plate was loaded with food.

Her mother had pulled out all the stops: carrots, honey-glazed parsnips, fresh green cabbage, petite pois, French beans, broccoli, plus roast potatoes, new potatoes, and Yorkshire puds.

'It's a real feast,' he added.

Her mother winked at her. 'All that's lacking are the pigs in blankets and the crackers, and this could be a Christmas dinner. We don't usually bother with a turkey; we have chicken and a joint of pork instead. Do you have turkey, Julian?'

He hesitated, a forkful of food halfway to his mouth. 'No.'

'What *do* you have?'

'It depends on what I fancy,' he replied.

Yvonne's eyebrows rose. 'Do you do the cooking in your house?'

'I have to, otherwise I wouldn't eat. If I don't fancy cooking, I'll have a meal out or a takeaway.'

Frankie caught her mother's gaze, and she looked down, pretending to concentrate on her meal.

Her dad took up the baton. 'Is it just you, or…?' He left the rest of the sentence hanging.

'Yep, just me.'

Arnie said, 'If you don't feel like cooking this year, you could come to us. One more won't matter, and I'll be glad of the company. There's only so many times a chap can watch *The Sound of Music* without going doolally. Yvonne's parents love it. I hide in the shed when it's on.'

'That's because you're a miserable old fart,' Yvonne said, but she was smiling as she said it.

Frankie added, 'I wouldn't mind if they actually watched it, but the pair of them sleep through most of it.' She turned to her dad. 'You do realise that you're not making Christmas dinner sound very appealing. Julian's going to think he'll be expected to stay til teatime to keep you company.'

Her father's eyes lit up. 'Would you?' he asked, a pleading expression on his face as he gazed at Julian.

'Leave the poor man alone, Arnie,' Yvonne commanded. 'Julian, my lovely, the offer is there. Come to us for Christmas lunch if you want – we'd love to have you – but don't feel obliged. I expect you've got other plans. Ones that don't involve old fogies and re-runs of dreadful sitcoms.'

Oh dear, her parents were really hamming it up. Neither of them would be in the running for an Oscar any time soon.

Julian's expression could best be described as stunned.

'Sorry,' Frankie said. 'They can get overexcited sometimes. They don't get out much.'

'Just because we like to be in bed by ten,' her mother retorted. 'Don't listen to her, Julian. We get out a lot. We both still work, for one thing. Though not for much longer, if we have our way. Arnie will be sixty in three years and he's thinking of retiring, which is why we wanted to talk to you about our investments.'

Frankie blinked. *Well played, Mum,* she thought, saying, 'I didn't know you had any.'

'We don't. We're thinking it might be a good idea to have some. What do you say, Julian?'

Frankie's dad stepped in. They mightn't be Oscar-winning actors, she mused, but they made a great tag-team.

'Let him finish his lunch first, Yvonne. We can pick his brains later. Anyway, I can't concentrate and eat at the same time.'

'Of course you can't, you're a man!' was her mum's swift retort. 'More stuffing, anyone?'

CHAPTER 9

That was weird. Nice, but weird, Julian thought as he left the Fox house, replete and with a tub of leftover chicken in his hand. He couldn't help feeling overwhelmed by their kindness.

It had been fun seeing Frankie with her parents. She'd turned into a cute combination of teenage girl and exasperated geriatric. One minute she'd been pulling embarrassed faces at their antics, and the next she'd sounded like a grumpy old woman having to deal with a couple of exuberant youngsters. It had made for an interesting family dynamic.

Julian had lots of experience when it came to family dynamics. Over the course of his young life, he'd been exposed to quite a few. And he wasn't sure he'd got to grips with any of them, though none had been as batty as Frankie's.

Might he have a different perspective because he was now an adult? He recalled how vulnerable he'd felt each time he'd been placed in a new foster home. How there'd always been new rules to learn, and new relationships to navigate. Nearly all his foster carers had made him welcome, and nearly all had tried their utmost to help him fit in, but he'd never felt at home in any of them.

The only time he'd felt at home since his mother had died, was when he'd had the keys to his very first place. It had been a rented bedsit, but his name had been on the lease. It had taken several years and total dedication to his chosen profession before he'd managed to buy a property, and even then, the mortgage company had owned the lion's share.

Things had moved on since: property-wise, at least. However, he still struggled with relationships, and although he'd had his fair share of them, none had been earth-moving or long-lasting.

Julian was abruptly struck by a loneliness so profound that it made him stumble.

Looking around to make sure no one had noticed him tripping over his own feet, he carried on walking, his route taking him through the park. As he passed Molly and Jack's cottage, he saw that the lights were on, but the curtains were not yet drawn, and his footsteps slowed. Even though he couldn't see inside because it was set too far back from the path, he could imagine the scene: a fire blazing in the hearth, the dog curled up on a rug in front of it, Molly and Jack cuddled on the sofa...

Julian's house was cold and dark, and he wished he'd thought to leave a lamp on before he'd gone out. As he hurried to do that now, he also popped the heating on, and while he was at it, he switched the TV on for company. It could get very quiet around here in the evenings.

He changed into his slouchies, made a coffee, then slumped onto the sofa and wondered whether Frankie was still at her parents' house.

She hadn't seemed in any hurry to leave when he was saying goodbye, so he thought she probably might be. He hoped he hadn't made too bad an impression on her parents, especially since he'd advised them against gambling on the stock market. Because that's what it amounted to – gambling. No shares could be guaranteed to increase in value, although if you knew what you were doing you could take an educated guess, and there were ways to mitigate the risk. But Frankie's parents were unfamiliar with the stock market, and his advice had been to steer well clear and to invest in an ISA instead.

Frankie had seemed very grateful when she'd seen him out, and he was pleased to have been able to help.

The meal had been lovely and so had they. They'd made him feel very welcome and Yvonne inviting him to join them for Christmas lunch was incredibly kind.

He wouldn't, of course. What he would do though, was send Yvonne a bunch of flowers to thank her for lunch today. And he'd also check out the Snow Globe she'd mentioned, because he found the thought of accompanying Frankie to her first ever skiing lesson rather exciting.

***

'I'm telling you now – he won't come.' Yvonne was adamant.

'He might.' Frankie guessed her mother was right, but she was trying to remain hopeful. She'd gone from feeling sorry for Julian for being on his own over Christmas, to seriously wanting him to spend Christmas Day with her. At her parents' house, obviously. She didn't mean just him and her, although now that thought had lodged in her head there was no shifting it, because she was imagining something far naughtier than mince pies and mistletoe.

Hmm, mistletoe… That was an idea.

There was definitely a spark between them, but whether she wanted to take it any further was something she would have to think about, and she reminded herself that the occasional date might be nice but anything longer term was out of the question. If she wasn't hell bent on pursuing a career away from Sweet Meadow, then maybe things would be different, because the more time she spent in Julian's company the more she liked him. He was the first man to seriously capture her interest in a long time.

'Earth to Frankie, come in, Frankie…'

'Huh?'

Her mother had her hands on her hips and was staring at her in exasperation. 'You haven't heard a word I've said.'

'Sorry, I was thinking.'

'About Julian?' Yvonne raised her eyebrows.

'About work.'

'You're dedicated, I'll say that for you. I hope Neil appreciates it.'

'It'll be worth it when I'm working for one of the big publications,' Frankie said. As a firm believer in the power of positive thought, she was well aware that she'd said *when* not *if*. She was determined she would land her dream job sooner or later.

'Anyway,' her mother continued, 'I reckon you're going to have to work on Julian a bit more if you're serious about him joining us for Christmas dinner.'

'Yeah, I think so, too.'

'I don't know why you're so determined about this.'

Neither did Frankie, but she feared that if Julian spent Christmas Day all alone, she wouldn't be able to enjoy hers. And yes, some of the driving force behind it was her libido. As long as Julian wasn't expecting wedding bells, was there any harm in a festive fling?

Returning to the subject of mistletoe, she remembered that some of the trees in the park had mistletoe growing on them. And there were also several holly bushes, resplendent with red berries, plus the park had tons of ivy.

And Julian had a front door that was simply crying out for a Christmas wreath.

***

'Tell me again why I'm doing this?' Julian muttered under his breath as he eyed the vicious spiky leaves. He'd already had one encounter with the holly tree and the damned thing had fought back!

When Frankie had messaged him to ask whether he'd like to make a wreath for his front door, he hadn't imagined having to forage for the stuff to make it. He'd assumed they would buy it from a shop like normal people, and he'd been quite looking forward to a return trip to the garden centre.

But Frankie had other ideas, which was why he was getting scratched to hell in the park this afternoon.

'It's satisfying,' Frankie replied. 'Stop grizzling.'

'Is this even legal?'

'I asked Molly, and she checked with Reuben, who says it is, just don't pick too much.'

There was no chance of that. Not with this tree's attitude. 'Who's Reuben?'

'He's the guy who saved the pond. A bit of an eco-warrior. That's a nice clump there.' She pointed to a branch with a cluster of bright red berries on it.

Julian sighed as Frankie slapped the secateurs into his hand in much the same way a nurse handed a surgeon a scalpel.

She continued, 'The council were going to drain it, but he discovered a rare species of newt living in it, so they couldn't.'

Julian snipped the slender branch, flinching as one of the prickly leaves penetrated his woollen gloves. 'Ow!'

'It was in the paper,' she added. 'I wrote the article.'

'Shouldn't you be at work right now? The garden centre is open until eight. We could go later and buy everything we need from there.'

'I don't have set hours as such. I go where the stories are,' she replied grandly.

'You won't find any stories here.'

'You forget that I'm supposed to be writing about the park.'

'Stealing foliage isn't anything to do with the Fayre,' he said, putting the cluster of berries gingerly into the bag she was holding open for him.

'It's getting me in the mood.'

'Would that be cold and muddy?'

They were currently in a part of the park that Julian hadn't ventured into before. The swathe of woodland ran for several hundred metres along the park's topmost flank and had a path running through it, which was muddy underneath the fallen leaves. It would have been a nice walk if he didn't have to fight spiky-leaved vegetation with attitude.

'Mum says thank you for the flowers, by the way. She also told me to tell you that you shouldn't have, and the offer still stand for Christmas lunch so there was no need to butter her up.'

'I wasn't!'

'She also asked if you could let her know sooner rather than later. So, *are* you coming?'

'I, er…'

'If you're not doing anything else, you should. It's worth it for the entertainment factor alone – although the food is pretty amazing, too.'

'I'm not sure.'

'About what you're going to be doing on Christmas Day, or whether you can face lunch with my lot?'

'Both. I mean, neither.' Hell, he was floundering about like a fish in a puddle.

She said, 'I'm not going to try to persuade you to do something you don't want to, Julian. Come, or don't come. It makes no difference to me. But it might make a difference to *you*.'

Feeling pressured, despite what Frankie said, Julian dithered some more before making up his mind. 'Yes, please. I'd love to have Christmas dinner at your parents' house.'

'Good, that's settled. Mum will be pleased.' She peered into the bag. 'I think we've got enough holly.'

'Thank God! Can we go now?' His fingers were going numb. Not only that, it would be dark soon. He didn't fancy being in the woods at night, even if night did happen to arrive at four-thirty in the afternoon.

'We don't have any mistletoe yet,' she informed him, and he groaned.

He didn't even know what a mistletoe tree looked like. At least holly berries were easy to spot. Mistletoe were a kind of milky white.

'If mistletoe trees are spiky, I'm going home right now,' he declared.

'Wimp.'

Julian glared at her. 'You're not the one getting your hands shredded.'

'There's no such thing as a mistletoe tree. They do grow *on* trees, though.'

Frowning, he asked, 'How does that work?' Frankie wasn't making any sense.

'It's a parasitic plant. It attaches itself to a branch and lives off the host tree's water and nutrients.'

'So where will we find it?'

'Up there.'

Julian followed her gaze. She was looking into the branches of a tall tree. Some of them were bare, and others had clumps of leaves clustered together where they forked.

'I'm not climbing up there.'

'It is a bit high,' she agreed.

'Garden centre it is, then,' he said happily.

'Nuh-uh. There's sure to be some growing lower down.' Frankie sauntered off, scanning the branches overhead.

Julian trailed behind her reluctantly.

'Here we go!' she cried, coming to a halt in front of a much smaller tree. Orange berries clung to its mostly bare branches.

'What are those?' he asked, pointing to them.

'It's a rowan tree.'

No spikey leaves he noticed. 'Why can't we use these instead of holly berries?'

'Because we need holly *leaves*. Our wreaths won't be the same without holly leaves.'

'Do you hate your postman that much?'

She narrowed her eyes and stuck out her tongue. 'Are you going to pick some mistletoe or not?'

'No, it's too high.' Even standing on tiptoe and stretching as far as he could, he wasn't going to reach.

'Can't you climb it?' she asked.

'Can't *you?*' he countered.

'I don't like heights.'

'What makes you think *I* do?'

'You're tall.'

Julian barked out a laugh. 'You'll be asking me what the weather's like up here, next. Don't bother, I've heard all the jokes. And FYI, being tall does *not* mean you like heights. Think about it, if I keel over I've got further to fall than you, plus it'll hurt more and there's a greater risk of injury.'

'You're not going to climb it, are you?'

'Not a chance.'

Frankie pressed her lips together and stared longingly at the mistletoe above their heads.

Julian wasn't swayed – there was no way he was climbing a tree, and as there wasn't a ladder handy, she was going to have to do without.

Or *was* she…?

'I've got an idea,' he said. 'How much do you want it?'

'It depends on what you have in mind.'

'Have you ever been to Glastonbury?'

'Er, no.'

'Any music festival?'

'One or two. Look, what's that got to do with mistletoe?'

Julian tapped himself on the shoulder. It took her a second or two to get his meaning, and when she did her eyes widened and she shook her head.

'Why not?' he asked.

'You might drop me!'

'I won't.'

'What if you can't take my weight?'

'I'll put my back out,' he replied deadpan.

'I'm not *that* heavy!' Frankie's outraged expression made him laugh.

He laughed even harder when she told him to crouch down. Obediently, he sank onto his haunches and planted his hands on the leaf-strewn path for balance. Frankie straddled the back of his neck and carefully lowered herself onto his shoulders.

Julian eased back and slowly straightened, his knees and thighs protesting. Bloody hell, he hadn't realised he was so out of shape. Time to get back to the gym. He hadn't been in months. He shouldn't have joked about putting his back out, because it was now looking like a real possibility.

'Can you not squeeze so tight?' he gasped. Her legs were on either side of his neck, and her thighs had him in a death grip. He couldn't work out whether she was trying to strangle him or break his neck. Either way, it was bloody uncomfortable.

'Sorry.' She loosened her grip, her fingers digging into his scalp instead, as she tried to keep her balance.

Julian began to worry she might rip the top of his head off. 'I've got you,' he wheezed, putting his hands on her thighs to steady her.

'Please don't drop me.'

'I'll try not to.'

'That doesn't inspire me with confidence.'

'You'll be fine,' he said, with more conviction than he felt. 'I'm going to take a step, so brace yourself.'

Frankie's bracing consisted of strangling him in a headlock again. Gritting his teeth and praying they wouldn't topple over, he took a tentative step, then almost unbalanced when she let out an almighty shriek.

'Bloody hell!' he cried.

'My hat!'

'What about it?'

'The tree has got it. Don't move, I'm going to…'

She shifted her weight, and he grunted. 'What are you doing?'

'Getting my hat. It was caught on a branch. There, got it.'

'Can I move now?'

'Yes, I'm good.'

Julian shuffled forward one step, then another, until they were directly beneath a ball of mistletoe.

'Pass me the secateurs,' she instructed, and he let go of her leg to reach into his pocket, passing them up to her. 'Are you OK?' she asked.

'I'm fine.'

'I'm not too heavy?'

'Get on with it.'

'I *am* too heavy. Do you want to put me down?'

No, he didn't, despite the strain on his shoulders and the ache in his neck. If he wasn't so damned uncomfortable and it wasn't so cold, he could have stayed like this for a good couple of hours. Maybe for the rest of the day.

It was a concern.

'Get on with it,' he repeated.

'OK, keep your hair on. No need to growl.'

There was some rustling, and she jostled a bit, then a clump of mistletoe landed at his feet. 'All done. You can put me down now.'

What if he didn't want to? 'OK, hold tight,' he said instead, and lowered himself awkwardly into a crouch.

Frankie dismounted, backing away and shaking out her legs. 'I've got cramp in my thighs.'

Julian glanced at them. Two seconds ago, he'd had his hands on those very legs. Swallowing, he said, '*Now* can we go?'

'Nope. Ivy.'

He pulled a face. 'God, help me. Where do we find ivy?'

'Here.' She tugged at a strand which was wrapped around a tree. 'There's some on the ground. We'll need a couple of metres, say six in all.'

'You've got the secateurs,' he reminded her, opening the bag and scooping up the fallen mistletoe. He continued to hold it open for the lengths of ivy.

'Good. Let's go,' he urged, when she placed the last piece of ivy into it.

'Not so fast,' she said.

Julian groaned. 'What now?'

'Pinecones.'

'*What?* You're kidding me? It's nearly four o'clock.' He glanced around anxiously. Under the canopy, it was getting dark fast.

'It won't take long and it's on our way home. There's a huge conifer near Molly's house, and a couple of oak trees. If the squirrels haven't stashed them all, we might find an acorn or two.'

Thankful that they were leaving the woodland, Julian picked up the bag. 'Lead the way,' he said, wondering whether the cafe was still open. A mug of hot coffee would go down a treat.

Twenty minutes, several pinecones and a handful of difficult-to-find acorns later, Julian discovered that the cafe was closed.

Disappointed he said, 'It doesn't matter, I'll be home in five minutes.'

'More like fifteen for me. I walked.'

'In that case, you must come back to mine and warm up. I bet you're freezing. Have a hot drink, then I'll drive you home.'

'Or you could drive me home now, stay for tea, and we could crack on with making the wreaths?'

'Do you think I'm incapable of feeding myself?' he asked. She seemed to be forever suggesting food.

'Not at all. I expect you to help me cook, if you're going to be eating it.'

'Fair enough. Although I *did* do the lion's share of collecting the stuff for the wreath. I've got the scratched hands, the aching shoulders and the sore neck to prove it.'

'You can't cook, can you?'

'I can too!'

'Prove it.'

'I walked right into that.'

146

'So you did. We're having bangers and mash, with onion gravy.'

Real comfort food, he thought. 'What would you want me to do?'

'Chop the onions. I hate doing it. Makes me cry.'

'I can do that.'

'Make me cry?'

'Chop the onions, silly,' he replied, never once imagining that in the not-too-distant future, crying was *exactly* what he would make her do.

CHAPTER 10

'So,' Julian began as he sliced into an onion, 'do you always make your own wreaths?'

Frankie nodded. 'And if I had a staircase and a mantlepiece I'd make garlands for those as well.' She looked at him hopefully and was disappointed when he shook his head.

'No. Definitely not. You've already talked me into a Christmas tree and a wreath. Enough is enough.'

'You can't have too much Christmas.' She was positive about that.

'Yeah, so I see,' he said.

Frankie had to admit that she did tend to go overboard when it came to the festive season – even the kitchen had some decorations and Christmassy bits and pieces. OK, more than some, she conceded. But it was such a wonderful time of year that it needed to be celebrated properly, and for Frankie, the run-up to Christmas was as exciting as the big day itself.

'I know you said that you don't want to be writing about fayres in parks for the rest of your life, but reporting on the Festive Fayre must be right up your street,' he said.

He was blinking furiously and Frankie felt sorry for him. But not sorry enough to relieve him of his onion-chopping duty.

'It is,' she agreed, 'but unfortunately Sweet Meadow's Festive Fayre isn't going to be of much interest beyond the town itself. That's why I'm always looking for something else – a different angle or focus. The problem is, I'm all out of ideas, which is why I was hoping you were a spy or an assassin,' she added with a laugh, as she scooped the chopped onions into the frying pan. 'That would have been a coup. The world's most dangerous assassin discovered hiding out in a small Welsh town.'

'You do realise that if you discovered my identity, I'd be forced to kill you?'

'OK, maybe not an assassin. A spy who's in the witness protection programme?'

'Same thing, except it wouldn't be me who you'd be in danger from, it would be from the foreign governments who I've been spying on. They'd kidnap and torture you to get to me.'

Frankie chuckled. 'That escalated quickly.'

'Yeah, you'd best stick to reporting on when the gritters will be out next.'

'The gritters?'

'It's supposed to dip below freezing in the next day or so. The roads will be icy.'

'Did you know that gritters have names?' she asked.

'Like what?'

'*A View to a Chill, Grit and Bear It, Blizzard of Oz…*'

'You're joking!'

She shook her head. 'It's a thing. My favourite is *Skid Vicious.*'

'Dear Lord.' Julian looked incredulous. 'It's quite witty, though.'

'Do you have a name for your car?' she asked.

'No one in their right mind names their car.' He paused. 'Please don't tell me you do?'

'Peapod.' Frankie finished frying the onions and began to make the gravy. The sausages were warming under the grill, and the potatoes were ready for mashing.

'Good grief,' he groaned.

'It suits her. She's little and green.'

'You're weird.'

Frankie grinned at him. 'But in a nice way. We'll have to think of a name for yours.'

'Absolutely not. I refuse to name my car.'

'What if I think up some names and you can say yes or no?'

'I won't answer you.'

'Aw, go on, it's just a game. Or don't you like games?' With the gravy made, she was ready to dish up.

'It depends on the game.'

'We've already established that you don't like many sports. Do you like card games? I bet you're ace at poker. What about roulette?'

'I haven't got the face for poker, and I've not got the nerve to play either of them.'

'Because it's gambling?' She put the plates on the table and grabbed some knives and forks.

'You've got it,' he said, sitting down.

'How about Monopoly? You'd play with pretend money, wouldn't you?'

'That's different.' He began to eat. 'Mmm, this is lovely.'

'What's your favourite board game?'

'Cluedo.'

'Murder? Why doesn't that surprise me.'

'We're back to the assassin thing again, aren't we? I bet *your* favourite is Scrabble.'

Frankie stuck her nose in the air and refused to answer. Was she that predictable?

'It is, isn't it?' he persisted.

'Words are my thing,' she said haughtily. 'In fact, I challenge you to a game. I've got a Scrabble board around here somewhere.'

'Challenge accepted. It'll be better than making wreaths.'

'Oh no, matey. You're not getting out of making a wreath. We'll play Scrabble after. And I'm going to beat you, so you might want to think about a forfeit.'

'A forfeit?'

'It's no fun if there aren't any stakes.'

'What happened to the simple pleasure of taking part?'

'Nah. If I win you've got to give your car a name.'

'OK…'

Frankie could tell that he thought he was getting off lightly. She could also tell that no matter what name she came up with, he would never refer to his car by it. Time to up the stakes.

'*And* you've got to get a decal printed with the name on and put it on the rear bumper,' she added.

'No way!'

'Chicken. You know you're going to lose.'

He narrowed his eyes. 'We'll see about that. And if *you* lose – which you will – you've got to take all your Christmas decorations down and not put them up again until next Christmas.'

'That's harsh.'

'Not so confident now, are you?' he crowed, popping the final piece of sausage into his mouth.

Frankie pressed her lips together. 'Finished?'

He placed his knife and fork neatly on the plate. 'Yes, thank you. That was delicious.'

Frankie snatched his plate away. 'Good, because we're going to make those wreaths and then I'm going to whip your ass, so you may as well start thinking about names now!'

***

Frankie propped up the finished wreaths and sat back to admire them. The table was covered with leaves, glue, glitter and ribbon. Julian had more gold paint on his hands than on his pinecones, and Frankie had fake snow in her hair.

'It's good,' she said, staring at Julian's wreath and hoping he couldn't tell that she was fibbing.

'It isn't,' he replied. 'But never mind, I'll hang *yours* on *my* door since you won't be able to. It would be a shame to waste it.'

OK, gloves off, she thought. 'I take it you didn't do art in school?'

'I was more into maths.' He didn't appear at all bothered by her comment.

'When I'm done with you, you might wish you'd been more into English.'

'I did English as well, and I was rather good at it.'

'Hmm, we'll see. Can I interest you in a mug of cocoa?'

'Not hot chocolate?'

'I haven't got any cream.'

'I'll drink it without.'

'Not on my watch, you won't. Cocoa or coffee?'

'I'll risk the cocoa, and if you've got a heated throw and some slippers I can borrow…?'

'Are you making fun of me?'

'I didn't realise you were an OAP.'

'Don't knock a heated throw until you've tried it, and slippers are *comfortable*. Don't you own a pair?'

'No, I wear sliders.'

'Boring!' she sang, glancing down at her reindeer slippers, which were now covered in glitter from a small spillage. She wasn't bothered – by the time Christmas was done and dusted, her little flat would be covered in the stuff. She'd still be vacuuming it out of the carpet come Easter.

Under her instruction, Julian helped her clean up the mess, then she made the cocoa while he set up the Scrabble board.

'Mince pie?' she offered, plonking a plate on the table. 'They're the iced ones. Extra yummy.'

He took one and bit into it, holding a cupped hand underneath his chin to catch the crumbs.

Frankie took a bite out of hers, then picked up the bag of tiles and shook it. 'Pick a tile.'

Julian chose one. 'M,' he said, showing her.

Frankie slipped her hand into the bag. 'X. That means you have to go first.' She was pleased about that, in case she wasn't able to make a word out of her tiles.

In between munching on mince pies and sipping hot cocoa, they each selected seven tiles and placed them on their stands.

'Ready?' she asked.

'Let battle commence.'

Julian sounded far too confident, and she wished she knew what tiles he had on his rack.

He paused for a moment, then put down his first word. SLUNG.

As he totted up the points and wrote them down, Frankie said, 'I'm trusting you to add them up properly, Number Boy.'

'*Number Boy?*' He glared at her.

Frankie smiled innocently back.

'OK, Wordy Girl, your turn. By the way, I've checked the Snow Globe's opening times. Are there any days or times you can't do?'

'Weekends are better for me. Now shush, you're distracting me.'

'Sorry, I don't mean to.' He mimed zipping his lips closed and after a moment she put her tiles on the board, then dipped her hand into the bag to select three more.

She was trailing two points behind, which wasn't a brilliant start, but neither was it a disastrous one.

Four goes later, the gap had widened and not in her favour.

Frankie watched Julian as he studied the board: the concentration on his face, the little line between his brows, the way he nibbled at his bottom lip when he was thinking, then the slow deliberate placing of the tiles with his long fingers. Desire shivered through her. Sitting here in her little flat, just the two of them, with music playing in the background and a drink at hand, felt very intimate.

OK, so Brenda Lee's *Rockin' Around the Christmas Tree* wasn't the most romantic song in the world, and the second mug of cocoa was hardly the drink of choice for a seduction scene, but she could imagine him leaning across the table to kiss her and entwining those long fingers in her hair.

Frankie cleared her throat self-consciously and tried to think of the least sexy topic of conversation imaginable. 'Did I thank you for advising my daft parents against dabbling in the stock market?'

'You did.'

'Right. Thank you again, anyway.'

'You're welcome. If it's any consolation, I don't think they were serious.'

'Why's that?'

'They didn't have the first clue about it. People generally have s*ome* idea. They normally want to know which company's shares are on the up, or whether a certain company is worth investing in.'

'If I were to ask you that, would you tell me?'

'I'm a little out of touch.'

'Your sabbatical?'

He shrugged, which Frankie took to mean yes.

'How will you get back into it when your sabbatical is over?' she asked.

Alarm flitted across his face, swiftly masked. 'I'll have to get myself up to speed, I suppose.'

'Will it take long?'

He appeared to be concentrating on his tiles, because he didn't answer for a moment. 'I'll have to study the market. It moves fast. Too fast.'

'Will you go back to it after your *sabbatical?*' Her emphasis on the word was deliberate. Something wasn't right here. Was he being investigated for fraud? Had he made a major cockup? Had he lost someone lots of money and was now in hiding? The 2008 financial crisis had been caused by the collapse of an investment bank and had led to a global recession, hadn't it? Maybe Julian had been doing some dodgy dealing or had invested unwisely.

'I don't know,' he replied. 'I'd like to think so.'

'What are you doing here, Julian?'

'Playing Scrabble.'

Frankie put her elbows on the table and rested her chin on her hands. 'You know what I mean.'

'Hunting for a story? Because if you are, I'm not your man. I'm not a spy, or an assassin, or anything else exciting. I'm merely a financier who has lost his mojo.'

'What do you mean?'

He looked away, his gaze on the Christmas tree, his focus turned inwards. 'I had a crisis of confidence,' he replied quietly.

Frankie's tone was equally soft. 'We all get those.'

'You don't understand. I couldn't hack it. I couldn't do it anymore. I had an… episode, I suppose you'd call it. Not just the one. Several. My therapist,' his laugh was bitter, 'yes, I had a therapist – she said they were panic attacks. She mentioned anxiety, a mental health crisis, or what some people would call a nervous breakdown.'

When his gaze turned back to her, Frankie was dismayed to see the anguish in his eyes.

'I'm sorry,' she said, aware that the apology wasn't sufficient. If she hadn't insisted, he wouldn't be so distraught.

'You weren't to know. I suppose it's in your nature to keep pushing until you get your story. Burnout wasn't what you were expecting, I bet.'

'I didn't know what to expect,' she replied honestly.

'But you knew there was something, right?'

'I had an inkling. You were too evasive.'

He pushed back from the table, making the racks of tiles wobble and she knew she'd upset him. 'Not everyone wants to broadcast their private lives to all and sundry,' he snapped.

Frankie was disconcerted to discover she was hurt. 'I didn't realise I was all and sundry.'

Julian exhaled slowly. 'You're not. But it takes time to get to know someone.'

She studied him, her eyes searching his face. 'Did you think I would judge you?'

'Why not, when *I* do?'

'I don't, and you shouldn't, either.'

'You don't understand.'

'Then explain it to me.'

'I don't know if I can.' He lapsed into silence and when he eventually spoke again, he changed the subject. 'Whose turn is it?'

'Yours, if you still want to play.'

'I'm winning – of course I want to play.'

'Not by much!'

'A win is a win, whether by one point or a thousand.'

'You're jumping the gun, Number Boy. You haven't won yet. Put your money where your mouth is and put your tiles on the board.'

They played for a while longer, Julian's lead slowly and steadily increasing, much to Frankie's irritation, and eventually, despite her best efforts, she was forced to concede defeat.

'I hate you,' she announced.

'No, you don't. You hate *yourself* because you lost to a guy who plays with numbers for a living.' He hesitated, then amended, '*Used* to play with numbers.' And once again the atmosphere grew sombre.

'The Festive Fayre leaflets looked good,' she said, trying to lighten the mood.

'Unfortunately, they don't pay the bills.'

'What are you going to do?'

'I honestly don't know. I can't sit on my backside and wallow forever.'

'Would you go back into finance?'

'I might.' His reply was cautious.

'How long has it been?'

He smiled ruefully. 'You can't *not* ask questions, can you?'

'I'm nosey. I think journalists have to be.'

'I had my first episode, or panic attack – call it what you will – about a year ago. But before that I'd been having issues: I couldn't sleep, I'd lost my appetite, I felt sick, anxious, was unable to concentrate. At first I thought I was coming down with something, but it went on for too long and I didn't feel unwell, as such. Just, not quite right.'

Frankie packed away the game as he talked, glancing at him now and again to show that she was listening.

He carried on. 'I began making mistakes, which led to me doubting and second-guessing myself. And every time it happened, I lost confidence. The crunch came when I was with a client – an important client – and I suddenly found I couldn't breathe, my heart was thumping and everything grew dark. I thought I was having a heart attack, but it was a panic attack.'

'What caused it, do you know?'

'Morag – that's my therapist – gave it some fancy name, but the upshot is burnout.' He pressed his lips together. 'Apparently, I had to learn something called a *"work-life balance".* He did air quotes. 'I'd heard of it, I knew what it was, but I didn't think it applied to me. I was invincible, you see, a high-flyer, destined for great things. Just call me Icarus.'

'Are your wings burnt to a crisp or merely singed?'

'I honestly don't know.'

Frankie couldn't put her finger on how she knew this, but she had a feeling he was too scared to find out which it was, in case he didn't like the answer. 'Do you feel any better?'

He went quiet and she could tell he was considering her question seriously. 'If you'd asked me that a couple of weeks ago, I'd have said no, but do you know what – I believe I do.'

'What do you attribute it to?'

'I feel like you're interviewing me,' he joked weakly.

'I'm just curious.'

He lifted one shoulder in a half-shrug. 'Getting away from it all, I suppose. I did think about an extended holiday, but Morag suggested that I would only be delaying the inevitable, that the problems would still be there. She advocated a total reset.'

'So, Sweet Meadow?'

'Yes.' His smile was more of a grimace, but at least he'd tried, she thought.

They stared at each other for a second, then Julian got to his feet. 'Time to claim my forfeit,' he announced, to her dismay.

She'd been so engrossed in his story, that she'd forgotten all about it. 'Oh, no! You're so mean,' she wailed, as he picked up her lovingly crafted wreath, very warily, she noticed, and she silently hoped that the holly would avenge her.

'Where do you want to start?' he asked, looking meaningfully at her gorgeous tree.

'Can't I do it tomorrow?' she begged.

'I don't trust you. You'll say you've taken your decorations down, but you'll be lying. I want to watch you do it – that's half the fun.'

'You're horrid.'

'You'd be equally as horrid if *you'd* won.'

'I wouldn't!'

Her protest fell on deaf ears, as Julian stood there tapping his foot. Anyway, he was right: she would have insisted on him putting a decal on his car.

'OK,' she sighed, giving in with bad grace. It was her own fault for insisting on a forfeit in the first place. But she'd been so confident that she would win. She'd always won when she used to play with her parents. Or had they *let* her win? They had, hadn't they? Bummer.

Nevertheless, it was a reasonable assumption that she would be able to beat Julian, because she was the player who used words for a living, not him.

Sadly, she got to her feet. Christmas simply wouldn't be the same if she didn't have her decorations up.

'You don't want to take them down, do you?' he said.

'No,' she pouted and gazed at him from under her lowered lashes, hoping she looked so pathetic that he'd take pity on her and at least let her leave the tree up.

'I tell you what,' he said. 'You can keep your decorations if you promise to do something else for me instead.'

Frankie lifted her head, her body tense. If he asked her to do anything remotely sexual, she'd shove that wreath so far up his backside that he would be spitting berries for a week! She might fancy him rotten, but there were limits.

'Take me shopping for a Christmas jumper,' he said. 'If I'm going to be having Christmas dinner at your mum and dad's house, then the least I can do is make an effort to look festive on the day.'

Frankie's spirits lifted. 'I could kiss you!' she exclaimed. 'Going shopping for a Christmas jumper is right up my street!'

Then she blushed, because she *really could* kiss him – and it had nothing to do with buying jumpers!

CHAPTER 11

Her attention on her laptop, Frankie put her mobile on speakerphone and balanced it on the arm of her chair. Harper's disbelieving voice issued from it.

'I can't believe you had the delectable Julian in your flat and you played Scrabble. *What's wrong with you?*'

'You think Julian is delectable?' A twinge of jealousy coiled in Frankie's stomach.

'No, but *you* do. He's not my type.'

'I didn't think I had a type,' she replied.

'You *do*. Intelligent, that's your type.'

Julian was definitely intelligent, and Frankie was definitely attracted to him – and not only to his mind. She was also attracted to him physically. His mind was a bonus.

Thinking about his mind, she carried on scrolling. For the past hour she'd been reading everything she could find on the phenomenon crudely referred to as burnout.

'Frankie, are you there?'

'I'm here.'

'You've not heard a word I said.'

'Sorry, I'm in the middle of something.'

'Anything exciting?'

'Not sure yet.' She had a vague glimmer of a subject for an article, but nothing concrete. She needed to do more research, which was what she was doing now. 'Did you know that there's something called a Type A personality? It's characterised by being driven, competitive, ambitious, goal-orientated—'

'Are you describing yourself?'

'I'm not like that!'

'You can be. You're certainly ambitious.'

'There's nothing wrong with being ambitious,' Frankie protested.

'I didn't say there was. But from what you've told me, you could be a candidate for that type of personality. What are the others?'

'B, C and D, apparently.'

'Which one are you, then? Actually, which one am I?'

'I haven't paid much attention to the others. Type A's tend to be more susceptible to burnout.'

'What has got you started on this road?'

'Somebody mentioned it, and it got me thinking how some people seem to have it together on the outside, yet on the inside they're struggling. Burnout is insidious. It creeps up on people and they often try to push through it, to keep going until they can't keep going anymore and it's too late.'

'Sounds interesting,' Harper said, clearly not meaning it as she unsuccessfully stifled a yawn. 'Are you sure you and Julian only played Scrabble?'

'I'm sure.'

'That's a waste of an evening, if you ask me. You go on awful dates, yet as soon as you get within sniffing distance of a decent fella, you play board games. Or was that the problem, were you bored? Get it – *bored*? B.O.R.E.D. not B.O.A.R.D.?'

'I get it and no, I wasn't bored.'

'Didn't he even *try* to kiss you?'

'No.'

'Has he got a girlfriend? A boyfriend?'

'No to both.'

'Then you must be sending out the wrong signals.'

'Maybe he simply doesn't fancy me?'

'Pft! Have you looked in the mirror? *Of course* he fancies you.'

Hmm, Frankie had sensed the odd spark or two, but an occasional spark didn't necessarily lead to a flame. From what she'd discovered these past couple of hours, Julian mightn't be in the right frame of mind for a fling. Or any other kind of relationship. Apparently, a loss of libido was one of the many consequences of burnout. If she and Julian did happen to get it on, it would indicate that he was on the road to recovery.

The thought of being physical with him was a heady one (he was extremely sexy in an understated way) but any such encounter would have to be initiated by him. And that wasn't because she was old-fashioned in that regard, because she absolutely wasn't. It was because she liked him too much. If she made a move that he wasn't comfortable with or wasn't ready for, she would jeopardise their friendship and she might set his recovery back.

Frankie recalled the first time she'd met him, scuffing aimlessly through the park, looking like he had the weight of the world on his shoulders. She also recalled his shocked expression when he'd offered to help Molly with tracking the financial side of things – as though the words had left his mouth before he'd had a chance to consider what he was saying. In hindsight, there had been a quiet desperation on his face, followed by a flare of something that could have been relief when Molly had accepted his offer.

Frankie had also noticed that Julian had come out of his shell somewhat since then. There was a liveliness in his step and a twinkle in his eye that had been lacking, and she wondered how much of this was due to his involvement in the organisation of the Festive Fayre, or was that merely a coincidence? Whatever the reason, she wanted to explore it more thoroughly, because she had an idea for an article that might, *just might*, take her career to the next level.

***

Julian leapt out of bed, keen to start the day. OK, maybe "leapt" was an exaggeration, but he did throw the covers off, stretched, then got out of bed with far more enthusiasm than he'd done of late. He had a busy day ahead: a meeting of the Festive Fayre group in the cafe, followed by Christmas jumper shopping.

He'd been looking forward to it all week, which was mad since he was never usually keen on shopping, especially at Christmas when the shops were filled with people buying presents for friends, family and loved ones.

Julian didn't buy presents. He had no one to buy them for. But perhaps that should change this year – he could hardly turn up at the Fox household empty-handed. However, he knew nothing about Frankie's parents and very little about Frankie herself, so trying to guess what any of them might like as a present would be nigh on impossible. Maybe he'd get her parents a hamper?

As they'd frequently done over the past few days, his thoughts lingered on Frankie. He still found it hard to believe he'd confided in her. Apart from a couple of senior staff at the bank, the HR manager and his therapist, Frankie was only the fifth person who knew. And the *only* person in Sweet Meadow. It was strange, but he felt better for telling her. It was a cliché, but it was as though a weight had been lifted. When he'd told Frankie that he felt better, he'd actually meant it.

Julian wandered into the cafe a couple of hours later feeling more at home than he'd done the last time. And more confident. Partly because he knew everyone, and partly because he'd been helping Bill construct the countertops for the stalls, ready for them to be put together. The construction had consisted of Julian being told what to do by Bill, while Bill supervised. It was work that needed to be done ahead of the final job of putting the stalls together a few days before the Fayre.

Julian was pleased to see Frankie already there, and after he'd ordered a drink, he sat down next to her. Sitting on the other side of her was a woman he didn't know. Roughly the same age as Frankie, she was small, dark and vivacious, and was wearing a pair of beige overalls.

'This is my friend, Harper,' Frankie said. 'She's an electrician and she's going to be doing the lighting.'

'Hi,' he said, conscious of the woman's scrutiny.

Harper smirked. 'I've heard a lot about you.'

Nervously, he met Frankie's eyes.

'All good,' she said, and he realised she was trying to tell him that she hadn't mentioned anything personal about him to her friend.

Harper said, 'I would have made her take her decorations down. You do realise that going shopping isn't a punishment for her, especially for something Christmas-related?'

'I know, but I don't own a Christmas jumper, so it seemed a good idea.'

Harper laughed. 'She would have gone with you anyway.'

'I'm seriously reconsidering our friendship,' Frankie said. 'This isn't what bezzies do.'

Harper replied, 'Yeah, but you love me.'

'You're lucky I do,' Frankie retorted, as Molly called the meeting to order.

After updating the group on what had taken place over the previous week (quite a lot, apparently), one of the teenagers asked, 'Is Father Christmas going to be there?'

Fiona reached across the table and gently patted Liam's hand. 'I don't like to be the one to burst your bubble, my dear, but Father Christmas isn't real.'

Liam gave her a scathing look. 'I *know*, but little kids still believe.'

'They do,' Madeleine agreed.

Bill said, 'My neighbour's little granddaughter, Tamsin, certainly does. She's seven. It might be nice to have a Father Christmas.'

'Are you thinking of a grotto?' Molly asked.

Gavin groaned. 'Please don't say that you expect me to make one out of pallets!'

Liam said, 'Nah, my dad's got an old shed he wants to get rid of. We can use that. Connor and I will do it up, won't we Connor?'

The other boy nodded. 'I'm good at art.'

Bill nudged him and winked. 'Graffiti?'

Connor blushed. 'I don't do that anymore. I do proper art now.'

Jack asked, 'Who will we get to play Santa?'

Liam said, 'Bill can be Santa. He's, like, *really* old.'

Everyone turned to Bill, who looked horrified.

Harper said, 'You'd make a good Santa.'

'Because I'm *old?*' Bill spluttered.

'Because you've got twinkly eyes,' she said.

'I have?'

'And you're old,' Liam repeated. 'Kids can tell.'

Molly chuckled. 'I thought anyone over twenty was old to a child?'

'Nah, there's old and there's ancient. Santa has to be...' He flicked Bill a glance then trailed off.

'Now he's calling me ancient!' Bill grumbled. 'The cheeky blighter.'

Molly asked, 'Would you do it?'

'If I must.' He sounded reluctant, but Julian could tell that the old guy was chuffed to be asked.

The meeting broke up shortly afterwards, with Jack having been tasked to check at the council offices whether anyone had a Santa costume they'd be willing to loan them.

'Back to work for me,' Harper said. 'Enjoy your Christmas jumper hunt. I don't envy you going shopping on a Saturday afternoon. Cardiff will be heaving.'

'Is that where we're going?' Julian asked Frankie.

'Better selection,' she said. 'Shall we have a spot of lunch here before we head off? Harper is right, Cardiff will be busy. It'll be easier to eat before we go, and I don't know about you but I'm starving.'

'I suppose I could manage a little something.'

'Want to join us, Harper?'

'Can't. Promised a chap I'd install a couple of new sockets in his kitchen this afternoon. He's got fitters coming in on Monday. You two have fun. If you fancy meeting up in the Farmers Arms for a drink later, you can tell me all about it. You too, Julian. Gavin will be there, so it won't be all girl-talk.' She waggled her fingers as she headed for the door. Gavin, who had bought a coffee to take away with him, held it open for her, and they went outside together.

Julian caught the speculative look in Frankie's eye and said, 'I didn't think they were a couple.'

'They're not, but they should be. What do you say about going for a drink later?'

'I wouldn't want to intrude.'

'It won't be just Harper and Gavin – there'll be others there, more's the pity. Those two look good together. Maybe we can set them up?'

'Are you matchmaking?'

'I wouldn't phrase it quite like that. Putting opportunity their way, shall we say?'

'I'll go for a drink, but don't involve me in your scheming.'

'Not the romantic type?'

'I can be romantic when I want to be,' he retorted, but wondered whether that was true. Romance hadn't featured very highly in his life so far and none of his girlfriends had held his interest for long.

But there *was* one woman who was holding it, one woman who he was becoming more captivated by with every passing day, and that was Frankie.

Suddenly his gaze landed on her lips. They were curved into a smile, and he wondered what it would be like to kiss them.

It was right there, right then, that he knew he would have to find out. And it was also right there, right then that Julian realised he was feeling much, *much* better.

***

Cardiff city centre was bustling with shoppers searching for that perfect gift or party outfit, or simply having a mooch with friends. Every restaurant and cafe Frankie passed was full, and she was so glad that Julian had agreed to have food at the cafe in Sweet Meadow Park before they'd left. She loved the hustle and bustle of the Welsh capital, but she hadn't wanted to have to wait ages for a table – not when there was shopping to be done.

'I'm not sure how much choice we'll have,' she said, grabbing his sleeve and pulling him towards a display of red and green jumpers. 'The best ones will have already gone.'

'When you say *we,* you don't mean *me*, do you? I get the feeling *you'll* be choosing this jumper.'

'I do have considerable experience in selecting Christmas jumpers,' she said, pointing to her chest. Her jumper of choice today was a Fairisle, in navy, cream and red. It didn't scream Christmas, but if one took the time to look, the red bits were reindeer. It was understated, stylish, and warm.

Julian peered at it. 'I didn't realise those were reindeer. Nice.'

'I have more.'

'I don't doubt it. How many more?'

'Seven. Or it could be eight.'

'Don't you know?'

'It'll be eight if I buy another today. We could have matching ones.'

'We'd look like a pair of bookends.'

'I thought we could wear them to the Snow Globe tomorrow. It'll be fun.'

'We'll have coats on.'

'Not all the time. They've got a restaurant.'

'I had noticed.'

'It's called The Igloo.'

'I know.'

'The food looks good.'

'It does.'

'So, can we?'

'I'm beginning to realise that you're a slave to your stomach.'

Frankie was affronted. 'I like food. I like it even better when I don't have to cook it myself, and we'll be hungry after being on the slopes.' She'd done her research and was trying to get to grips with the terminology.

'I was planning on us having lunch there anyway, because I've booked us a tubing session in the afternoon.'

Frankie's eyes widened: she'd read about that, plus the other activities in the Snow Globe. 'We deffo need matching jumpers,' she declared. 'And hats.'

'I've got a perfectly good hat, thanks.'

'With a pompom?'

'No.'

'With antlers?'

'Absolutely not.'

'A Santa hat, then?'

'No.'

'So how can you say you've got a perfectly good hat?'

'Because I bought it specifically for skiing and it fits under a helmet.'

'A helmet?'

'Mandatory in the Snow Globe. Sorry.'

Frankie absorbed the information. If silly festive hats weren't an option, maybe she could talk him into wearing a headband in the pub later?

Or maybe not, she thought catching his sombre expression. She reminded herself that he wasn't as enthused by Christmas as she was, and that he mightn't feel as festive.

'How about this one?' She held up a snazzy red jumper with bands of white Christmas trees and snowflakes. 'Or this?' It was navy with a huge reindeer on the front. Its nose flashed.

Julian shuddered. 'I prefer the first one.'

'I thought you might. Shall we get it?' She held it out.

'You're determined to have us wear matching ones, aren't you?'

'It'll be fun,' she insisted, picking up another and holding it against herself, wondering whether it would be too big. Oh, what the hell, she liked her jumpers baggy.

Julian rolled his eyes and stalked towards the till. Frankie hurried after him.

'Shall we wear them out tonight?' she asked, after they'd paid for their jumpers and were on their way home.

'Tonight?'

'The pub? You are coming, aren't you? You said you would.'

'I think I'll give it a miss. Another time maybe?'

'Oh, OK. No worries.' Frankie was disappointed, but she made a point not to show it. She didn't want to put any pressure on him, and neither did she want to appear too keen. And it wasn't as though she wouldn't be seeing him again for a while, because they would be spending the day together tomorrow and Frankie couldn't wait!

CHAPTER 12

Julian was pleased to see that Frankie had dressed warmly and was carrying a pair of gloves and a sensible woollen hat. The Snow Globe might be an indoor venue, but due to its very nature it was going to be cold.

'Ready?' he asked.

'As I'll ever be. If I break a leg, I'm going to blame you.'

Mildly alarmed, Julian said, 'You don't have to do this, if you don't want to.'

'I want to. I've got to try it once, haven't I? You never know, I might be a natural!'

'You're having a two-hour complete beginner lesson,' he told her, hoping she wasn't expecting to be hurtling down the slope today. If she learnt how to slow down, turn, and stop without falling over, she would be doing well.

'I assumed *you'd* be teaching me,' she said.

'It's best if you learn the basics from a qualified instructor. Anyway, you won't be allowed on the snow on your own until you reach a certain standard.'

'Are you having a lesson with me?'

'I've got a lift pass booked for the same time, which means I can use the slope unsupervised. We'll meet up again afterwards. It'll be fun, I promise. You'll enjoy it. And I'll be keeping an eye on you.' Although never having been to the Snow Globe, he couldn't guarantee that he'd be able to see the nursery slope from the main run, but he hoped he would.

Julian stayed with Frankie while she was being kitted out (he'd brought his own boots and helmet), then he collected a pair of skis and headed off to enjoy his session. Unfortunately, the beginner slope and the recreational one were totally separate, so he couldn't keep an eye on her as he'd promised, and after less than an hour he gave up and went to sit in the viewing area.

Although he'd quite enjoyed his session (it felt good to be on the snow again), the run itself was short and busy. He'd been spoilt being able to ski in the Alps, or his favourite place, Andorra. Skiing outside was a totally different experience, and he hoped Frankie would one day get to experience that for herself – if she enjoyed skiing, that is. It wasn't for everyone. But at least she could now say she'd tried it.

There she was, her cheeks pink, her face glowing.

Frankie was travelling slowly down the gentle slope, the front tips of her skis pointing inwards to control her wobbly descent. She was bent over too far, and her knees were stiff, but she had the biggest smile on her face.

Julian grinned in response, even though she hadn't noticed him. She looked so happy that it made his heart sing. God, she was gorgeous! But that was the problem. All day yesterday, he'd felt the urge to take her in his arms and kiss her senseless – which was why he hadn't gone to the pub last night. He'd wanted to put some distance between them, to give himself time to evaluate his growing feelings for her. It wasn't simply physical attraction: it was more than that.

One of the coping mechanisms Morag had suggested was that he try to take a step back from any situation which might trigger a panic attack– even if it was only a mental step. And although his feelings for Frankie and the re-awakening of his libido wasn't a bad thing, he didn't want to jump into anything. Especially since he liked her a lot. She was sparky, fun, intelligent, and very, very sexy, and he wanted her more than he'd wanted anyone.

Did she feel the same way? He hoped so. Several times he'd sensed a delicious tension between them, a hint that their growing friendship might develop into something more. Did he have the courage to make the first move? What if he'd got it wrong, and she rebuffed him? It was this worry that held him back. Or was part of the reason. The other part was his concern that he wasn't ready for that kind of relationship. His confidence had taken such a knock, and his belief in himself was at such a low that—

Julian froze. Was it?

It *had* been, but was it any longer? He was feeling so much better about himself lately, more in control, more optimistic, and was beginning to feel more like his pre-breakdown self.

And he was becoming restless. The lethargy had gone, his anxiety had diminished, and these days he looked forward to getting out of bed in the morning. His reset button had been well and truly pushed, and the dark cloud that had hung over him had lifted considerably. There was still the fear that it might be hovering high above his head, too high to be seen, like a satellite. But it was no longer oppressive, and life finally had colour again.

The challenge was to not slide back.

Julian understood that being busy and feeling useful probably had something to do with it and might also be contributing to his growing restlessness. But being in charge of Sweet Meadow Park's spreadsheet and posting about the Fayre on social media was no longer enough. Neither were the meetings, nor the stall construction sessions. And as much as he was enjoying these excursions with Frankie (and he really *was* enjoying them), he needed something else to occupy him.

He needed a *job*.

Finally, after all these months, Julian felt ready to return to work. Now all he had to do was find one – which, in a niche market like his, mightn't be easy.

Surely he had some transferable skills? It was time to start looking. Maybe put a feeler or two out.

Movement caught his eye, and he realised Frankie had spotted him. She was waving.

Julian waved back, and her grin grew even broader. It warmed his heart to see it. She was having such a good time and when her lesson ended, those were the first words out of her mouth. The next were, 'My bloody legs are killing me. You never said that skiing was such a workout.'

'It didn't occur to me.' Thinking back, his first time had been a bit of a shock to his legs, too. He'd forgotten that. 'Would you go skiing again?' he asked.

'Try and stop me! I want to have a go on the big slope.'

Julian chuckled. 'You'll get your wish after lunch. We're going tubing, remember?'

'I haven't forgotten, but I want to *ski* down it.'

Her enthusiasm was infectious, and Julian had a vision of blue skies, high mountains and powdery white snow, with Frankie skiing by his side. The image was a compelling one.

He cleared his throat. 'Lunch?'

'Yes please, I'm starving,' she announced, linking an arm through his.

He stiffened at her touch, then relaxed into it. 'You're always hungry.'

'I've got a healthy appetite, Anyway, I'm sure we'll burn it off later.' She squeezed his arm, her smile wicked, and he gulped.

'We *will?*'

'I'm assuming that tubing won't be as energetic as skiing, but it'll be a darn site more physical than splatting on a couch.'

Oh, *that's* what she meant. Her smile hadn't been wicked at all, and the disappointment he felt surprised him.

The restaurant was warm and busy, and after they'd found a table, Julian shrugged off his coat.

Frankie's shriek made him jump.

'You're wearing your Christmas jumper!' she cried. 'So am I. We're jumper buddies!' she chortled, as she removed her coat to reveal her matching jumper, much to the amusement of the diners on a nearby table.

Julian had had a feeling she might wear hers. His cheeks felt warm, and he didn't think it was solely due to the increase in temperature. She looked utterly delectable.

Sitting down, he picked up a menu and focused on it. 'What do you fancy?' he asked after a few seconds.

'I don't know. You?'

Gah! He wished she *did* fancy him. Something about seeing the joy on her face earlier, was doing strange things to him.

'There's a festive pizza,' he said, not caring what he ate.

'Where? I can't see it.'

Julian leant across the table and pointed it out on her menu. As he did so, he caught her eye. She wasn't looking at the menu: she was looking at *him*. Her pupils were large, her eyes luminous and her cheeks were flushed.

He hastily looked away and sat back. When he plucked up the courage to look at her again, he realised she was still staring at him.

'What?' he asked, hoping he didn't have dirt on his face or a spot on his nose.

'Has anyone ever told you that you look like Alexander Skarsgård?'

'Who?'

'The actor in *True Blood*. The Viking one. I've been watching re-runs.'

'No.' He had no idea who she was talking about. *Please don't tell me he's a gargoyle*, he begged silently.

'He's tall, blonde and good-looking,' she said.

Julian's mouth dropped open. 'You think I'm…?' He couldn't say it.

She nodded, the glow in her cheeks deepening. She was blushing like mad, he realised.

So was he.

'I think we'd better order before I—' He stopped abruptly.

'Before you what?' She was gazing at him with an intensity that made his heart trip.

'Kiss you.' There, he'd said it.

'Is that what you'd like to do?'

Mutely he nodded.

'Then why don't you?' she murmured, leaning forward, her lips parting.

He couldn't breathe and his heart pounded fiercely as she drew him towards her, the pull of her undeniable.

His face was only inches from hers when the scrape of a chair across the floor jolted him out of whatever trance he was in.

His half-closed eyes shot open, and he inhaled sharply. 'Oh, boy,' he muttered.

Frankie's laugh sounded nervous. 'Yeah, we don't want to get thrown out. I don't think they'd appreciate us snogging across the condiments.'

'Not the best place for a first kiss,' he agreed shakily. He stared at the menu, which lay forgotten on the table.

'Pizza for me,' she said, following his gaze. 'The Christmas one.'

'I'll go order.' He leapt to his feet.

'And a cola!' she called after him.

Cola? He needed a stiff drink, but opted for cola as well, and by the time he returned to the table he'd managed to compose himself.

'Tell me about Andorra,' she asked, after taking a sip.

So he did, grateful for the change of subject. If there was any more talk of kissing, he might blow a gasket.

The conversation was light all through the meal, as he entertained her with stories from his various skiing trips.

'Do you usually go on your own?' she asked as they waited for the empty plates to be cleared.

'Most of the time. Went with a couple of guys from work once or twice.' By a couple of guys, he meant Tristan and some of his mates.

Tristan was an ex-colleague at the bank, who had left to join another financial institution a month before

Julian had his first panic attack. He was a year or two younger than him, and he was the person who had introduced him to skiing. His family owned a chalet in Andorra and Tristan used to go out there for a couple of weeks every January or February with some of his friends. When he'd casually invited Julian along, Julian's initial response had been to refuse, but he hadn't – and wasn't he glad about that, because he'd thoroughly enjoyed it and he'd skied every season since.

He wondered what Tristan was doing now. Their friendship had kind of fizzled out when Tristan got engaged and had dried up completely by the time he'd got married.

'Doesn't it get lonely?' she asked.

'Not particularly.' He was lying. It had been lonely on occasion, mostly in the evenings when he'd watched couples, families and groups of friends having fun together. But invariably someone would strike up a conversation with him, and he wouldn't feel lonely for long. Skiers were a friendly bunch, on the whole.

Dessert came and went, and they were drinking coffee when Julian realised the time. They were going to be late for their tubing session if they didn't hurry.

If he hadn't already known that Frankie was competitive, Julian would have been in no doubt by the end of their time on the snow. From the second she plonked her backside in the inflatable ring, she was determined to get to the bottom of the slope faster than him.

Squealing with glee, she hurtled down it, her control over the tube better than his, as he too often spun and ended up going down backwards. As soon as she hit the buffers at the bottom, she scrambled out of the ring and dashed towards the escalator to go back to the top for another go. She had a technique for pushing off, he noticed, and he laughed out loud at her enthusiasm.

After they'd had their final turn and had taken their tubes back, Frankie exclaimed, 'That was so much fun!'

'Better than skiing?'

'Yes, because my legs didn't hurt.' She was hobbling as they made their way back to the car.

'You need a nice hot soak in the bath,' he advised.

'Ooh, that sounds good. A hot bath, fluffy pyjamas and something good on TV. That's my evening sorted. Thanks so much for today. I've had a brilliant time.'

So had Julian. It was a pity it had to end. But end it must, and after he'd dropped her off at her flat and drove back to his place, he found he was missing her already.

CHAPTER 13

'Damn, bugger and blast!' Frankie muttered, going through her pockets for a second time, panic beginning to take hold. Where the hell was her phone? She wished she could remember when she'd last had it. Definitely after lunch because she remembered checking that the zip of her pocket had been fully closed before their tubing session.

And she remembered feeling it in the *same* pocket when she went hunting for a tissue on the way home, which meant it had either fallen out in Julian's car, or she'd dropped it in the street.

Hurrying downstairs, Frankie scoured the narrow hallway, then opened the door and peered onto the pavement. For several minutes she trawled up and down the same small stretch of paving slabs, hoping in vain that her phone would miraculously appear. Losing her mobile was bad enough, but what concerned her more was the loss of the bank card that she kept tucked behind it.

'Bugger, bugger, bugger!'

'Are you all right, love?' a middle-aged chap asked.

Frankie straightened. 'I'm fine, thanks.' He gave her a dubious look and carried on walking.

However, Frankie was far from fine. She was beginning to hyperventilate. She was also shivering violently because it was close to freezing and she was standing in the street without her coat. Cold and worried sick that someone had found her phone, she dashed back upstairs, stuffed herself into her coat and grabbed her keys.

The drive to Julian's house was short, but it seemed to take forever as she imagined some nefarious bastard playing fast and loose with her card. She didn't have a lot in her bank account, but she had a hefty overdraft limit, and she could all too easily imagine it going deeper and deeper into the red.

Practically throwing her hatchback into a space near Julian's car, she leapt out and hurried over to it.

Cupping her hands around her eyes, she peered inside, and although the streetlight illuminated the passenger seat well enough for her to be able to make out that her phone wasn't on it, she couldn't see into the footwell.

Julian was surprised to see her when he opened his front door to her frantic knocking.

She was equally as surprised to see him, because he was wearing nothing but a white towel around his waist. Her phone momentarily forgotten, she stared at his chest.

'Frankie?'

'Oh, er, I've lost my phone,' she stuttered, dragging her gaze away, panic reasserting itself. 'It's got my bank card in it. I'm hoping it's in your car.'

'Let me fetch my keys.' Clutching the towel, he retreated to the living room, returning with them a moment later.

'Let me,' she said, holding out her hand. 'You've not got anything on your feet.'

He gave her the keys and she hurried to unlock the car. Scrabbling around, she shoved her hands down between the seats, her heart sinking when she failed to find it.

She was about to give up when her fingers touched something hard and flat.

There it was! She'd found it. With a little cry of relief, she worked her hand in further and managed to gingerly retrieve it with two fingers, and when it was safely in her hand, she cradled it to her chest.

'Have you found it?' Julian called.

Frankie backed out of the car. 'Yes, thank God.'

He'd swapped the towel for a pair of jogging bottoms she saw, when she handed him his keys back, but the rest of him was bare. He had a very nice chest. Very nice indeed.

'Sorry I disturbed you,' she said.

'I'd just got out of the shower. Would you like to come in? You look frozen.'

She was. She was still shivering, and her teeth were chattering. She also felt shaky, but that was from the relief of having found her phone. Her bank account was safe.

'A cup of tea to warm you up?' he offered.

She thought of her chilly flat (she hadn't left the heating on this morning) and compared it to the warmth seeping out of Julian's house.

'Just a quick one,' she said, conscious that by standing there dithering, all that lovely heat was escaping into the street.

Julian padded into the kitchen, and she followed, her eyes on the smooth skin of his back. For a tall slim bloke, he was surprisingly muscular. He flicked the switch on the kettle, then glanced at her over his shoulder and caught her ogling him.

Frankie blushed. 'Sorry about this.' She held up her phone. 'You've probably seen enough of me for one day.'

'Not at all. I'm just glad you found it. Anyway, you've probably seen enough of *me!*'

Not nearly enough, she thought, forcing herself to keep her eyes on his face. 'I'll drink my tea, then go,' she said, thinking that she shouldn't have taken him up on his offer.

'Are you feeling any warmer yet? You've stopped shivering, at least.'

So she had. She'd gone from being frozen to feeling incredibly warm. Hot, even.

She shucked off her coat and draped it over a chair. But her temperature continued to rise as she watched him take a couple of mugs out of a cupboard and pop a tea bag in each. It was rising so fast that she was forced to shed her incredibly warm Christmas jumper.

'How do you like it?' he asked.

Long and slow. 'Um, milk, one sugar, please.'

'Weak or strong?'

'Strong.' *Definitely strong. Oh, God…*

'Do you want anything with it?'

You…

'A chocolate biscuit?' he suggested.

'No thanks. Just the tea.'

'You surprise me. I'm offering you something to eat and you're turning it down?'

If he offered something else, she wouldn't turn *that* down. 'It'll spoil my appetite,' she told him.

'I might have known. Mind you, skiing is hungry work. What are you having for supper?'

'Toast, probably.'

'Is that all?'

She shrugged. 'I hadn't thought about it.'

'Are you hungry?' He held a mug out to her, but when she reached for it, her fingers touched his. Flinching, she jerked away and hot tea spilt onto the floor.

Julian jumped back as it narrowly missed his bare toes.

'Oh, God, sorry!' she cried, grabbing the nearest thing to mop it up with – her jumper.

As she knelt to clear it up, Julian whipped a cloth from the draining board, and when he bent down, his head collided with hers with an audible crack.

The force of the collision knocked her off balance, her backside hit the tiles and the rest of the tea in the mug splashed over the floor. And *her*.

Frankie was soaked.

Ruefully, she rubbed her forehead. 'Ow.'

'Are you OK?' Julian put a finger to his and winced.

'I'm not seeing stars or anything, so I think so. You?'

'No stars. On a scale of one to ten, how wet are your trousers?'

'Six?' She was wearing fleece-lined leggings and in parts they were soaked through. It felt gross.

'You can't go home like that.'

'I'll be OK.'

'Why don't you borrow a pair of my joggers?'

'A towel will be fine.'

'Are you proposing to drive home with only a towel around your nethers?' His lips twitched.

'You're not painting a particularly flattering picture.'

'Oh, I don't know. You've seen me with a towel wrapped around my waist – maybe you should take a turn.'

'I'm not going to drive home in just a towel. I'll get cold. And arrested.'

He held out a hand and Frankie took it, letting him haul her to her feet. She looked down at her legs and grimaced.

Julian said, 'The bathroom is at the top of the stairs and straight ahead. Go get yourself dried off and I'll dig out a pair of joggers. There are fresh towels on the shelf, so help yourself, and if you need to rinse all that builder's tea off, feel free to hop in the shower.'

Frankie wasn't sure about that. It was one thing quickly changing her trousers, but getting completely naked and hopping in his shower was an entirely different thing altogether.

Even so, when she entered the bathroom and saw the walk-in power shower, her head was turned. Her shower was a dribble-and-spit affair with dodgy temperature control. Julian's looked as though it belonged in a posh hotel.

When she turned the dial, she had no intention of getting in it; she merely wanted to see how hot it got and how much water pressure there was, but when steaming hot water gushed out in a waterfall, Frankie couldn't resist.

Telling herself it would be easier to jump in for a second or two to wash off the sticky tea, than try to dab it off with dampened loo roll, Frankie checked that the lock on the door was working, then stripped off, grimacing as she peeled the wet leggings down her legs. Her socks were damp too. Nasty.

The shower was sheer bliss and as Frankie stood under it, angling her head so as not to get her hair wet, she vowed that one day she would have a shower like this.

She could have stayed there all evening, but a knock on the door reminded her that it was Julian's hot water she was using.

'I've left a clean pair of joggers outside the door,' he called. 'I'll be in the kitchen if you need me.'

Grateful that he was thoughtful enough to make sure she knew that he wasn't going to be lurking around upstairs waiting for her to emerge, Frankie turned the shower off and grabbed a towel. It was thick and fluffy, and far more luxurious than the thin, scratchy things she owned. Julian definitely liked the finer things in life. So did Frankie, but the problem was that she couldn't afford them. Financing must pay well. Mind you, a lot of things paid better than *The Observer*, which was why she could only afford to rent a one-bed flat above a hairdresser.

True to his word, there was a pair of soft grey joggers on the floor outside the bathroom, Frankie saw, when she tentatively opened the door. Peering around it, she crouched down, reached out and snatched them up, relaxing when she heard noises coming from the kitchen.

She dressed quickly, thankful that her long-sleeved T-shirt had survived the tea incident, and checked in the steamed-up mirror to see if she looked as ridiculous as she felt.

From the waist up, she looked OK: from the waist down, it was a different story. The joggers were shapeless and far too long, so she was forced to roll them up.

To make herself feel a little less gruesome, she released her hair from the bun she'd been wearing, and shook it out, combing it through with her fingers until it fell in a curtain down her back. Her make-up was only a little smudged around the eyes, so she repaired the damage with a dab of water on a bit of loo roll.

It would have to do.

As she ventured down the stairs, a delicious smell wafted up her nose.

She found Julian at the stove, stirring something on the hob, and he glanced around and smiled when she entered the kitchen.

She said, 'I hope you don't mind, but I did have a quick shower.'

'Not at all.'

'And thanks for the lend of your joggers.'

'You're welcome.'

'I'll be off then.'

He stopped stirring and turned to face her. 'Aren't you staying for dinner? I'm cooking spag bol. Nothing fancy, but it's filling and tasty. I hope.'

'I'm sure it will be.' It smelled divine, and she realised she was hungry. Lunch in the Snow Globe seemed an awfully long time ago.

'You may as well stay,' he urged, 'unless you actually *prefer* toast?'

Frankie smiled. She most certainly did not prefer toast.

'It'll be ready in ten minutes,' he added.

'OK then, thanks. Is there anything I can do?'

'It's all under control. Do you want a bag for those?' He looked at the wet clothes in her hand.

'Yes, please.'

'Under the sink.'

She took out a carrier bag and shoved her leggings and socks into it, then sat at the table.

'What have you got planned for the week?' he asked, returning to his cooking.

'Nothing exciting. Unless something crops up.' Unlikely, she knew. She'd continue to work on her article, though. She intended to pitch it to several publications at the same time, in the hope that one of them would be interested. 'How about you?'

'Nothing much. Gavin says we can't do any more with the pallets until a couple of days before the Fayre, so I'm at a bit of a loose end.'

'I'll be doing more interviews with the stallholders this week. Two are online, but one of them is in person with a woman who makes gingerbread houses. Want to come with me?'

'Will your boss mind?'

'As long as the piece gets written, Neil won't care. Is Tuesday afternoon good for you?'

'Absolutely!'

He placed a bowl of aromatic pasta and sauce in front of her and Frankie inhaled. 'Mmm, this looks nice!' He'd even added mushrooms.

'Tuck in. Can I get you anything else?'

'No thanks.' She stabbed a fork into the middle of the bowl and twirled it.

As she ate, she wanted to question him about how he was feeling, but she couldn't see a way to work it into the conversation without it seeming as though she was interviewing him. He'd already accused her of that once, but she was genuinely interested. And concerned.

Deciding to leave it for the time being, she focused on enjoying her meal.

'This is so kind of you,' she said, after swallowing the final mouthful.

'We were both hungry. It seemed silly not to eat together, especially since I had the makings of a fabulous spaghetti bolognese and you were going to eat dry toast.'

'I was planning on buttering it,' she informed him seriously.

'Oh well, butter makes all the difference.'

'It does, actually. Hot, dripping, golden butter, running down your fingers.' She closed her eyes and licked her lips, murmuring, 'Mmm...'

'Don't.'

Frankie opened them.

Julian was staring at her mouth. His blue eyes had darkened to navy, and when he raised them to meet hers, she was taken aback: was that desire she could see?

Searching his face, she said, 'Don't what?'

'Tease.'

'I wasn't—' She stopped. Biting her lip, she realised she *had* been teasing him; or if not teasing, definitely flirting. They had almost kissed earlier over a different table. Was she attempting to reenact that?

His gaze locked onto hers and she couldn't tear herself away.

Without losing eye contact, she slowly rose and walked around to his side of the table.

Julian didn't move, but his pupils expanded until the blue nearly disappeared.

As she lowered herself onto his lap, he inhaled sharply and tensed, but he didn't push her away, and when she wrapped her arms around his neck, he grasped her waist, holding her in place.

'Do you want me to stop?' she breathed. Mutely, he shook his head, and she smiled. 'Then I won't.'

That first meeting of the lips was gentle, hesitant, a tentative taste, a flutter. But she was uniquely positioned to gauge the effect it had on him, and her breathing quickened at his unmistakable excitement.

Gripping the back of his head, her fingers digging into his hair, she deepened their connection, her tongue seeking his, and his groan sent desire shivering through her.

'Upstairs.' she urged.

Julian duly obliged…

CHAPTER 14

The sheets were a tangled mess, and it took Frankie a stealthy moment to disentangle herself. Easing out of Julian's warm arms, she shivered in the chill of the dark bedroom, hunting for her discarded clothing.

Dressing quickly, she crept downstairs and out of the house, pausing only long enough to send him a brief message.

Had to go. Work in the morning. Speak later?
X

She didn't want him to think she regretted what they'd done, but neither did she want to stay the night and do the walk of shame this morning, because someone would undoubtedly spot her. So, sneaking out in the small hours was the best option. Besides, she needed to go home and change anyway at some point, because she couldn't go to work wearing Julian's joggers and no socks.

Her flat was cold and unwelcoming when she got back, but at least she'd left a light on, so there was that. There was also little chance of going back to sleep. Not that she'd slept a great deal – she had been otherwise occupied.

Warmth infused her as she recalled how thoroughly and delightfully occupied she'd been, and she hoped Julian would understand why she'd left without waking him. Because if she had, she'd still be there now, being *occupied*.

Frankie made a cup of tea, smiling softly as she remembered that it was a cup of tea that had set the ball in motion last night, and as she sipped it, curled up on the sofa with a soft blanket wrapped around her, her thoughts turned to Julian.

To be fair, thinking about Julian was nothing new: she seemed to have been doing it a lot. And she had a suspicion that she would continue to think about him. Sleeping with him had kind of ensured that would happen.

Tea finished, she checked the time. Five-forty-five was too early to expect a reply. He was probably still asleep. When he woke, would he reach for her and be disappointed that she'd gone? Or would he be relieved?

No, she didn't think he'd be relieved. They had a connection – a very intense connection, and she wasn't just referring to the sex. Although that had also been very intense.

It went deeper than the mere physical.

She should have stayed. Too late for regrets now, though.

Restless and hoping she hadn't blown it by sneaking out, Frankie did the only sensible thing. Rather than sit and wallow, she got to work. She had an article to finish and now was as good a time as any.

***

The message from Julian must have come whilst she was away from her desk, because when Frankie returned with a mug of the dodgy office coffee in her hand, it was waiting for her.

You missed a bacon sandwich. And you forgot your jumper. I'm hoping it's not symbolic. Meet for lunch? Or are you busy?

Smiling, she saw he'd struck just the right note, telling her that he wanted to see her again, while at the same time giving her a get-out-of-jail-free card. She could pass up the invitation if she wanted.

She didn't want to.

'Good news?' Neil asked, followed by, 'You could have made *me* one.'

'You're on a health kick.'

'Given it up for Christmas. I'll start again in the New Year. Mince pie?' He held out an open box.

'Go on, then. Thanks.' She took one and bit into it, wondering whether he should be eating mince pies after his health scare. Surely he should be tucking into an apple instead?

She thought about Julian and his bacon sandwich. She should have stayed.

He asked, 'Why are you grinning like an idiot?'

Frankie didn't know she was, and she quickly rearranged her face. Was it even possible to grin like an idiot whilst eating a Mr Kipling's mince pie?

'You look...' Her boss scrutinised her. 'Smug.' His eyes widened. 'I know that look! It's a man!'

'Not necessarily. I could have won the lottery.'

'You wouldn't be sitting here if you had.'

'True. What do you mean, *you know that look*? What look?'

'The cat that's got the cream look. The wife has it after we... you know.'

'Ew. Stop talking, you're putting me off my mince pie.'

'I'm right though, aren't I? Who is he?'

'You don't know him.' Actually, Neil might: Neil knew Bill and Bill knew Julian, and Bill had told Neil that Frankie had gone to St Fagans to drum up vendors for Sweet Meadow's Festive Fayre, so Neil must be aware of who she'd gone there with. She hoped he didn't join the dots.

'Is it that Julian bloke?' he asked, joining them instantly.

'It's none of your business who I—' She caught herself in time, unsure whether she had been about to say something rude or something quite profound, such as *who I'm falling for*. Because she realised that was what she was doing, falling for Julian. He was getting under her skin like no one else ever had.

Hmm, she would have to be careful about that. She had ambitions and dreams that didn't include falling in love. A fling, a bit of fun, maybe a friend with benefits, she could cope with. But nothing serious, not when she intended to escape from Sweet Meadow at the first opportunity.

'You've gone all serious,' Neil observed.

'Just thinking. I do that now and again.'

'Glad to hear it. Hopefully you were thinking about work?'

'Always.'

'Fibber. I'd better get back to trying to sell advertising space.'

'Rather you than me,' she said.

Neil had started at the bottom in the days when *The Sweet Meadow Observer* was the only source of local news, aside from gossiping over the garden fence.

He'd done his stint as a reporter, then as an editor, and had finally bought the paper when the then owner had retired. That was way before she'd started working there, but in a way Frankie had grown up with the newspaper. Her parents had always bought a copy, and they still did, but she suspected they only did so now because she wrote a fair chunk of what was in it.

As she watched Neil trundle back to his office, guilt pricked at her. If – no, *when* she left for pastures new, what would he do? Would he replace her?

She suspected not. He'd mentioned more than once (it was his favourite topic of conversation) that it was getting harder and harder to turn a profit, and that the newspaper was "hanging on by the skin of its teeth". Maybe he'd welcome not having another wage to pay, but as he *was* currently paying her, she'd better stop procrastinating and do some work.

However, as her fingers hovered over the keyboard, she couldn't help her thoughts returning to the piece she'd completed this morning.

It needed one final read-through and then she'd pitch it to as many publications as she thought might be interested.

It was a scatter-gun approach, which hopefully would yield a result. And once she'd got her foot in the door, so to speak, she intended to fit the rest of herself through it, one way or another.

***

Julian was adamant that they took *his* car this afternoon, because Frankie's little Peapod was too cramped for his long legs. No matter how far back the seat went, his knees were up around his chin, and it didn't make for a comfortable journey. Anyway, he was more than happy to drive, which was why he was currently parked outside *The Observer's* office, leaning against his car as he waited for Frankie. They were going to see some gingerbread houses and to interview the woman who made them.

Well, *Frankie* would be doing the interviewing. He was just along for the ride. He didn't care where they were going or what they were doing, as long as he was with her. It was a state of mind he wasn't particularly comfortable with, having never experienced it before. He wasn't entirely sure how to behave or what was expected, or how to deal with the emotions flooding him.

Surely it couldn't be purely about the sex, could it? As amazing as it was, he'd had pretty good sex before. But he'd never been so… He didn't have a word for how he felt. It was disconcerting. But one thing was certain – Frankie wasn't in this for the long haul. She'd made it perfectly clear that Sweet Meadow wasn't her forever home.

Julian didn't think it was his, either. He was feeling so much better recently, more like his old self, that he was also fairly sure he wouldn't be in Sweet Meadow for much longer. Which was why he had put some feelers out this morning, a casual email or two, to former colleagues and acquaintances to test the water and see what was out there.

He'd also been looking through job sites, and the first thing that had struck him was that if he had any intention of getting his career back on track, he wouldn't be doing it by living in Sweet Meadow. He probably wouldn't be doing it in *Wales*. London was where it was at, was where he needed to be. So, for now, he would enjoy being with Frankie, whilst keeping one eye on the future.

Speaking of Frankie, there she was, emerging from a door with peeling green paint, a middle-aged man by her side. She glanced around, spotted Julian's car and gave a little wave. The man followed the direction of her gaze, then cocked an eyebrow at her. Her sigh was visible from here.

The two of them approached, and Julian uncrossed his legs, took his hands out of his pockets and straightened up.

'Hi,' Frankie said, hesitated, then leant in for a kiss. It was brief, barely a graze of her lips on his cheek. 'This is Neil, he owns The Observer. Neil, meet Julian. He's one of the Festive Fayre volunteers and he's coming with me today when I interview a stallholder. She's got a real heartbreaking story.'

'Our readers will like that,' Frankie's boss said, thrusting out a hand. Julian took it, and his arm was vigorously pumped. 'You're the fella with a head for figures,' he said.

'So they tell me.'

'I could do with someone like you to look over mine.'

'Don't you have an accountant?'

Neil shrugged, 'Yes, but he only does the actual accounts. The paper needs...' Another shrug, accompanied by a huff. 'I'm not sure *what* it needs.' He seemed to shake himself. 'See you tomorrow, Frankie,' he said, and nodded to Julian.

Julian nodded back.

Frankie's eyes were on Neil.

'Is everything all right?' Julian asked.

'What?' Frankie blinked. 'Yes, everything's fine. Shall we get on?'

The journey to the gingerbread house maker's house (try saying that quickly when you've had one too many, he thought) was along narrow county lanes once the dual carriageway had been left behind, and Julian, whose car was satnav deficient, had to rely on Frankie guiding him via the maps app on her phone.

'So, what's the story with the gingerbread house woman?' he asked. 'You look gorgeous, by the way.'

'This old thing?' She tugged at her woollen coat. 'I've had it ages.'

'You were wearing it the first time I saw you.'

'In the cafe?'

'In the park outside the cafe.'

'You remember that? You seemed lost in a world of your own.'

'Not so lost that I didn't notice a vision with long blonde hair trotting through the leaves.'

'I didn't realise you were a romantic.'

'I'm not. You looked...' He wasn't sure how to describe her. 'Full of life.'

'And you weren't.' Her voice was gentle.

'Not as such.'

'I thought you seemed weary. Not physically perhaps, but mentally.'

That was the perfect way of describing how he'd felt: weary. Drained, exhausted, everything too much bother, worn down, worn out... He could keep going. 'I was,' was all he said.

'Sweet Meadow hadn't worked its magic on you yet?'

'Not yet.'

'But it has now? Funny, I never thought Sweet Meadow had any magic.'

'Maybe you're too close to it, having lived here all your life. You don't know how lucky you are. It's quiet and peaceful, the pace of life is slower here.'

'*Too* bloody slow,' she muttered. 'Take the next left.'

Julian took it. It was another country lane: they were all starting to look alike. He supposed she had a point. Nothing much happened, but that was what had drawn him to the town in the first place. It had been a complete contrast to London, and Morag had advised that he needed that contrast in order to heal. Living life in the fast lane had been responsible for him burning out.

He tried again. 'Look at all this glorious countryside, and you don't even need to drive somewhere to enjoy it, because there's plenty of countryside outside our own front doors. If the park is too small, there's the mountain, and all the little valleys around with nothing in them but sheep and a few wild ponies.'

'That's my point.'

'The people are lovely,' he persisted.

'Do you have any friends here? I'm only asking because I haven't heard you mention anyone.'

Julian pulled a face, debating whether to tell her, before deciding he would. 'It's taken me a while to get to know people, but that's my own fault. How could I get to know anyone when I hardly left the house, apart from the obligatory walks or to buy groceries? And even when someone spoke to me, I mostly kept my head down.' Out of the corner of his eye, he could see her studying him and he hoped he wasn't coming across as pathetic as he feared.

'It couldn't have been easy.'

'It wasn't. But, hey, I'm over the worst. You were telling me about the gingerbread woman?'

'Oh, look, we're here.' Frankie pointed to a house set back off the road, with a gravel drive and a large garage to the side.

'I can't remember her name,' he hissed, even though they hadn't got out of the car yet and the windows were up. She'd filled in the online form he'd devised and had paid for the stall, but all he could remember was her company's name, Home Sweet Home.

'Ellen,' Frankie reminded him.

'Ah, that's right, and there she is, I believe.'

A woman in her forties had emerged from the house and was walking towards them.

'Ellen?' Frankie called, getting out of the car. The two women chatted for a moment, then Frankie introduced him.

Aware that this was a working trip for Frankie, Julian made sure to say little and remain in the background as the woman showed them around her workshop. Or was it a kitchen? He wasn't sure what to call it.

Home Sweet Home produced houses made out of gingerbread, but with a twist: they were all in kit form and there were several different designs. They weren't just for Christmas either, although the majority of the ones that Ellen would be bringing to the Festive Fayre would be well… *festive*. The kind that was usually associated with Christmas.

Frankie asked, 'I know you've already given me a quick explanation, but could you tell me again why you started making gingerbread houses?'

'My daughter loved them,' Ellen said, pointing to a small, crude and haphazardly decorated specimen inside a glass case. 'Decorating a gingerbread house was one of her favourite things to do at Christmas. When she left us,' she hesitated, taking a deep breath, 'I never thought I'd be able to celebrate Christmas again, but for some reason I wanted to make a gingerbread house. Even though Caitlyn wasn't here to help, it made me feel closer to her. I made one, then another, then another. I couldn't seem to stop. So Dominic, that's my husband, suggested I sell them. I mean, what else could I do with them? We certainly couldn't eat them all, even if we wanted to. The money from every sale went to charity, less the cost of the ingredients, and the business grew from there.'

'What's the name of the charity?' Frankie asked.

'The Home Sweet Home Trust. Its aim is to help raise awareness of mental health issues in young people. You see, Caitlyn took her own life, and if I can help prevent another family from going through what me, her dad and her bother have been through – what we are *still* going through – her death won't have been in vain.'

Julian froze, ice seeping through him. The pain in the woman's voice echoed the pain in his heart, and he closed his eyes to centre himself.

They were only closed for a second, but Frankie noticed, and she sent him a questioning look. Mutely he shook his head. He wasn't ready to share that with her yet and even if he had been, now wasn't the time.

The rest of the interview passed in a blur, as he tried not to listen. He had pain enough of his own to cope with. Someone else's was too much. He did, however, buy a gingerbread house. It was the least he could do.

'Gosh, that was so sad,' Frankie said when they were on the road again. 'I hope she does well at the Fayre. It was kind of you to buy a kit. You'll have to show it to me when it's finished.'

'It's for you,' he said.

'For *me?*' she sounded delighted. 'That's so sweet, but I insist on you helping me make it.'

'Arts and crafts aren't my thing. You saw the mess I made of the wreath.'

'You've *got* to help,' she insisted. 'What are you doing later?'

'Making a gingerbread house,' he sighed, resigned.

The look she gave him was pure seduction as she said, 'Would that be before or *after* you make love to me?'

***

Frankie lay on her side, Julian curled around her, one arm anchoring her in place and a long leg hooked over her thigh.

She wasn't asleep, and neither was he, but she didn't think either of them had the strength to move. Not after what they'd just done. Her bed was warm and comfy, and she was enjoying being spooned far too much.

A loud burble disturbed the silence.

'Was that your stomach?' she asked.

His arm tightened around her. 'Ignore it.'

It rumbled again.

'You're hungry.'

'Only a little. Not so you'd notice.'

'*I* noticed. It sounded like you haven't eaten for a week. Did you have any lunch?'

'Can't remember.'

'That means no.' She considered the contents of her fridge. 'How about tomato soup and cheese sandwiches? Or boiled eggs and soldiers? Or we could make that gingerbread house?'

He stiffened, his body tense against hers.

'Yeah, silly idea,' she agreed. 'It'll take ages to bake and then it'll need decorating, and I don't think I'll want to eat it if it looks good. Tomato soup, then?'

He didn't answer.

'Julian, are you asleep?'

'No.' His voice sounded strange.

'I might have a tin of vegetable soup, if you don't like tomato.'

'It's not that.'

'What is it?' She turned over to look at him. The soft light from the lamp in the living room illuminated his face enough for her to see the tension in his eyes.

'My mother,' he said shortly.

Frankie waited, a growing suspicion stealing through her.

Taking a deep breath, he said, 'She took her own life.'

Frankie didn't know what to say or how to comfort him. It explained why he'd been in foster care, and it also explained why he was so insular. 'Oh, Julian. I'm so sorry. How old were you?'

'Nine.'

'I expect you want to know what happened?'

'Not if you don't want to tell me.'

'You may as well know.' His eyes on the ceiling, he said, 'Once upon a time there was a little boy whose mother was poorly. She was often sad and cried a lot. Sometimes she didn't want to get out of bed, and sometimes she found it hard to take care of him. When that happened, the little boy had to take care of *her*. It wasn't easy, but he learned fast because hunger and fear were stern teachers. He became very good at managing his mum's money and he found maths easy in school.'

Frankie had tears in her eyes as she listened to the rest of his story, and her heart went out to him.

The pieces of him fell into place, a puzzle she'd been trying to solve since the first time she'd set eyes on him. It all made sense now.

Her heart full, she held him tight.

But as she cuddled him, her mind was whirling, and she realised she'd found her perfect story.

CHAPTER 15

Julian studied the selection of hampers online, feeling out of his depth. There were so many to choose from that he didn't know which to pick. Should he get the "traditional hamper" with the cognac butter and vintage port, or the "family hamper" with three different wines and chocolate coins? Then there was the one with champagne truffles and clotted cream biscuits, or the one with Boxing Day pickle and Scottish smoked salmon.

All of them sounded lovely.

In the end, he settled for a medium-priced hamper with a good range of products which wasn't too heavy on the alcohol. He selected delivery for the Monday before Christmas and hoped it wouldn't be late.

Now, should he get Frankie a gift? A proper gift – the kind of gift a boyfriend would give his girlfriend?

But *were* they boyfriend and girlfriend? What *was* their relationship?

Julian wasn't sure. The only thing he was sure about was that they were beyond the friendship stage – *way* beyond. It made the breath catch in his throat when he thought just how far beyond friendship they were. But he could hardly refer to her as his lover, and "partner" was too formal and not entirely accurate.

Should he have a chat with her about it, or would it be too weird?

Deciding that it probably would be weird, he returned to the conundrum of what, if anything, to buy her. Despite having spent a considerable amount of time together since Sunday, he realised he didn't know her that well. He knew she liked Christmas, that her favourite flavour of ice cream was butterscotch, and her favourite pizza topping was chorizo, but they'd only met a short time ago and he had no idea what perfume she liked to wear or whether she preferred gold or silver jewellery. She didn't wear a lot, but he didn't know whether that was due to preference, or because she didn't own much.

Aside from perfume or jewellery, what else could he get her?

A gift voucher?

Too impersonal.

A bag or a purse?

Julian wrinkled his nose. He wouldn't have a clue where to start. Ditto for items of clothing such as a scarf or gloves.

After spending an inordinate amount of time fretting about it, Julian put it on the backburner and logged into his emails, his heart leaping when he saw he'd had a reply from Tristan. Julian had dropped him a quick email earlier in the week to say hi and let him know he was still alive.

Wondered where you'd got to. Got lots of news. Call me? the message said.

Julian hesitated, then thought what the hell. What did he have to lose?

'Hi, mate!' Tristan cried down the phone. 'Good to hear from you.'

'Is now OK, or should I call back later?' Julian was half-hoping he would tell him to call back later.

'Now's fine. I heard you'd moved on. Where are you now?'

'Wales.'

'Hell, man, what are you doing *there?* It must have been one hell of a promotion.'

'No promotion, I decided to take a few months out.'

'Cool. I wish I could do that. Have you heard?'

Julian was relieved that Tristan didn't press him for more details. 'Heard what?'

'Me and Paris have split up.'

'Oh, hell. I'm so sorry. Are you OK?' Julian shook his head as he answered his own question. 'Of course you aren't. What a stupid thing to say.'

'I'm all right. Back to being single again, and you know what that means – party time! Are you going to join me or what?'

'I live in Wales now, remember?'

'Like, permanently?'

'I bought a house.'

'Aw, man, what happened to your flat?'

'I sold it.'

'No worries. If you fancy popping back to the Big Smoke for a bit, you can crash at mine. Paris has moved out and I've got a spare room.'

'Why did…?' Julian stopped. It was none of his business why Tristan and his wife broke up.

'Irreconcilable differences,' Tristan said.

Julian guessed Paris had probably caught him cheating. He had always been a bit of a lad.

Tristan said, 'Come back to London. We used to have a laugh, didn't we, me and you? It could be like old times.'

Julian didn't remember that much laughter, but he did recall a lot of boozy nights after work. Tristan and his mates used to work hard and play even harder, and Julian had been more than happy to tag along: it had been better than sitting at home alone all evening and staring at the view. It had been a fab view, but he hadn't wanted to look at it all night, every night.

'What do you say?' Tristan urged. 'Come up for a weekend. Or longer, if you get bored with living in the sticks. As I said, I've got a spare room.'

'Maybe after Christmas.' There was silence for a second or two, then Julian said, 'I'm, um, looking for a job and putting out a few feelers.'

'Felt anything tasty?'

'Not yet.'

'If I hear anything, I'll give you a shout.'

'Thanks, I appreciate it.'

Before Tristan hung up, Julian heard a voice in the background say that shares in Dragonfly Pharma were up, and a wave of nostalgia hit him. He remembered the company floating shares on the stock market years ago, and how everyone had scrambled to buy them. He used to be so good at this, *so good.* Until he wasn't.

And he'd enjoyed it.

Until he didn't. He'd let the stress and responsibility wear him down.

He had been like Tristan once, although Julian had worked harder. Far harder. And had played less. Because, unlike Tristan, Julian hadn't had the advantage of a father who worked in corporate finance. And when Julian said "worked" he meant "held controlling shares". Julian wouldn't go as far as to say that Tristan's career had been handed to him on a plate, but he'd had a head start, whereas Julian had fought for his every step of the way.

Tristan's offer to go up to London and stay with him was something to seriously consider. If Julian wanted to get his career back on track, he'd have to live in the city, and without a base there, he'd struggle. If he did stay with Tristan for a bit, it would give him time to sell up here and look for something there.

A pang caught him unawares, and it took him a second or two to realise what had caused it.

Leaving Sweet Meadow meant leaving Frankie. But then, she'd made no secret that she would be off the first chance she got: Sweet Meadow was too small, too provincial for her, and with her gone there wouldn't be anything to keep him here – not now that he was better. He had to do something with his life. He couldn't stay here forever, and neither could he let his escalating feelings for Frankie hold him back.

***

Some kind of weird techno crap with *Silent Night* dubbed over it, was playing over the speakers when Frankie strode into the supermarket after work on Thursday evening.

On Monday it would be the first of December, and everyone knew what that meant – Advent calendar time! She had to buy one today (two actually, since *she* wanted one to open as well) because if she left it until the weekend, all the good ones would be gone, and Frankie was very particular about her Advent calendar.

She was also very particular about the pyjamas she wore on Christmas Eve. She always had a new pair. It was a tradition.

Frankie was reaching for an avocado when she paused. Should she get Julian a pair of festive PJs? Would he wear them? Would she wear *hers* this year?

Not if she slept at his, obviously, because PJs would only get in the way.

On the nights she spent with Julian (and that had been every night since Sunday) she slept naked. *When* she'd slept, which wasn't much, because eight hours of uninterrupted slumber went out of the window when there were far nicer things to do in bed.

She was looking forward to the weekend though, because she was hoping to have a lazy lie-in. With Julian, of course.

Frankie hesitated again, her hand hovering over the dark green fruit. Were they seeing too much of each other? She was rather concerned that she couldn't seem to get enough of him. It wasn't healthy. Not when she didn't want to get too involved. There was no point. She wasn't going to be around long enough. Hopefully.

Frankie thought about the article she'd written and had emailed to as many publications as she'd thought she stood a chance with. It was her best work yet, and she had high hopes one of them would take it up. When that happened—

'Excuse me.' She was nudged out of the way by a grey-haired woman in a smart grey coat who picked up two of the loose avocados, and Frankie realised she'd better get on.

She couldn't stand here all day dreaming – she had shopping to do. And she wanted to pop home to shower and change before she went to Julian's for her tea. And other things...

Enjoy it for what it is, she told herself, deciding not to buy any avocados after all. This wasn't going to last forever, but it could be fun while it did. She just had to make sure she didn't do anything silly, like fall in love, because she had a feeling that Julian Blade would be a very easy man to fall in love with.

***

'They always go in pairs,' Gavin said to Julian, as Frankie and Harper got to their feet. 'Haven't you noticed?'

The four of them were enjoying a drink in the Farmer's Arms, and Frankie and Harper were off to the loo.

Frankie felt a warm glow when Julian's eyes met hers and he smiled.

'I can't say I've noticed,' he replied.

'Well, they do. It's like they need moral support, or someone to stop them falling in.'

Harper said, 'What us girls need is five minutes alone so we can talk about what a pain in the arse men are.'

Gavin raised his pint and winked at her. 'You wouldn't be without us.'

'Don't bet on it,' she muttered, stalking off.

Frankie shrugged and followed her. Gavin was right – women often seemed to go to the loo in pairs.

Harper rounded on her as soon as they entered the ladies' toilets. 'Give me all the goss,' she demanded. 'And don't try to tell me that you haven't done the dirty with him, because I can tell that you have. It's as plain as day. When? Where? How? Scrap that last one – I don't need to know *all* the gory details.'

'Sunday, after—'

'*Sunday*!' Harper screeched. 'You slept with him on *Sunday* and you didn't think to tell me? That's a whole week ago.'

'Six days.'

'Stop splitting hairs. I can't believe you kept it from me.' She headed into the nearest cubicle.

'I didn't keep it from you.'

'If you didn't, how come I didn't know?' Harper called, from behind the door.

Frankie took a lipstick out of her bag. 'Because I didn't want to say anything until I saw you.'

'You could have seen me any time. You've had all week to see me.' She flushed the loo and walked over to the sink.

'I've been busy,' Frankie said, pouting at her reflection.

'Doing what?' Harper's brows shot up. 'Doing Julian!' she cried. '*Every* night?'

Frankie nodded.

Harper said, 'He must be good.' Her eyebrows, which had come down a little, went back up again.

Frankie refused to respond to that. Instead, she told her, 'You know we went to the Snow Globe? After Julian dropped me off, I realised I'd lost my phone, so I drove to his house in case it had fallen out in his car and—'

'Had it?'

'Yes.'

'Then what happened?'

'If you stop interrupting me, I'll tell you. I kissed him and took him to bed.'

231

'Woo hoo! Go, girl!'

'Somebody had to make the first move,' Frankie said dryly.

'How many—?'

'I'm not telling you and you shouldn't ask.'

'Did he—?'

'Nuh-uh. You're not getting any more info.'

Harper looked at her. '*Every* night?' she repeated.

'Yes.'

Her friend sobered and her expression became solemn. 'Does he know you're not sticking around?'

'He knows.'

'And he's not bothered?'

'Should he be?'

'I'm only mentioning it because he seems really into you.'

'He's into me as much as I'm into him,' Frankie's reply was deliberately cryptic. She assumed Julian liked her, but it was difficult to tell exactly how much. 'Speaking of not sticking around, I've written a damned good piece,' she announced, spritzing perfume in her hair and on her wrists, before rubbing the pulse points together like some kind of fragrant praying mantis.

'What is it about?'

'The effects of suicide on the people left behind.'

'Blimey, that's not very festive.'

'It isn't meant to be.'

'How did you come up with that?'

'I interviewed a stallholder, the one doing the gingerbread houses, and she told me she makes them because they used to be her daughter's favourite thing to do at Christmas. She lost her to suicide, so she set up a fund, and all the profits go to helping families cope with the effects of losing a child, grandchild or sibling in this way.'

'Oh, that's awful. The poor woman. I must buy one of her gingerbread houses.'

'I sent the article off a couple of days ago, and although it's too soon to hear back, every time I open my emails my heart is in my mouth.'

'I've got my fingers crossed for you.'

'Me, too. I was going to write about something else – in fact, it's written – but this piece is better. I think. *I hope.*'

'What was the other one about?'

'Societal expectations that people need to work hard to do well and earn lots of money, and how that ingrained work ethic can be detrimental to one's mental health.'

'Is that why you were wittering on about Type A personalities the other day?'

'I wasn't wittering.'

'You were. It sounds good though. We're all chasing the dream, aren't we? Few of us are happy with what we've got – most of us strive for more.'

'And that's not a bad thing,' Frankie said. 'But too much striving and not enough self-care is bad for our mental health.'

'I should think either one of those articles could do well.'

'Enough talk of work – self-care, remember? We'd better get back out there before they send out a search party. We've been in here ages. Anyway, what's with you and Gavin? You seem very pally all of a sudden.'

Harper immediately went on the defensive. 'We're not pally.'

Frankie bumped her with her hip as they went back to the table. 'But you'd like to be,' she teased.

'Maybe. I'm not sure yet.'

'You've known him, like, forever. We were all in school together. How sure do you need to be? Just think, when a sparky and a builder get together, their offspring could be baby plumbers!'

'Has anyone ever told you that you're strange?'

'Plenty of times, and they'd be right.'

'There you are!' Gavin exclaimed when he saw them. 'We were about to send out a search party.'

Frankie met Harper's eye, and they burst out laughing.

'What on earth do you talk about in there?' he asked.

'Believe me, you don't want to know,' Frankie replied, as she snuggled up next to Julian. And when his arm came around her and he kissed her hair, she put the article and her hopes for it to the back of her mind – for now, at least.

Tonight was for enjoying herself and that's what she intended to do. The future was for another day.

CHAPTER 16

Julian wasn't keen. Cute films aimed at kids didn't do it for him, no matter how festive it was nor how much they tried to make it appeal to adults. But Frankie wanted to see it, so he said he'd go with her – with the proviso that he could choose the film next time.

It started at six-thirty – well, it would, wouldn't it, because it was a film for little children who needed to be in bed by nine at the latest – so he suggested she have a late lunch at work and he'd do the same (not at work, obviously) and they'd have dinner afterwards, if they didn't fill up on crap from the kiosk in the foyer. Popcorn was obligatory, but they squabbled good-naturedly over whether it should be sweet or salt, ending up with two separate buckets (sweet for her and salt for him), and they shared a large fizzy drink and a bag of Maltesers. They were going to be buzzing from all the sugar and additives by the time they'd worked their way through that lot, so he wasn't entirely convinced that they'd be able to fit anything else in afterwards, and certainly not a full meal.

'Back row?' he suggested as they entered the dimly lit theatre.

Frankie's look was scathing. 'We're not teenagers.'

'Yet you're dragging me to watch a film aimed at under-tens?'

'This will be one of those iconic films that'll be shown for years to come,' she argued. 'You can tell your kids that you remember going to see it when it first came out.'

What kids, he mused. He hadn't thought about having children. There hadn't seemed any point. There still wasn't. He'd have to meet a woman who was going to stick around long enough to have them with first and Frankie, by her own admission, *wasn't* that woman.

In the end, he enjoyed the film, although he'd never admit it and probably wouldn't watch it again. Frankie, however, was on a high after it ended, but that might have been from all the sugar she'd consumed. It hadn't curbed her appetite though, and Julian discovered he was also peckish.

There were a couple of eateries nearby, and as he eyed them speculatively Frankie said, 'Shall we eat here or grab some fish and chips on the way home?'

Eating fish and chips on the sofa sounded good. 'Your place or mine?' he asked.

'I don't mind, but you're the one with the power shower.'

'You're planning on staying the night, are you?' he teased.

She threaded her arm through his and cuddled into him. 'If you want me to.'

'You only want me for my power shower,' he murmured.

'And a few other things.' She stretched up to nibble his ear.

'Like what?' Desire flared as her teeth gently nipped his earlobe.

'You've got a coffee machine.'

'Anything else?'

'Your bed is bigger than mine.'

'Is that all?'

'Why don't we go to yours, and I'll show you?'

'I thought you wanted fish and chips?'

'I want *you* more.'

Her breath was warm, her lips urgent as her mouth found his. This woman was driving him crazy.

All thoughts of food forgotten, he drove home and took her to bed. And afterwards, lying there with their limbs entwined, he wished they could stay like this forever.

***

Just as she arrived at the library and said hello to the senior librarian, Frankie felt her phone vibrate with an incoming email. Longing to read it, but aware that she'd be rude if she did, she pushed it to the back of her mind and turned her attention to the task in hand, guessing that the email probably wouldn't be anything exciting anyway. Neither was this, but she had a job to do, and she'd better get on with it because Chris Jones was looking at her expectantly. He was about to give her a tour of the updated facilities and details of the festive treats the library had in store in the run-up to Christmas. The library had recently undergone a major refurbishment and now had several new features, all of which Mr Jones was keen to showcase.

'We've got a Welsh language section for both literature and non-fiction,' he was saying, as they strolled around the ground floor. 'The Welsh Assembly Government is keen to promote the Welsh language so we're doing our bit. Speaking of the council, there's a drop-in office on the first floor where people can pay their council tax or order a new wheelie bin – but we'll get to that in a minute. I'd like to show you our Christmas Corner first.'

That was more like it, she thought, as the librarian proudly indicated a cheerily decorated area filled with festive books for both young and old, from picture stories for the tiniest children to seasonal cookbooks for the adults. It also had a small seating area, and he explained that people were encouraged to sit and read, rather than simply choose books and leave.

All in all, the library was a well-thought-out and pleasant place to be, and it wasn't just about books. People could borrow board games too, and Frankie remembered how Julian had trounced her at Scrabble. Maybe she could borrow a Monopoly set or Cluedo, and they could have an evening playing games?

Frankie took several photos and made copious notes, and when she thought she had enough for a good write-up, she thanked Mr Jones for his hospitality and headed back to the office. It wouldn't take long to put this together, then she'd stop for lunch.

As soon as she was outside, she retrieved her phone from her pocket. It was a week since she'd pitched the article and although it was early days, she'd already had one reply. It had been a thanks-but-no-thanks response, which wasn't unexpected as she was aware that not everyone would want it. She only needed *one* editor to like it.

Three emails were sitting in her inbox. One was a notification of a new blog post that she sometimes read, but the other two were responses to her pitch. Unfortunately, both were rejections.

Trying not to feel disheartened, Frankie squared her shoulders. There were still a few more to hear back from, so she wouldn't give up hope just yet.

With spirits slightly lower than when she'd started the day, she trudged back to *The Observer's* office to concentrate on the job she *had*, and not the one she was *hoping* to have.

***

Recovery, Julian knew, wasn't linear. Whether the issues were mental or physical, the path wasn't level or straight. Nevertheless, this morning he was dismayed at the return of the familiar lassitude, the can't-be-arsed feeling that went deeper than simply not being bothered. It was akin to a sense of pointlessness, and he felt a lurking panic hiding behind it.

Frankie had left early this morning, her focus on the day ahead. She had a thing on at the library and was then going to see a fella about the state of the pavement outside his house. Thankfully she hadn't noticed his deflated mood, and Julian had been able to keep up the pretence of being sleepy until he'd heard the front door close.

Lying in bed afterwards, he'd stared blankly up at the ceiling until the postman shoved something through the letter box.

Although Julian hadn't wanted to get up, he knew he couldn't stay there all day. But apart from seeing what brand of junk mail had landed on his mat, what was there to get up for? He had nothing to do, nowhere to go, and no one to talk to when Frankie was at work. He'd felt a bit like this yesterday, but it was worse today.

'Stop it,' he muttered aloud. 'Get up off your arse and *do* something.'

Easier said than done when there wasn't anything *to* do. The house was clean, Frankie was going to her parents this evening so he wouldn't be seeing her until much later (if at all because, let's face it, they'd been in one another's pockets for the best part of a fortnight), and the thought of watching daytime TV depressed him even more than he was already. He didn't feel like reading, he couldn't care less what was happening with the stock market right now (even though he *should* if he wanted a job where an interest in the vagaries of stocks and shares was integral) and he didn't have any hobbies. His friends in Sweet Meadow weren't friends, they were acquaintances, and his relationship with his girlfriend was temporary until her career took her away from here. He was one sad git.

Julian fell back on asking himself what Morag would say?

He knew what she would advise, so with a sigh, he rolled out of bed, pulled on a pair of scruffy joggers and a fleece, and padded downstairs to see what the postman had left.

As he suspected, it was junk, a flyer for a local burger joint, and he threw it in the recycling.

Food would be a good place to start, he decided, so he made a plate of scrambled eggs and wholemeal toast and ate it with little interest. It was fuel, that was all, something to keep him going for a while. Mechanically shovelling it into his mouth, he thought about Frankie and the way she relished her food, and he smiled. She relished other things too, and when he thought about her enthusiasm and passion in the bedroom, he felt a stirring of lust. Thank God *that* hadn't fallen into the hole of black despair. It was well documented that desire was generally one of the first things to be affected, so perhaps it wasn't as bad as he thought. He was having an off day, that was all.

Abruptly, he realised the reason. Or what he *hoped* was the reason.

He was *bored*.

As he'd noted earlier, he had nothing to do and nowhere to be, so there was no incentive for him to go anywhere or do anything. But he knew of somewhere he *could* be, and something he *might* be able to do.

After putting his dirty dishes in the dishwasher, he went upstairs to get dressed.

***

'A pinny suits you,' Fiona said, and Julian grinned, doing a twirl.

'I wasn't sure whether it was my colour,' he joked, picking up an empty cup and saucer and giving the table a quick wipe over.

The cafe in the park was surprisingly busy for a cold Thursday in December, and it was becoming a real hub for the local community, especially dog walkers. The humans enjoyed a hot drink, a pastry and a chat, while their canine counterparts enjoyed a complementary dog biscuit and seeing their doggy friends.

Mums, dads and grandparents were known to pop in after dropping the kids off at school or meeting for a cuppa before collecting them in the afternoon, and a couple of joggers usually ended their runs in the cafe, probably undoing all the good work they'd done in the process. The carry-out service was popular too, especially at lunchtime, and when Julian had stuck his head around the door and asked whether he could lend a hand, Madeleine had almost bitten it off.

'You don't fancy volunteering on a more formal basis, do you?' Fiona asked, pushing the chairs back into position ready for the next customer.

'Sorry, no, but I don't mind helping out now and again if I've got some spare time.' He didn't like to admit that spare time was something he had an abundance of. Anyway, he was hoping that might change in the New Year, when he began job hunting in earnest.

It felt good to be busy and delivering food and drinks to tables and then cleaning them afterwards, was surprisingly hard work, because he was constantly on the move and he had to interact with people, something he'd not had much practice in recently.

And he must admit that he did feel better than he'd done this morning, possibly because he didn't have time to dwell. Heck, he didn't have time to *think*, except to ensure he gave the right order to the right customer.

He couldn't understand why he hadn't followed his own intuition after the first Festive Fayre meeting. He'd already worked out that he needed to keep busy, but he'd forgotten it in the whirlwind of the past couple of weeks since he and Frankie had gone from friends to lovers.

And what wonderful weeks those had been. But they wouldn't last, and even if they did, he needed more.

The sooner he returned to real life the better.

It was getting dark, and the cafe would be closing soon. Customers were thinning out as people's minds turned to home and dinner, and after Julian had cleared away the table nearest the door, he realised Madeleine and Fiona would be fine without him now. They had probably been fine for a while but hadn't liked to tell him.

'Do you want a coffee before you go?' Madeleine asked. 'There's a scone with your name on it, too. Please say yes, because it'll only go to waste. I always bake fresh every morning.'

'In that case…' Julian said, moving towards the counter to fetch it.

'Sit down, I'll bring it to you.'

He would have insisted on making the drink himself, but he didn't know how to operate the fearsome-looking machine, and with Madeleine and Fiona already behind the counter, there wasn't room for three.

Despite feeling awkward that he was being waited on, his feet were grateful, and he sank onto a chair with a sigh. Taking his phone out of his pocket, he decided to have a quick gander at *The Financial Times* whilst he enjoyed his scone.

However, he didn't get the chance.

Or rather, he would have done, if he hadn't noticed an email from Tristan containing an offer he wasn't sure he could refuse.

***

'You're quiet,' Frankie said to Julian, wondering whether something was wrong. They were having a drink in the Farmer's Arms with Harper and Gavin, who seemed to be making a regular thing out of being together without *being together*, if that made sense.

Could he be upset because Frankie had opted to go home yesterday evening after having tea with her parents instead of going to his, or was he upset that she hadn't asked him to come along. She had considered inviting him, but she hadn't seen her mum and dad since the other Sunday when Julian had come to lunch, and she'd thought they mightn't appreciate her dragging him along.

'Have you two had a row?' Harper asked bluntly.

'Not at all,' Julian replied, draping his arm around Frankie's shoulders.

Frankie snuggled into him, relieved. The last thing she wanted was for him to be upset with her.

'What's up then?' Harper persisted. 'You've got a face like a slapped arse.'

'You know…'

He was hedging and Frankie sent Harper a look, warning her to lay off. If it was something serious, she hoped Julian would tell her, and even if he didn't, she had no right to pry. She might share his bed, but that didn't mean he was supposed to share his innermost thoughts with her. Everyone was entitled to an off-day, and from what Julian had told her, he was more entitled than most.

Harper didn't let it lie though, asking again when the pair of them visited the loo – together, naturally. 'You're not a bundle of laughs, either,' she said. 'Are you sure you and Julian haven't squabbled?'

'I'm sure. I suppose I'm a bit disappointed because I've had some replies from the piece I pitched – no takers yet, I'm afraid.'

'Oh, hun, I'm sure there will be. You haven't heard back from everyone yet, have you?'

Frankie shook her head.

'Well, then! Chin up and let's forget about work for this evening. I tell you what – I'll buy you a drink.'

Frankie elbowed her. 'It's *your* round anyway.'

'It is? Damn. OK, half a shandy?'

'Bugger off. I want wine. A large one.'

Julian had perked up by the time the girls returned, and although he couldn't be described as the life and soul of the party (which he never was anyway, as far as Frankie could tell) he was lively enough. And he was certainly lively enough in the bedroom later, leaving her breathless and satisfied. It was only when they were in that gentle, dreamy state between spent passion and exhausted sleep, did Frankie find out what was on Julian's mind.

'I've, um, had an email,' he began hesitantly, and Frankie stiffened. From his tone, whatever he was about to tell her wasn't going to be good.

'It's from a mate in London,' he continued. 'I asked him to put some feelers out and let me know if he heard anything. We used to work for the same bank, but he moved on before my…' He paused. 'Anyway, the place he's at now is looking for someone with my skill set. He wants to know if I'm interested.'

'Are you?'

She felt him shrug. 'I think so.' He paused again. 'No, I *know* so.'

'London?'

'Yes. I asked if he could set me up with a meeting.'

'Wouldn't you have to apply?'

'Not necessarily. The old boys' network is alive and kicking, and its often who you *know*, not *what*.'

'When do you think the meeting will be?'

'After Christmas, probably.'

Frankie felt an unexpected and rather sharp pang. The thought of Julian not being around dismayed her. She'd clicked with him the first time they'd met, and friendship had turned into something much more, especially when they'd started sleeping together. She would miss him. *Badly.*

Which was silly, considering she didn't intend to be around for much longer herself, if she could help it. She also had plans for her future, and no matter how much she liked Julian, he didn't feature in it. So why did she feel so sad?

CHAPTER 17

Julian had to get out of the house. They wanted to see him next week. He was to give a presentation, and if they liked what they saw, there was a start date of the third of January. "They" was the financial institution Tristan worked for. Tristan had put in a good word – 'sang your praises' was the term he'd used. Followed by 'don't let me down, mate.'

Julian had been so convinced that nothing would happen this side of Christmas, that Tristan's phone call this morning had taken him by surprise. He'd said he'd be there, but the adrenalin was already starting to kick in and he was fidgety.

A walk into town to buy a copy of *The Financial Times* should help – he preferred the real thing, to reading on screen, especially since he wanted to make notes and highlight stuff. And he'd pick up something nice for dinner at the same time, because Frankie was coming to his house after work.

Frankie…

What a strange relationship they had. Intense, passionate, exclusive, yet time limited. It almost felt like a holiday romance, both of them knowing it wouldn't last, yet intent on making the most of it while it did. He would miss her, he realised. He would also miss Sweet Meadow. His fondness for the little town had grown in recent weeks. It was ironic that just as he was starting to put down roots, he finally felt well enough to leave and return to his old life. His *real* life.

He wondered what Morag would make of that, what insight she would be able to give him. When he was settled, maybe he'd give her a call and have one final session to show her how far he'd come. He hadn't had an appointment with her since before he'd left London.

Quite a while before he'd left, actually. His last session with her had been shortly before he'd put his flat on the market, after she'd suggested that he needed to take a step back and re-evaluate his life. He'd had another session booked, but she'd been forced to cancel due to a bereavement, and he hadn't rearranged, too caught up by the speed with which his flat had been sold. The first person to view it had put an in offer, and before he knew it he'd moved to Sweet Meadow and the rest was history.

Julian was on his way back from town with his purchases (a crusty sourdough loaf to make a sandwich for lunch, and two nice pieces of steak for dinner, plus a copy of *The Financial Times* that he'd had to visit two shops to find), and he was walking through the park when he spied a familiar figure up a tree.

Harper wasn't *in* the tree as such, she was on a ladder – a very long ladder – threading lights through its branches.

'Do you need a hand?' he called.

'I need several. This isn't a one-man job, or even a two-man job. Wait there!' She climbed down, breathing hard.

'That's one hell of a Christmas tree,' he said, gazing up at the large fir. It was a perfect Christmas-tree shape, but incredibly tall.

'Jack persuaded someone at the council to let him borrow a spare set of outdoor tree lights, so I said I'd put them up.'

'Couldn't you find anything bigger?' he joked. The tree was in a prominent position inside the park's main gates. Decked out in coloured lights, it would be magnificent.

'What I need is a cherry picker,' she grumbled. 'I'm not sure whether a set of ladders will do it. I've got the end of the lights secured to the top branch, but the rest is proving tricky.'

'I hope you've checked them to make sure they work.'

Harper's glare was scathing. 'You stick to spreadsheets and leave the 'lectrics to the professionals.'

'Sorry. I was remembering that Frankie made me check the lights on my tree before we decorated it.'

'I'm *not* decorating this monster. The lights will be enough, so don't you dare suggest it. Molly's got enough daft ideas of her own. Anyway, you'd need *huge* baubles.'

'It would look good, though,' he said. 'Frankie would love it.'

'Frankie can get lost, and so can you. I've got enough to do with these damn lights.'

'Can I do anything to help?' he offered again.

'Not unless you've got a long ladder,' she replied gloomily.

'Would Gavin have one?'

'Yes, but I expect he's busy.'

'Why don't you give him a call?'

'You're full of suggestions today, aren't you? OK, I will, but I'm going to ring him from the comfort of the cafe. I need caffeine, sugar and a sit in the warm, and if you're not doing anything you can keep me company and tell me why you were such a miserable fecker in the pub on Friday.'

'I wasn't miserable,' he protested, falling into step with her as she strode towards the cafe.

'You both were. I thought you'd had a row until Frankie told me her reason. What was yours?'

Julian held the door open for her, the warmth hitting him along with the smell of freshly ground beans and baking.

'Not that it's any of my business,' she added when they approached the counter, and she bent down to see the selection of cakes. 'You can tell me to bugger off, if you want.'

'Bugger off,' he said, with a smile to show he was joking, but his thoughts were on Frankie.

He'd also noticed that she'd seemed a little quiet in the pub, and when he'd asked if she was OK (worried that it might have something to do with her visit to her parents the evening before) she'd assured him she was fine. Work, she'd said, and he'd left it at that, not wanting to pry.

Julian and Harper sat at one of the tables near the window so Harper could keep an eye on her ladder (she could just about see it after she'd scooted her chair around) and waited for their drinks. And as they did so, she said, 'Hopefully Frankie will have some good news this week. I'm keeping my fingers crossed for her.'

Julian had no idea what Harper was talking about, but not wanting to show his ignorance, he plastered a sympathetic look on his face and nodded.

Harper continued, 'It'll mean the world to her if the article gets picked up by one of the nationals. I'm not sure how it works, but she seems to think that if they publish one, they're more likely to publish more from her, as well as standing her in good stead if job comes up. She said something about getting a foot in the door.'

'She mentioned that to me as well,' he said, smiling as Madeleine approached with their order.

'It sounds good,' Harper said. She picked up the sugar tongs and dropped a cube into her cup.

'What does?' Had he missed something?

'The article, of course — although I did wonder whether just before Christmas was really the best time to be talking about suicide, or burnout, which was the other piece she's been working on. I would have thought people would prefer happy, jolly stuff. Then again, what do I know? And maybe they wouldn't put it in the paper or magazine until January. I don't know enough about this kind of thing. Do you?'

Suicide? *Burnout?* Julian couldn't speak. It was pretty clear where Frankie had got her inspiration from, and he used the pretence of taking a sip of hot chocolate to give himself time to think.

When he finally found his voice, it was strained, and he had to force the words out between stiff lips. 'No, I don't. Why would I?'

Harper's eyes widened. 'Sorry, I—'

'Never mind.' Julian got to his feet, feeling sick. His stomach was churning, his thoughts whirling. How could Frankie do that to him? He mightn't have sworn her to secrecy or told her in confidence, but it felt like a betrayal nevertheless. She'd written about his pain for all to see.

'Julian?' Harper looked concerned.

'Got to go,' he choked out.

'Are you all right?'

'I'm fine. Forgot I've got a delivery coming.'

'Oh, right. See you,' she called after him as he lumbered towards the door.

Filled with disbelief and dismay, Julian went home, unable to believe what Frankie had done. Harper must have got it wrong, surely? But he very much feared she hadn't.

He knew what he had to do, the only thing he *could* do, and his mobile phone was in his hand before he could change his mind. 'Tristan, it's Julian.'

***

'Frankie, Vince, can I have a word?' Neil looked and sounded serious.

The pair of them exchanged glances as their boss went back into his office. 'Any idea what this is about?' Frankie whispered.

'Not a clue, but he doesn't look happy.'

Neil was sitting behind his desk when they entered, his arms folded. 'Sit down, both of you.'

Vince jerked his head at the chair nearest the desk, indicating that Frankie should take it, and he dragged a second from near the door.

'I've got some bad news,' Neil said solemnly.

Frankie's first thought was that he was ill, that his heart problems had resurfaced, and she had a sinking feeling in her stomach.

He cleared his throat. 'I'm sorry to say that the paper will fold after Christmas. The final edition will go out on the thirty-first of December.'

'What?' She screwed up her eyes as she stared at him, certain she must have misheard.

Vince must have thought so too, because he said, 'Paper folding? That joke is as old as I am.'

'It isn't a joke. *The Observer* can't go on. It hasn't made a profit for months.' Neil was shaking his head. 'I'm so sorry. I'd hoped it wouldn't come to this, but it's run its course. I can't afford to keep it going any longer.'

Frankie was dumbstruck. Her mind was numb. She'd heard what Neil had said, but the words didn't make sense. *The Observer* had been going since forever. It couldn't simply stop.

'I hate to break the news to you just before Christmas, but I've got no choice.' Neil seemed near to tears.

Frankie knew how he felt.

Vince looked stunned. 'We could take a cut in wages, couldn't we, Frankie? Or go part-time or something?'

Neil was shaking his head. 'I've got no more fight left in me. I'm close to retirement and my health isn't the best, as you know. It's time I packed it in.'

'But what about the people of Sweet Meadow? What will they do? What will *we* do?' Vince demanded, pointing to himself and Frankie.

Frankie was wondering the very same thing. It was inconceivable that Sweet Meadow would no longer have a newspaper. It was inconceivable that she would no longer have a job.

Neil said, 'If the residents of Sweet Meadow were so concerned they should have bought more newspapers.' His tone was sharp, softening when he added, 'I'll give you both an excellent reference, and I'm sure you won't have any difficulty finding new employment.'

Frankie wasn't. Jobs in journalism weren't exactly ten-a-penny, especially around here, and the thought of doing an admin job and being tied to a desk all day filled her with dismay.

What was she going to do? How was she going to pay her rent?

She tuned back in to hear Neil say something about a redundancy package, but she knew it wouldn't be much. It might keep her going for a few weeks if she was very, very careful.

As upset as she was for herself, she was also upset for Neil. He'd put his heart and soul into the paper for the best part of forty-five years, and he must be devastated to have to give it up, knowing that this was the end of it.

In a daze she stood up, leant across the desk and patted him on the shoulder.

Pressing his lips together, his mouth downturned, he nodded once, a jerky movement. His eyes were damp, and her heart went out to him. He was finding it just as difficult to tell her and Vince, as they were finding to hear it.

Wordlessly she returned to her desk and stared unseeingly at the screen. Four more editions, then *The Observer* would be no more. It would be the end of an era, and Sweet Meadow would be the poorer because of it.

***

A shadowy figure detached itself from the dark recess of the doorway, making Frankie jump. The hairdresser wasn't open on a Monday, so who the hell was lurking outside?

It stepped forward and Frankie stiffened, relief flooding through her when she recognised Julian.

'What are you doing here?' she asked. 'I thought I was supposed to be coming to yours?'

'Were you ever going to tell me?' His voice was gruff.

'Tell you what?'

'Your article. Or should I say, *articles*? Plural.'

Oh, hell... Sheepishly, she wondered whether she should have told him what she was working on. She'd deliberately not said anything because she'd not wanted to burst the little bubble of happiness they seemed to be in when they were together, in the same way that lovers who had met on holiday didn't want to acknowledge that the romance would be over when the holiday ended. To Frankie, it was as though her career and the budding romance with Julian were two separate entities, and she hadn't wanted the prospect of her leaving Sweet Meadow to sour it. Maybe she should have told him she was a step closer to her goal, but she didn't think he'd be this upset about it.

'You used me,' he spat.

'What are you talking about? What do you mean, used you?' She was confused – he had been well aware that she wasn't interested in a long-term thing. But saying that she'd used him was a bit harsh. Anyway, he was talking about moving back to London, so *he* was just as guilty of using *her,* if that was the case.

His tone colder than the night air, he said, 'Using what happened to me, what I've been through, to further your career.'

'It's not like that—' she began, realising what he meant and appalled that he could think that of her.

He didn't let her finish. 'I trusted you. No wonder journalists have a crappy reputation – they deserve it.'

Hurt and anxious to show him what she'd written, to put his mind at ease, Frankie said, 'It's cold; come inside, and while I get changed you can read them.'

'I don't *want* to read them.' He shook his head, disgust on his face. 'You take the biscuit, Frankie.'

'But there's nothing—'

Once again, he didn't let her finish. 'I'm done with this conversation. I'm done with *you.*'

He turned to walk away, and Frankie called after him, 'Julian, wait! Let me explain,' but he kept going.

She wondered whether she should run after him and force him to listen to her. She hadn't *used* him. She'd written a story that needed to be told but it hadn't been about him, guessing from the way he'd been so reluctant to open up to her that he wouldn't appreciate the publicity, even if she didn't mention him by name. However, Ellen from Home Sweet Home was a different matter entirely, since she was selling her gingerbread houses to raise awareness.

Upset and weary, Frankie watched him go. She'd speak to him tomorrow when he was calmer, and when she had more energy. Because right now, all she wanted to do was curl up in a ball and lick her wounds after the crappy day she'd had.

Tears imminent, Frankie let herself into her flat. Throwing her coat and bag on the sofa, she plopped down next to them, leant back and closed her eyes, willing herself not to cry.

She would take a moment to compose herself, then she'd get changed, have something to eat (even though she wasn't hungry), and after that she'd start job hunting. It might be the wrong time of year to look for another job, but she had to start somewhere, and it would give her something to do this evening, rather than wallowing in her own misery.

However, when she reached for her phone to speak to her mum to tell her that she'd soon be jobless, she discovered that misery hadn't finished with her yet.

Frankie's article had been passed over for a final time. *No one wanted it.*

Tears came then, and she couldn't prevent herself from giving in to them. What a crappy, crappy day.

***

Julian propped the suitcases by the front door as he did a final check. He'd packed most of his clothes, all of his toiletries, his electronics, and his shoes. He didn't think he'd forgotten anything vital, but if he had, he could come back for it. Or buy another. He wasn't sure that coming back to Sweet Meadow would be good for him. He would have to return at some point obviously, to sort out the house. But that could wait until the New Year.

He started upstairs, quickly opening the drawers and the wardrobes, then moving to the bathroom, before going down to the kitchen. He'd already thrown out anything that might spoil and had emptied the bin. After making sure that the kettle and the coffee machine were unplugged, and that the heating was set to come on only when the temperature dropped below five degrees (he didn't want the pipes to freeze or the property to get damp), he went into the living room.

The unlit Christmas tree in the bay window seemed to mock him as the memory of decorating it with Frankie popped into his head.

Angrily he brushed it aside. He'd like to take the damn thing down, but he didn't want to waste the time. He needed to get on the road, as it was a three-and-a-half-hour drive to London. He should have set off earlier while it was still light, but he'd wanted to see Frankie one last time. He'd wanted to see her face when he accused her of using him, to make her understand how upset he was. But he hadn't seen much beyond his own angry tears.

He'd ended up walking away before they fell.

Tristan had been delighted when Julian had asked if he could impose on him this evening, and Julian hoped his mate wasn't expecting him to paint the town red every night. A pale pink was all he'd be able to manage. He simply wasn't in the mood.

Hopefully, he soon would be when he was back in London. He'd quickly be back in the swing of things, and he could forget all about Sweet Meadow and Frankie. He had a bright future ahead of him and, as he'd always told himself, there was no point in looking back.

CHAPTER 18

Frankie had hoped to feel more positive this morning as she hurried through the park and out the other side, but if anything, she felt worse.

She was supposed to finishing off a piece for Thursday's edition, but she'd sneaked off when Neil went out. He probably wouldn't have minded, because she and Vince were in and out of the office continually and didn't have set working hours as such, and as long as everything was in on time that was all he was concerned about. But Frankie didn't want him to think she was taking her job any less seriously now that it was about to end. She intended to give it her best, right up to the very last day. Neil had been good to her over the years, so it was the least she could do.

The park was quiet, which wasn't surprising given the dull, dismal weather. Frankie hoped it wouldn't be like this on the day of the Fayre, but as there was a week and a half to go, and the weather could change on a penny, it might be snowing by then for all Frankie knew. A dusting of the white stuff might be atmospheric.

Today's weather reflected her mood perfectly though, as she turned into Julian's street and a gust of wind hit her in the face, making her eyes water. Blinking, she stomped up the pavement, dabbing at her eyes with a tissue and cursing. She didn't want to arrive at his house looking as though she was crying. It was bad enough that her eyes were still sore from her sob session last night.

When she'd told her mum about her awful day, Yvonne had come straight over with a frozen lasagne and a hug. Frankie hadn't wanted the lasagne, but the hug had been very welcome, as she'd bawled her eyes out. Then after her mum had (very reluctantly) left, Frankie rang Harper and told her the news.

Harper had turned up shortly afterwards with a bottle of wine and another hug. She'd also had a confession.

'I'm sorry, I think it's my fault Julian was upset,' her friend had said, and had gone on to explain.

Frankie had been quick to reassure her that she'd done nothing wrong, and the pair of them had ended up having a hug-fest on the sofa.

'I'll go see him tomorrow,' Frankie had said. 'I'm sure he'll be fine about it after I've explained.' She'd even printed out a copy of the article this morning, so he could see for himself.

She might be hopeful that she'd be able to patch things up with Julian, but she still felt incredibly down, and for once the Christmas decorations failed to cheer her. Most people in Julian's street had put theirs up, she noticed, but seeing them didn't bring her any joy.

Julian didn't have his Christmas lights on though and knowing that he wasn't as enthusiastic about Christmas as she was, Frankie wasn't surprised. More than once it had been left to her to switch them on when she'd gone to his house.

It was as she pressed her finger on the bell, that she realised his car wasn't there. Bugger, he was out. How long would he be, she wondered, debating whether to hang around for a while or to message him. But she wanted to speak to him in person, which was why she was standing on his doorstep in the first place.

Deciding to come back later, she turned to walk away, hunching deeper into her coat, and almost tipped over a small white and tan dog.

'Patch?' She looked up and saw Bill.

'Off to do a shift in the cafe,' he said. 'Gotta do my bit, especially when there's pulled pork and apple pasties on the menu. That's my lunch sorted. Have you tried them? They're delicious – one of Fiona's creations. Anyway, how are you, my lovely? If you pardon an old man's impertinence, you look a bit peaky.'

'That's OK, Bill. I'm fine, honestly. Tired, that's all.' Neil hadn't asked her and Vince to keep news of *The Observer's* imminent demise quiet, but she didn't know whether he would want it broadcast yet. 'You wouldn't happen to know what time Julian went out, would you?' she asked.

Bill scratched his chin. 'Let me see... About six-thirty, I believe.'

'I wonder where he was off to so early?' she mused.

'Not six-thirty this morning: six thirty *last night*. I'm surprised he managed to get that amount of luggage into such a little car. You can barely fit Patch in it.'

Frankie's stomach dropped. 'What luggage?'

'Two big suitcases, a briefcase, a few other bits and pieces. Off on holiday, is he? I hope he'll be back in time for the Fayre. It'll be a shame if he misses it after the work he's put in, and it'll be all hands on deck for a couple of days before, to set it up.'

Frankie didn't say anything. She couldn't, because she knew in her heart that he wasn't coming back. Julian had gone, and he hadn't even said goodbye.

The realisation that she wouldn't see him again, and that whatever they'd had was over, hit her. The pain was unbearable.

***

'We've got to celebrate you being back in town, man,' Tristan said, slouching on the sofa, his arm across the back of it. He burped loudly. 'When did you learn how to cook?'

'Can't remember. Years ago.'

'I'm stuffed.' Tristan patted his stomach. 'Still got room for a few snifters, though.'

Julian had room too, but only because he hadn't eaten a lot as he didn't seem to have much of an appetite. He didn't fancy going to a bar, but the alternative was to stay in and think of Frankie, and he'd been trying hard not to do that all day.

Unfortunately, he hadn't succeeded. She'd been on his mind constantly since he'd fled Sweet Meadow yesterday evening and he couldn't believe how much he was missing her, despite the way she'd treated him.

In hindsight, he should never have left London. Thinking he could make a new start in a small rural town had been idiotic. However, he was used to new starts. Far too many of them, as he'd moved from foster home to foster home. And when he'd turned eighteen and had been on his own, he'd made a fresh start at university, and another when he'd landed his first job in the bank.

And here he was, making yet another. Or taking up where he'd left off. He wasn't sure anymore. The only thing he was sure about was the ache in his chest whenever he thought of Frankie, which was all the time. He couldn't *not* think about her.

'OK, I'm game,' he said. 'Got anywhere in mind?'

'There's a new place opened up around the corner. They do great cocktails.'

'You? Cocktails?' Julian raised his eyebrows.

'A vesper martini, shaken not stirred,' Tristan said, in an appallingly bad imitation of James Bond. 'It's popular with the ladies.'

'A vesper martini is?'

'The *bar*.'

'You're not on the pull, are you?'

'Course I am. Aren't you?'

'Your divorce hasn't come through yet.' After Julian had arrived last night, they'd stayed up late, talking. Tristan had told him that his wife was seeking a divorce.

'What's that got to do with it? We're separated, so technically I'm single.'

'Technically, you're still married,' Julian pointed out.

'I'm not looking for a long-term relationship. Bin there, done that, gotta pay the solicitor. A one-night stand will do me.'

He was looking at Julian as he said it, as though laying down a challenge, and Julian realised that his role in Tristan's social life would be to keep him company until he found a willing partner for the evening. It wasn't something he relished, but if it was the price he had to pay to stay in Tristan's spare room, Julian guessed he'd have to pay it.

Once again, he lamented his stupidity in selling his flat. Why couldn't he have kept it on, got a tenant in if necessary, and rented somewhere in Sweet Meadow instead of buying?

Sometimes Julian could kick himself.

***

The woman was attractive, but Julian wasn't interested. She was bubbly and chatty, but Julian wasn't listening. As he suspected, Tristan had made a beeline for two unaccompanied women, perched on precariously high stools at one of the equally high tables dotted around the trendy bar.

His opening gambit had been, 'You ladies look lonely. Would you like some company?'

The pair of them had looked Tristan up and down, and then Julian, who had smiled politely.

'Pull up a stool,' the woman with masses of curly brown hair said, adding, '*After* you buy us a drink.'

Tristan had been more than happy to oblige, which was why Julian was sitting next to the blonde one, on what must be the most uncomfortable stool in the world, and wishing a different blonde woman was sitting next to him.

'Bankers, eh?' the dark-haired one was saying, tossing her head and flicking her hair. 'Am I meant to be bored or impressed?'

Tristan was in his element. 'I can assure you, you won't be *bored*.'

The woman giggled and fluttered her eyelashes. The one Julian was sitting next to rolled her eyes. 'Is he always like this?' she asked.

Julian honestly didn't know. Tristan used to be a bit of a charmer, but he seemed to have got worse. 'Too many martinis,' he said dryly.

'Is that what you're drinking?'

'Jack Daniels and cola.'

'Can I have a taste?'

Julian pushed his glass towards her. 'Be my guest.'

She took a dainty sip, and he wished he could remember her name. Not that he was particularly interested, but it would be polite.

'Nice, but I think I'll stick to this.' She was drinking something pink with a coating of sugar around the rim of the glass.

Julian wondered whether he would be expected to escort her home if Tristan copped off with her friend. Then a thought occurred to him – would Tristan invite both women back to his place? And would they expect to stay the night?

Thankfully, after a couple more drinks the women made their excuses. 'You guys might be able to party all night, but we've got work in the morning, haven't we, Bree?'

Bree, *that* was the blonde's name.

Tristan, understandably, wasn't ready for them to leave. 'You can't go, the evening hasn't started yet.'

It was eleven-twenty. As far as Julian was concerned, the evening was almost over.

'I know a nice little club we could go to,' Tristan suggested.

'Maybe another time.' Bree looked as reluctant as Julian felt.

'I'll hold you to that,' Tristan said, but Julian noticed that no phone numbers were exchanged. Now that sex wasn't on offer, Tristan had lost interest. Julian was relieved, and he was even more relieved when Tristan decided he'd had enough, and they should go home.

'Gotta save ourselves for the weekend, eh? Do you remember Si and Cody? They've got a thing at this club, and I said I'd go. Open bar, they said, so of course I'm gonna be there. They won't mind if you tag along.'

There was a time, not too long ago, when Julian would have been well up for it. But now the thought made him feel tired. He was so out of practice, he felt like he'd aged thirty years and had become middle-aged overnight.

Abruptly Julian hardly recognised himself, and he didn't like it.

'Sod saving ourselves,' he said rebelliously. 'Where's that club you were on about?' It was time he started living again.

***

'So, Liam, Connor, what does the Festive Fayre mean to you?'

'Bunking off school,' was Liam's reply as he shovelled a slice of chocolate, orange and cranberry cake into his mouth.

Frankie sighed. 'Come on, guys, you've got to give me more than that.'

It's true. Sir said we can have Thursday and Friday off to help Gavin put the stalls together.'

'He only it that because that Friday is the end of term and we wouldn't be doing any work anyway,' Connor pointed out. 'Half the kids don't turn up for the last day, and we'll only be sat in the hall singing Christmas songs. It's *boring.*'

Frankie changed tack. 'What do you enjoy about helping with the Festive Fayre?' She was putting together the final pre-Fayre piece that would go out next week, and had left interviewing the two lads until last, hoping that the article, combined with a photo of kids enjoying themselves on the pop-up ice-rink that was being erected this Saturday, would generate interest from Sweet Meadow's younger residents. Not that many of them would read the newspaper – and that there was the problem, the reason she would shortly be out of a job.

After a few more questions, which resulted in Frankie finally getting a quote or two she could print, she wrapped it up. The lads were getting restless anyway, now that they'd scoffed their cake, and were keen to get off home. She hoped it hadn't spoiled their appetite for their tea.

The time was coming up to four o'clock and the cafe was about to close. Frankie should leave too, but she couldn't summon the energy, so she sat there for a while staring into space as Madeleine cleared up around her.

'Finished with that?' Madeleine asked, pointing to Frankie's empty cup.

'Yes, thanks.'

'Is everything all right? You look a bit down.'

A bit down was an understatement. She'd never felt this low in her life.

'It's a busy time of year,' she replied evasively, hoping she was giving the impression that she was tired, not broken-hearted. Because that's what she had – a broken heart. Without realising it until it was too late, she'd given her heart to Julian.

She didn't blame him: it was *her* fault she'd fallen in love, not his. She'd never intended for it to happen. Frankie hadn't wanted love. She'd wanted a bit of fun. Unfortunately for her, she'd got more than she'd bargained for and was now paying the price.

How could she have been so stupid? Love had never been part of the plan. She didn't want to be tied down: not because she didn't believe in love (she did), but because she hadn't been ready for it. Love was something that would happen in the future, when her career had taken off and she was living her best life. This *was not* her best life.

Wearily she got to her feet and put on her coat.

'See you Saturday,' Madeleine said, hovering near the door, obviously keen to lock up. 'They're putting the ice rink up and I reckon the park will be busy.' She looked excited at the prospect.

Frankie tried to muster some enthusiasm. 'I'll be there,' she said. 'Wouldn't miss it for the world.'

'Does your Julian skate? I heard he's a skier.'

Hearing his name sent a lance of pain through her. 'I don't know.' And he wasn't *her* Julian.

He never had been. This sleepy little town would never have been enough for him. He'd been used to the bright lights of London and the excitement the city had to offer. Sweet Meadow was too provincial. His departure had been inevitable. It was just a pity he'd taken her heart with him when he'd left.

Conversely, Frankie felt both empty and brimming with pain. She'd never experienced hurt like it. The old adage of playing with fire and getting burned, swam into her head. She'd played with fire by getting to know him, and she should have realised that sleeping with him was a bad idea. At the risk of mixing metaphors, she'd paddled in what she'd assumed to be shallow water, only to find herself in over her head. And now she was drowning.

Her heart was filled with the pain of never seeing him again, and her soul was awash with despair.

God, she should have been a bloody romantic poet, not a journalist, with the crap she was spouting.

But however she described it, whatever label she gave it, didn't lessen the reality – Frankie's heart was broken.

CHAPTER 19

Saturday was one of those crisp, bright December days that made the middle of winter sparkle.

Unfortunately for Julian, he'd drunk far too much last night and felt as sparkly as a broken lightbulb. He'd gone out on the lash again, talked into it by Tristan who, now that his brief stint at matrimony was over, was acting like a student during Freshers' Week.

Julian, despite being unemployed and able to spend the mornings after the nights before in bed recuperating, couldn't keep up with him.

This morning wasn't a *staying in bed and ignoring the hangover* kind of morning. Not with the noises coming from Tristan's bedroom. How the guy had the energy and stamina to do what he was doing after the amount he'd drunk, was astounding. Especially since Julian could barely crawl out of bed.

He was in desperate need of coffee, but he didn't want to hang around in the flat long enough to make one in case he bumped into the woman Tristan had brought back last night, so he splashed his face with cold water, got dressed and headed outside.

He didn't know this part of Kensington well, but he was getting to know it fast – mostly via the bars and during the hours of darkness. It would be nice to see it in daylight. Tristan's flat wasn't in the poshest part, but it was within walking distance of Kensington Palace and Hyde Park, so he decided to explore.

Feeling sluggish, Julian went in search of coffee and breakfast, then he'd go for a walk. Admittedly, it would be a *long* walk, but considering that the last one he'd taken had been nearly a week ago (lumbering from one bar to another didn't count) he decided some exercise was overdue. And in all the years he'd lived in London, he'd never visited Hyde Park.

Feeling more human after his breakfast, Julian entered the park from Bayswater Road and was soon strolling along a wide tree-lined path running through an area of parkland. It felt good to be in nature again, with the sun shining through the bare branches and the air chill and relatively fresh. It reminded him of Sweet Meadow Park, although on a considerably grander scale. The place was huge. He'd been aware of that, but knowing something wasn't the same as seeing it with his own eyes, and he was impressed. He was also quickly lost, as he came to a crossroads and wondered which way to go.

Left, he decided, for no particular reason.

Another fork in the road soon appeared, this time with a metal signpost and a monument. He gave the monument a cursory glance, then took the path leading to the Italian Fountains, because they sounded nice.

He'd walked quite a distance already and was beginning to think he'd never get there, when the parkland finally gave way to formal gardens with several ornate ponds with a fountain in the centre of each. There was also a large building which, after a bit of digging, he discovered was a Victorian pumping house that used to contain a steam engine to power the fountains. Even in the depths of winter it was a pleasant place to be, but Julian couldn't help comparing it to Sweet Meadow's pond, tiny yet filled with wildlife, and the battered old bandstand that had seen better days. To his surprise, he knew which park he preferred, and it wasn't this one. For all its impressive space and history, he felt Hyde Park was lacking in something, but he wasn't sure what. A sense of community, maybe?

He was probably being silly. It was unfamiliar, that was all. He was sure it was lovely, and there was no doubt it was popular. Lots of people were out for a stroll or a run, and he thought he'd seen the occasional cyclist in the distance. People rode horses here as well, but he hadn't seen any.

He lingered by the fountains for a moment, before moving on. It was too cold to hang around.

Julian wasn't sure how far he'd walked or for how long, when he realised that the park had grown progressively busier, and it took him a moment to realise where many of the people were heading – Hyde Park's Winter Wonderland.

He was close enough to hear the music and through the scattered trees he could see glimpses of the huge black wall encircling the site, as well as some of the rides rising into the air. Was that a roller-coaster? He could even smell a faint aroma of food.

Abruptly, he did and about-turn. He didn't want to see it. He didn't want to be reminded of Christmas fayres, or ice rinks, or stalls selling festive goods, because he didn't want to think about Sweet Meadow's own Festive Fayre, or the woman who was reporting on it.

He didn't want to think about Frankie, because it hurt too much when he did.

***

'Your dad and I took you ice skating one Christmas in Cardiff. Do you remember?'

Frankie, her mum and dad, along with many others, were watching the construction of the ice rink, and her dad was particularly fascinated. The aim was to get it up and running by this afternoon, when the Christmas lights on the large fir tree near the park's main gates would be switched on as soon as it grew dark.

'Frankie? Do you remember?' her mum repeated, putting her arm around her and giving her a squeeze.

Frankie's chin wobbled. It should be Julian with an arm around her, not her mother. He should be here.

But he wasn't. He was in London, where he belonged. And she was so miserable she could cry. Again.

'Aw, love, don't fret. It'll be all right,' Yvonne said. 'You'll soon find another job, and if push comes to shove, we haven't converted your old bedroom yet.'

'I hope it won't come to that.' She was aware that it might, though.

'So do I – I want to turn it into an en suite and a walk-in wardrobe.'

If her mum had been hoping to raise a smile, she was disappointed, because Frankie didn't have the energy, although she did appreciate her mum's attempts to cheer her up, as well as the offer to move back into the family home. At the moment, she was struggling to think that far ahead. She could barely think beyond today.

She knew she should get a move on and start looking in earnest for another job, but she didn't want *another* job. She liked the one she had.

The insight startled her.

She *did* like her job – more than she'd realised. And she understood that she was more attached to Sweet Meadow's newspaper than she had admitted. It had been her first proper job, and she remembered how proud she'd been. Yes, she'd had her eye on bigger things, and when she'd been studying for her degree, she hadn't been naïve enough to think that she'd waltz straight into a job with *Vanity Fair* or the like. She'd been fully aware that she'd have to work her way up. She'd viewed reporting for *The Sweet Meadow Observer* as a stopgap, but now that it was about to be taken away, she realised just how much the newspaper meant to her, and she felt like crying.

Molly walked towards her, a beaming smile on her face. 'Isn't this great! I can't wait to have a go, though Jack is being a scaredy-cat and flatly refuses to put on a pair of skates.'

'I'm looking forward to taking some good photos,' Frankie said, hoping her sadness didn't show.

Neil wanted a double-page spread in next Thursday's paper, with the following Thursday (a special that would be out on the day before Christmas Eve) carrying photos of the Festive Fayre itself. It would be the last proper edition, and Neil wanted to go out on a high. Vince would also be around on the day, and between him and Frankie they should get some decent shots. Despite no longer feeling Chrismassy, Frankie was determined to do her best. Just because she was feeling miserable, there was no need to allow her sadness to affect her work.

Molly said, 'Have you heard from Julian?'

Frankie flinched. 'Not since Monday. Have you?'

'Same. He messaged me to say he wouldn't be able to help anymore.' Molly gave her a keen look. 'His leaving was a bit sudden, I thought.'

Thankfully Yvonne intervened, because Frankie was struggling to hold back tears. Every time his name was mentioned, it as though she was stabbed in the heart.

'Job offer,' Yvonne explained. 'He couldn't turn it down.'

When Molly opened her mouth to say something and closed it again without speaking, Frankie wondered whether everyone could tell how devastated she was. Thank God Julian didn't know how she felt about him, because that would be a humiliation too far. She wished she didn't care so much, but she couldn't help how she felt, and right now she suspected she might never be happy again.

Her dad was shuffling from foot to foot like an excited schoolboy, and craning his neck to see what was going on. 'Fascinating, isn't it?' he said. 'I've never seen the workings of an ice rink before. You should write an article on it.'

'It's not *that* interesting, Dad. Anyway, even if I did, there won't be a paper to write about it in for much longer.'

'I know, Sweetpea, but something will turn up. You've just got to keep trying and not give up hope. Those people don't know what they're missing. You're a bloody good journalist.'

'You're biased, but thank you, anyway.' She squeezed his arm and gave him a small smile. Bless him, he was trying his best.

'It's true,' he insisted.

'It really isn't. If I were as good as you say I am, my work wouldn't be turned down all the time.'

'Neil thinks you're good.'

'If you hadn't noticed, *The Sweet Meadow Observer* is going out of business.'

'It's not a reflection on your writing, though. It's because Neil is old-school and didn't move with the times. What that paper needs, is someone young and dynamic in charge, someone with loads of ideas and enthusiasm.' He paused. 'Someone like *you*. Could you take it over? Run it instead?'

'If Neil wanted that to happen, he would have said. He's had enough, Dad. He wants to retire. He doesn't want the worry, because no matter who he appointed, he wouldn't be able to sit back and let them get on with it. He'd still be involved, and with his health…' She stopped, an idea beginning to form.

She'd have to think about it properly, but even as she warned herself not to get too carried away, she couldn't help feeling excited.

The question was, would she be able to pull this idea of hers off?

***

Frankie winced when the battered, green-painted door squeaked as it swung shut behind her. One of these days she'd bring that can of WD40 to work and fix it, although she seemed to have grown rather fond of it recently.

Pausing for a moment, she scanned the room where she and Vince had their desks, her eyes briefly coming to rest on Neil's office. The door was closed, but she could see through the glass window that he was in there.

Dropping her shoulder bag on her desk, Frankie plopped into her chair, and it groaned as it took her weight. The arms wobbled, the mechanism to adjust the height of the seat no longer worked, and the fabric was threadbare, but she *loved* that chair.

Vince bounded in, bright-eyed and bushy tailed. He was grinning, but when he spotted her the wattage dimmed. 'Alright, Frankie?'

'Yeah. You?'

'I'm good.' He sat at his desk and turned his computer on. He was still smiling.

'Who is she?' Vince was divorced, and Frankie was aware he dated now and again, but they rarely came to anything.

'It's not a woman,' he said.

'What is it, then? Won the lottery, did you?'

'I've got a new job.' He looked pleased, excited and guilty all at once. Frankie guessed that the guilt stemmed from her having yet to find one, despite it being early days on the job-hunting front.

'Where?'

'In Newport, working for an insurance company. My brother put in a good word for me.'

'Old boys' network?' she asked, dryly.

'Pardon?'

'Never mind.' Julian was right; it often boiled down to who you knew, not what you knew.

'It's more money,' Vince said. 'Not too keen on the commute, though. I've had it easy working here.'

'Given a choice, if the paper wasn't closing, would you stay at *The Observer* or would you go?'

'Definitely go. I've been thinking about leaving for a while but couldn't be arsed.'

'Fair enough.'

'You?'

'I'd stay.'

His eyebrows rose. 'You surprise me, I thought you'd be off the first chance you got.'

'So did I.'

'What changed?'

'Shall we say, I've learnt to appreciate what I've got.'

'Yeah, right. Pull the other one, Frankie.'

She got to her feet. 'I'm making a coffee. Do you want one?'

'That would be great, thanks.'

Frankie made one for Neil whilst she was at it. When she took it into his office, he was on the phone and he gestured for her to put it on the desk, mouthing 'Thanks,' at her.

She set the mug down, but instead of leaving, she took a seat, sitting in the same chair that she'd sat in when he'd broken the news that *The Sweet Meadow Observer* had run its course.

Neil peered at her over the top of his glasses when he finished his call. 'What's up, Frankie?'

She leant forward nervously. 'I've got a proposition for you.'

CHAPTER 20

Julian went over his notes for the hundredth time, double and treble-checking his figures. This wasn't an interview. As he'd said to Frankie, this was more of a confirmation that he was the right man for the job. As far as he was aware, no one else was being considered.

He'd dressed in his sharpest suit, his crispest shirt, and his tie was understated. He'd had his hair trimmed yesterday and he'd given himself an exceptionally thorough shave this morning. It was imperative he looked confident, capable and in control, even if he didn't feel it. A lot was riding on this, and he'd woken with butterflies in his stomach. Not that he'd slept much anyway since he'd left Sweet Meadow, and over the past two days the nerves had started to creep in which had made his insomnia even worse.

Tristan had been quite blasé this morning, when he'd wandered into the open plan lounge and kitchen to find Julian leaning against the island, staring into space.

'You'll be fine,' he'd said dismissively. 'You know your stuff. Not sure I'd advise buying assets in Darklite – it's a bit risky if you ask me – but I'm sure you'll convince them. Anyway, it's a paper exercise. They just want to see what you're capable of.'

'Bankrupting a client?' Julian joked with a wan smile.

'We're all capable of doing that,' Tristan replied casually, scratching his bare chest.

And that was the very thing Julian was worried about. He'd suggested Darklite, an up-and-coming, acquisition-hungry IT company, precisely *because* it was risky. He wanted to prove that he hadn't lost his nerve, that he still had it – whatever *it* was. But now he was beginning to doubt himself.

Damn! It was too late to amend anything. He'd have to hope he hadn't made a grave error.

In the interest of not arriving flustered, Julian eschewed the tube and took a taxi to the steel and glass building, glancing up at it as he paid the driver.

His stomach churned and his mouth was dry, but that was to be expected. He was aware it wouldn't be the end of the world if they didn't like him and that there would be other opportunities, but this position was perfect for him and he was keen to get back in the saddle.

He was even more keen to find a place of his own to live. It was very good of Tristan to allow him to kip at his place, but Julian didn't want to impose for long. Tristan was too much of a party animal, and although Julian used to be just like him once, he wasn't any more. Going out every night was exhausting, and Julian couldn't keep up. And even if he could, he didn't want to. His heart wasn't in it and hadn't been for a while. Not since that awful time when—

Julian stopped himself. Thinking about his breakdown wasn't going to get him anywhere, especially not today. Taking a deep breath, he walked towards the entrance and straightened his shoulders.

The interior was modern, calm and reeked of money. There wasn't a cash machine or a teller in sight and there never would be. It wasn't *that* kind of bank. The money in this establishment was invisible, numbers on a screen, usually very *large* numbers, and although Julian had never been inside this particular building, it was nevertheless familiar.

He relaxed a little. He could do this. A sliver of doubt lingered, but it was only a sliver. The crippling fear had gone, and although he mightn't ooze the same confidence he'd once possessed, enough remained to carry this off.

He was collected from the atrium by a young man in an equally sharp suit, and Julian followed him to the lifts. There was no small talk on the way to the twelfth floor, just an awkward silence. The man indicated for Julian to step out ahead of him, then led him along a plush carpeted corridor flanked by quiet offices. It smelt of money and privilege.

Nerves fluttered in his stomach, but he ignored them.

It was perfectly natural to feel out of his comfort zone. He didn't belong here; he belonged in front of a computer, buying stocks and selling shares, predicting what would go up and come down, using gut feeling and knowledge gleaned from endless hours studying the market, neither of which prepared him for this.

Tristan had been born into this world. Julian had shoehorned himself into it by hard work and instinct. Right now, his instinct was telling him to run.

The room was large, an impressive boardroom with more than twenty chairs around an oval table. Three of them were occupied. Two men and one woman were seated at the far end. They looked expectant and sombre.

Julian swallowed nervously. His palms were damp, and the blood rushed in his ears.

Plastering a confident smile on his face, he stepped forward, holding out his hand to the nearest suit.

'Julian Blade, pleased to meet you,' he said – and that was as far as he got. He couldn't breathe. His heart began to race, and he felt hot and sweaty.

No, not now, please not now.

Feeling dizzy, he grasped the edge of the table, dimly hearing someone say, 'Are you going to faint?'

He didn't know. *Was he?*

He had to get out of there. Dread enveloped him, a black cloud of foreboding and fear, and he stumbled to the door. His legs felt weak, and he worried he wasn't going to make it. Then the handle was in his hand, and he wrenched the door open, gasping for breath.

'We need a first aider to the twelfth-floor boardroom *now!*' he heard the woman say as he staggered through the door.

'Is he having a heart attack?' someone else said. The man sounded curious rather than concerned. 'He's a bit young, isn't he?'

'Panic. Attack,' Julian managed to gasp, then he didn't remember much about the next few minutes as he focused on his breathing, trying to slow it down.

One of the coping mechanisms Morag had suggested was counting floor tiles or reciting a poem. "Distraction technique" she'd called it, so Julian attempted to distract himself by trying to name as many of Queen's hit singles as he could. He got to nine before his heart rate began to slow. Then he couldn't think of any others so he moved on to Coldplay, and all the while, a first aider fussed around him, telling him to breathe slowly and trying to get him to drink some water.

When he finally felt able, he made his apologies and fled, embarrassed and mortified.

He didn't return to Tristan's flat. Tristan wouldn't understand. But there *was* someone who would, and Julian needed to speak to her urgently.

***

'Morag won't see you without an appointment.' The therapist's receptionist was firm.

'Please can you tell her I'm here? I used to be a client. She might be able to squeeze me in. I don't care how long I have to wait.' Julian hated to beg, but he was desperate. He felt as though he was floundering in heavy seas and was about to capsize. 'Please,' he pleaded, close to tears.

The receptionist relented. 'She's with a client, but when they leave I'll tell her you're here. I can't guarantee she'll be able to fit you in, though. Her schedule is pretty tight.'

'Thank you, I appreciate it.'

Feeling somewhat calmer now that there was a chance he might get to speak with her, Julian took a seat. It didn't look like a typical waiting room: it was more like a trendy living room with weird-shaped chairs and abstract artwork. The style reflected the hefty consultation fees.

He waited for a long time, until well into the afternoon before Morag was finally able to fit him in.

A tall woman in her mid-to-late forties, with a mop of grey-stranded dark hair, and kindly eyes set in a stony face, Morag gestured for him to sit in an upright armchair.

She took the one opposite, crossed her legs and tilted her head to the side, gazing at him. She only ever asked one question when she began a session, and it was the same question every time.

'Tell me,' she said, then waited for him to speak.

So he did, beginning with when he decided to move to Sweet Meadow and ending with the embarrassing scene earlier today. He left nothing out, especially how he felt about Frankie. He spoke fast and succinctly, knowing he wouldn't have long.

When he'd finished, she was silent for several seconds, then she said, 'It's nothing to be ashamed of.'

He didn't ask what she meant. He knew. She was referring to mental health in general.

She was right, it wasn't, but it didn't alter the fact that he didn't want the state of *his* to be broadcast to the world.

'You said Frankie had offered to let you read the article. Why didn't you?'

Because he hadn't wanted to see his failings in black and white.

As the session went on, Morag gently probed and questioned, helping him to understand why he felt the way he did and when it ended, she asked him the most significant question of all. 'What makes you happy?'

He had one answer. *Frankie*.

***

'You gotta do what you gotta do, man.' Tristan was sprawled in his customary place on the couch, a bottle of beer held loosely in his hand, and had yet to look him in the eye.

Julian had waited for him to come home from work to tell him that he was going back to Sweet Meadow, and the reason why.

He'd kind of expected this reaction. Tristan had gone out of his way to secure that meeting, and Julian had blown it big time. He was probably eager to get rid of him and was worried that Julian's panic attack would reflect badly on him.

The realisation gave him pause. Morag was right – Julian *was* ashamed and embarrassed. And so, it seemed, was Tristan. He hadn't said as much, but Julian had the impression that Tristan was worried it might be catching, like measles. So maybe Frankie *was* right to air it. She hadn't had the right to use his story, and certainly not without asking him first, but it was a subject that needed to be discussed, otherwise people like Tristan would never understand.

Morag had helped him realise that he needed to go back to Sweet Meadow, that London and a return to his former life was unfeasible. He wasn't ready: he might *never* be ready. Morag's advice all those months ago, coupled with his instinct to flee, had been correct. He *had* needed to put time and distance between himself and what was causing his panic attacks.

It suddenly struck him that he didn't *want* to go back into finance. He was done with it – or *it* was done with *him*. The high-stress, fast pace no longer suited him. He wasn't convinced it ever had. He'd been kidding himself. And he knew why.

Julian recognised that his career in finance and his drive to make money stemmed from his childhood and the loss of his mother. He had been determined to prove himself, to never have to worry where his next meal was coming from, to be secure.

But perhaps what he'd been searching for was something else entirely. Maybe he'd been searching for love.

And he'd found it.

Unfortunately the woman he loved would also leave him, and he'd known that from the start. Frankie had made no secret of it.

However, he'd never been happier than these past few weeks in Sweet Meadow. Molly, Gavin, Harper and the rest had made him feel welcome, valued, a part of the community. He missed them, damn it. And he missed his house, and the park, and the little things he'd been able to help with.

Frankie might be anxious to leave, but he was anxious to return. He belonged *there* now. Not here. And as for Frankie, he'd take what he could get, even if she would be out of his life soon, because he missed *her* most of all.

CHAPTER 21

Returning to Sweet Meadow felt like coming home and some of the tension Julian had been carrying eased. It was good to be back.

The first thing he noticed was the Christmas lights and he was pleased that Harper had managed to decorate the big tree near the park's gates. Seeing it gave him a warm feeling as he drove past. The second was the ice rink. He didn't get a good look at it because it was set too far back from the road, but he would check it out tomorrow.

Even though it was gone ten o'clock when he opened his front door and struggled into the hall with his cases, within a couple of minutes he was outside again. There was someone he needed to see.

A soft glow emanated from the windows of Frankie's flat, and he hesitated on the pavement, staring up at them.

He'd spent the entire journey from London rehearsing what he was going to say, running through all her possible reactions and scenarios in his head, but now that he was here, he was too nervous to go through with it. Would she want to speak to him? Would she be pleased to see him? Or would she be mad?

Maybe he'd leave it until tomorrow. Turning up without warning mightn't be the best idea. He'd go home and send her a message instead.

He began to walk away, then froze.

Frankie was coming towards him, her head bowed, her shoulders hunched and her hands in her pockets. She hadn't noticed him yet as she scuffed along the pavement, but she would. Any second now…

'Julian?'

He searched her face, seeing her shock and disbelief. He'd been hoping for a more positive emotion.

'What are you—?' she began and stopped.

They stared at one another, the silence growing. He didn't know what to say. His mind had gone blank. All he could do was drink her in. He ached to hold her, but he couldn't move. He wanted to tell her how he felt about her, but he couldn't speak.

She bit her lip, then looked away as she took her keys out of her pocket. 'Do you want to come in?' she asked, without meeting his eye.

'If you want me to.'

'I wouldn't have offered if I didn't.'

He followed her up the stairs to the flat, his mouth dry, his heart racing. He didn't get the impression she was pleased to see him, but at least she hadn't told him to sod off.

She slung her bag on the sofa and turned to face him, her expression unreadable.

'You've not got your Christmas lights on,' he noticed. *Really?* Was that what his brain had decided to go with? What an inane comment.

'I thought you'd left,' she said, ignoring the unlit tree.

'So had I.'

'When do you start your new job?'

'I don't.'

She made a sympathetic face. 'I'm sorry.'

'I'm not.'

'You turned it down?' she asked, sounding surprised.

'Not exactly.'

Her eyes were narrow as she continued to stare at him, and he wished he knew what she was thinking.

'Can I get you something to drink? Tea, Coffee?' She sounded so formal, so polite that it hurt.

'Water will be fine, thanks.' His mouth was still dry, but at least his pulse no longer raced.

Frankie poured him a glass straight from the tap and placed it on the counter. 'There you go.'

He drank half of it in one gulp.

'Have you got anything else lined up?' she asked.

'Not right now.'

'It's the wrong time of year to job hunt.' There was an edge to her voice that he couldn't decipher. 'Something will turn up,' she added. 'How was London?'

'Not good.'

'In what way?'

'It wasn't Sweet Meadow.'

'I thought that was the point?'

'London isn't all it's cracked up to be.'

She pressed her lips together. 'Is this sour grapes because they didn't offer you the job?'

'I had a panic attack.'

Her expression softened. 'I'm sorry. Couldn't you have rearranged?'

'They witnessed it.'

'Oh, I see.' Her tone was flat. 'Give yourself a couple more weeks. You can try again in the New Year.' She glanced at the kitchen window. The blind hadn't been drawn and the building opposite was in darkness. 'It's late,' she said. 'Thanks for stopping by to let me know you're back.'

'That's not why I'm here. I mean, it is, but...' He was floundering. 'I want to apologise. I shouldn't have had a go at you. I was out of line.'

'You were.' She crossed her arms.

Apology not accepted, he guessed. 'Have you heard from any more papers or magazines? Harper told me you'd had a couple of rejections.'

'I have,' she confirmed. 'You'll be pleased to know they've all passed on it. No one wants it.'

'I'm sorry to hear that.'

'Huh!' She uttered a disbelieving snort, her mouth pressed into a thin line.

'I mean it.'

'You've changed your tune. Last week I was the spawn of the devil for writing it.'

'I never called you that.'

'Your face did.'

Julian spluttered, '*My face?*'

'It can be quite expressive when it wants to be.'

'You do realise that it's part of me? It's not a separate entity, with a mind of its own.'

'That's what I mean. Your face told me what you were thinking.'

Despite himself, Julian was amused. 'What's it telling you now?'

'That you're an idiot.'

'I can't argue with that. I have been an idiot. I overreacted and I'm sorry. It was a shock to learn you were writing about me. If you'd given me the head's up—'

'So it's *my* fault, is it?'

'That's not what—'

'You're blaming *me* that you went off on one and wouldn't let me explain?'

'You should have asked my permission to use my name, or at least warned me!' he cried.

'I didn't use your name.' Her reply was calm, her expression cold.

'Maybe not as such, but you used my experience to—'

'I did not!' Frankie stamped her foot. She was losing her temper, and he flinched. This wasn't good.

'But your article is about—'

'I *know* what my article is about!' she shrieked. 'I wrote the bloody thing. It wasn't about you. Sorry, hotshot, but you didn't get a mention, oblique or otherwise. However,' her tone was pure sarcasm, 'Ellen from Home Sweet Home *did*. She gave me permission to use the personal stories on her website.'

'But—'

'But nothing! You should have read the bloody thing when I told you to. You jumped in with your size twelves, all guns blazing and wouldn't let me get a word in edgeways, and I'd had an awful day and all I wanted was a cuddle!' Her chin wobbled, and she bit her lip.

'I'm so sorry.' At the risk of getting his head bitten off, he said, 'I can give you a cuddle now, if you like?'

'Sod off. If you think you can just walk back into my life and pick up where you left off, you need to think again. I'm not going to be your friend with benefits for the duration, until you decide to bugger off again. It's time you went. Off you pop – I want to go to bed. On my *own*.' She made shooing motions with her hands.

'I will, but not before I tell you something.' He had to tell her, to convince her that he was here to stay. That he'd come back to Sweet Meadow because he was in love with her, and not just because he hadn't been able to hack it in London.

'If you say you're sorry again, it won't wash,' she warned.

'I love you.'

'I don't care how sorry you are, you're not getting into my knickers.' She stopped and frowned. 'Say that again?'

'I love you.'

Frankie shook her head slowly as her eyes flashed with sudden fury. 'I don't believe it. How can you sink so low?'

'I swear to you it's true. I've stupidly fallen in love with you.'

'*Stupid?* Falling in love with me is *stupid?* I'll show you stupid!' Letting out an irate screech, she picked up the glass and hurled the water in his face. Thankfully for him, she kept hold of the glass, otherwise he might have had a lump on his head the size of an egg.

Julian gasped. He stood there, water running down his face and trickling down his neck inside the collar of his jacket.

Frankie looked stunned, her eyes wide, her mouth opening and closing. A blush leapt into her face, flushing her cheeks scarlet. 'I, er, I'll get you a towel.'

'No need. I'm fine.'

'You're soaking.'

It didn't matter. Nothing mattered. She didn't believe him. She seemed to think he was only saying he loved her to get her to sleep with him. That he would leave Sweet Meadow again as soon as he could.

Abruptly, he realised that even if she did believe him and they resumed their relationship, he would only be delaying the inevitable. He must be out of his mind to think he was strong enough to carry on a relationship with her, when he knew he would lose her sooner or later.

She didn't love him and even if she did develop feelings for him, she'd never allow them to get in the way of her dreams. And he wouldn't let her, because if he did, he knew she'd end up resenting it – and him – and that would be worse.

He'd severed their ties once – it was probably better if they stayed severed, because he'd only be opening himself up to even greater heartache when she did eventually leave. How could he be satisfied with a few weeks or a few months? He wanted her for forever, not just for now. And as much as it hurt to say goodbye, he had to.

Walking away from her a second time broke his heart all over again, but it was the only thing he could do.

***

Frankie was furious. How dare he come strolling into her flat after the stunt he'd pulled, thinking that an apology would make her fall into bed with him. And when that failed to work, he'd had the audacity to tell her he loved her! She shouldn't have thrown water over him, but he'd flippin' well deserved it.

'I hate him, hate him, *hate* him,' she muttered as she mopped up the water. Her method was unconventional, but it worked. She'd dropped an old towel on the floor, stood on it and was shuffling back and forth, using her feet to rub the towel over the lino. She called it the floor-mop-shuffle.

As she worked out her temper on the floor, she couldn't help wondering if he'd actually meant it. Did he love her, or had he only said it to get into her knickers?

Frankie stopped her frantic shuffling, her anger finally giving way to tears. He'd had the cheek to accuse her of using him, yet that was what he would have done to her: sleeping with her until he felt well enough to bugger off back to London again. Because he *would* leave again. She knew it in her bones. She'd sensed how bored he'd become, realised that he wasn't cut out for doing nothing. He needed to be busy. And she could empathise with that, she really could; idleness didn't suit her either.

The hardest thing she'd ever done had been to let him walk away. She'd been so incredibly tempted to pretend to believe him, to pretend that everything was all right between them, that they could continue their relationship as though nothing had happened, but…

He would leave at some point. It might take a few weeks or a few months, but sooner or later, he'd go – leaving her broken-hearted for a second time.

Tears trickling down her face, Frankie knew she'd done the right thing – the *only* thing – in letting him go.

CHAPTER 22

The pounding on his front door had Julian hurrying to answer it. It was Bill.

'You're back then.'

'So I am.' Julian bent to give Patch a pat on the head.

'How long for?'

'For good.'

'It didn't work out? Molly said something about a job.'

'Unfortunately – or fortunately – not.'

'Which is it?'

'Fortunately.'

'Good. We missed you. Frankie especially, I reckon. It'll cheer her up having you back, after the news she's had.'

Julian stiffened, forcing his mouth into a polite smile. 'What news?'

'*The Observer*, of course.'

'What about it?'

'It's shutting up shop. The final one is out on New Year's Eve.'

Julian was aghast. 'Why?'

'Dwindling readership, apparently. Not enough copies being sold.'

'Oh, hell! Poor Frankie. What's she going to do?'

Bill shrugged. 'I'm sure something will turn up. She's young and bright, and she's got bags of enthusiasm.'

Why didn't she tell me last night, Julian wondered. Mind you, between declarations of love and water being thrown, there hadn't been a great deal of opportunity.

'You're looking peaky, lad,' Bill said. 'Are you coming down with something? You need to take care of yourself.'

Julian had already come down with it, and he didn't think there was a cure for heartbreak.

Bill carried on, 'I hope you haven't caught anything from Frankie. She's been looking peaky too.' He took a step back. 'Whatever it is, I don't want to catch it.'

'I'm not ill.'

'You look it.'

Julian knew he did. He'd seen his reflection in the mirror this morning and it hadn't been nice. Having had little to no sleep, didn't help. He'd spent last night tossing and turning, unable to stop thinking about Frankie.

No wonder there had been an edge to her voice when she'd said it was the wrong time of year to job hunt.

He'd known that she'd be off soon, and he was doubly sure now, after hearing the news. With *The Observer* gone, she'd have even less reason to stay. As Bill said, she was young and bright and had bags of enthusiasm. She was also ambitious, and wanted more out of life than Sweet Meadow could provide. She needed a challenge. She wanted to write about more than cats stuck up trees or litter on pavements. She wanted to write about hard-hitting subjects, and she hadn't been able to do that while working for *The Observer*.

His heart went out to her, remembering the expression on her face last night when she'd informed him that the article she'd hoped would take her career up a notch had been rejected. He wanted to pay every editor that had turned it down a visit and beg them to change their minds. She'd looked so crestfallen.

Maybe if her boss, Neil, allowed her to publish it in his paper—? Oh, wait, that wouldn't happen now because it wouldn't exist for much longer. Which was a shame – although Julian had to admit to not having read it until he'd got to know Frankie, so he was part of the lack-of-readership problem. Maybe he would have bought one if it had contained harder-hitting content. Saying that though, since he'd become more integrated into the town, stories about littering and graffiti, or reading about the goings on at the council offices held greater appeal. It was a pity the newspaper wasn't more up to date, then maybe it wouldn't be folding.

'Anyway,' Bill said, 'I've come to tell you that we're putting the stalls up this afternoon, if you want to lend a hand.'

'I'll be there,' Julian promised, but his mind was elsewhere.

It was on Frankie, and an idea that had popped into his head.

***

'This is very cloak and dagger,' the owner of *The Sweet Meadow Observer* said, as Julian ushered him into the house after glancing up and down the street to make sure no one had noticed the man's arrival. Julian didn't want anyone to know about this until after the deal was done. *If* it was done.

He'd phoned *The Observer* earlier and informed Neil that he wanted to speak to him urgently about a business proposition, but he'd refused to divulge any details over the phone. He hadn't wanted to go to *The Observer's* office for fear of bumping into Frankie and had pleaded with Neil to come to him instead. He'd also said that he'd appreciate it if Neil didn't mention this meeting to anyone.

'Thanks for coming to see me at such short notice. Can I get you a coffee?' Julian offered, motioning for Neil to take a seat in the living room.

'No, thanks. I'm intrigued to know what this is about.'

'I understand that *The Observer* is to cease trading,' Julian began. 'Liquidation or dissolution?'

'Why do you want to know?' His tone implied that it wasn't any of Julian's business.

'Would you consider selling it?' Julian asked, watching Neil's face.

The man's expression became wary. 'I might. I fact, I'm already in discussion with someone regarding this very matter.'

'So you *are* considering selling?'

'Yes, but not to you. You know nothing about the newspaper business.'

'I'm a fast learner.'

'You're not a journalist.'

'No, I'm a numbers guy. I'm good with money.'

'It's not just about the money. It's the passion for the job. I'd prefer to see *The Observer* cease trading with its integrity intact, than sell it to someone who'll make a pig's ear of it.'

Julian sighed, frustrated. He hadn't been expecting competition, and he certainly didn't intend to enter into a bidding war, even if Neil was happy to sell to him – which he didn't appear to be.

He rubbed a hand across his face, two-day-old stubble rasping under his palm. 'If I tell you something, will you give me your word it won't go any further?'

'It depends on what you tell me.'

'Spoken like a true journalist,' Julian said. Neil didn't respond. 'You're right, I don't know the first thing about the newspaper business, but I was hoping that Frankie...' He ground to a halt and Neil tilted his head to the side, so he continued, 'I was looking for something to get my teeth into, but *The Observer* clearly isn't it. I must have been mad to think for even a minute that I could run it.'

His eyes boring into him, Neil said, 'Are you aware that I've had a similar conversation with Frankie?'

'*Frankie?*' Julian was staggered.

'I take it she hasn't discussed it with you?'

Mutely Julian shook his head.

Neil chuckled. 'You two need to work on your communication skills.' He got to his feet. 'Talk to her. You'd make a good team. She understands what readers want, and you understand the financial side.

And no matter how passionate Frankie is, she won't be able to run the newspaper on her own. She'll need someone who can do all the behind-the-scenes stuff. You're going to want to digitalise it, set up a subscription system… All the tech stuff that I couldn't do, and Frankie doesn't have time for. Then there's selling advertising space, the layout and the—' He stopped. 'Neither of you are familiar with that, but as you said, you're a fast learner and I could stay on for a bit to show you the ropes.'

Julian held up a hand to stop him. Neil was getting ahead of himself, and he needed much more information before he could commit to anything, however Julian could feel the adrenalin coursing through him, and his excitement was beginning to build. It was a feeling he'd thought he'd lost.

But the main thought running through his head was that Frankie wasn't intending to leave Sweet Meadow after all. She was staying!

Telling himself to stay calm, he said, 'What did you say to her? Have you come to any agreement? And I asked whether the paper is going into liquidation or whether the business is being dissolved? Which is it?' The questions shot out of his mouth, and more whirled through his head.

'*Frankie* didn't ask that, and she should have done. This what I mean by you and her making a good

319

team. You've got the business sense, and she's got the creative flair.' He was smiling. 'I'm not going to answer any more questions until you speak to her.'

So that was what Julian did.

***

Frankie shoved her gloved hands into her pockets and stamped her feet. 'It needs to move a metre to the left,' she said, eyeing the newly constructed stall and trying to avoid catching Julian's eye.

Gavin, Julian and the two teenagers shuffled it into position, and Bill whipped out a tape measure.

'Perfect,' he announced, as the four of them turned their attention to the next one. With twenty-three stalls in total to be made and only two in position, it was promising to be a long job.

Gavin and Jack had finished work early to get started on it, Molly should be here any minute to lend a hand, and Harper would be along later, after she'd finished dealing with a family without power. Fiona and Madeleine were busy in the cafe, keeping the troops fed and watered, and Frankie, who had only turned up to take a few photos, had been roped in to help.

She'd been using a staple gun to attach the tarpaulin to the first stall, but it was a two-person job, so when

Molly hurried over saying, 'Sorry, I got caught up showing a couple around a house in Newsome Street,' Frankie shoved the staple gun at her.

'I'll hold, you tack,' she instructed, stretching a length of tarpaulin flat against a wooden upright and holding it in position.

By the time they'd successfully made a cover for the first stall and moved on to the second, the third was halfway to being completed. Soon there was a veritable production line going on, and as everyone became more confident in what they were doing, the work went faster.

Frankie, despite being cold and hungry, was disappointed when the growing darkness forced them to down tools. There was still some way to go, and the park was starting to get busy. The ice rink opened from five p.m. to eight p.m. every evening, and even if it had been light enough to see, no one wanted to be sawing and hammering with so many people around. They'd have to carry on tomorrow and hope everything would be done on time.

Frankie was about to set off home when Julian appeared beside her. 'Got time for a hot chocolate?'

She narrowed her eyes, unsure how to deal with this. She felt awkward and uncertain, unable to work out what he was playing at.

'Why?' she demanded somewhat belligerently.

'We need to talk.'

'I think we did enough talking last night.'

'Please, Frankie. I've spoken to Neil.'

She hadn't been expecting that, and it flummoxed her. 'Why?'

'I was looking into the feasibility of purchasing *The Observer.*'

'Why?' She didn't seem able to say anything else. What the hell was he playing at. Why would he want to buy *The Observer?*

'Because I found out it was folding.'

Should she tell him that she was planning to buy the paper herself – with her dad's backing because she wouldn't be able to raise the necessary funds by herself – but she decided to see what else he had to say.

'That's no reason to buy it,' she retorted. 'What will you do with it? You don't know the first thing about running a newspaper.'

'But you do.'

She could feel her temper rising. 'So you thought you'd buy it and I'd work for you? You'd be my boss?' She snorted. 'I don't think so!'

'I don't want to be your boss. I want to be your partner.'

'That's not going to happen if you own it and I'm an employee, is it?' she scoffed. 'I don't want your charity.'

'You won't be getting it. As I said, partners, not employer and employee, and since you're already looking into buying the paper...' He raised his eyebrows.

Oh, so he knew about that, did he? She said, 'I'm not looking for a partner. I can manage *The Observer* on my own.'

'You're not planning on sleeping anytime in the next couple of years, I take it?'

'I'll manage,' she replied stubbornly, although it had also been one of her father's concerns. She'd played down Neil's role somewhat and had been panicking ever since. *The Sweet Meadow Observer* didn't need three full-time members of staff. However, it did need *two*.

'Neil thinks we'll make a good team.'

'How, when you'll be in London, or wherever, and I'll be running the damned thing? I don't need a financial backer, thanks; and I certainly don't need a sleeping partner.'

His lips twitched.

'Not in any sense of the word,' she stressed, 'even if I am in love with... you.' She faltered. 'Oh, bugger. You didn't hear that right?'

'Heard what?'

'Nothing, it doesn't matter.' She felt sick; how did she let that slip out?

'Did you say—?'

'I said I don't need a partner,' she replied, hoping to deflect him.

Julian was grinning. 'You *did* just say that you're in love with me!'

'No, no, you've got it wrong. That's not what I said at all, and will you stop smiling? You're creeping me out. Why are you grinning like a prize idiot?'

'Because you love me.'

'I didn't say that.'

'Yes, you did. I heard you.'

'You only *think* you did.'

'I know what I heard.'

'You *think* you know, but that's not what I actually said.'

'OK, Word Girl, what you *actually* said was, and I quote, *I am in love with*—' he paused dramatically '—*you.*'

'Can we get those hot chocolates to go?' she asked. 'I don't think the cafe is the ideal place to have this conversation.'

'I agree. Shall we go to mine, since it's closer?'

They didn't say much on the way to Julian's house, Frankie sipping her hot chocolate, more for something to do than because she wanted it, or because she was concerned it would grow cold. Julian, she noticed, hardly touched his.

'Neil thinks it's a good idea for us to go into business together,' he repeated, once they were inside.

She didn't bother taking her coat off. 'You clearly weren't listening to me when I told you that I don't need a partner who won't be around.' She was cross with Neil for discussing it with him.

'I *will* be around. I'm not going anywhere.' He drew in a slow breath and let it out in a sigh. 'I thought I'd made it clear – Sweet Meadow is my home.'

'Until you get bored.'

'I won't get bored if I own *The Sweet Meadow Observer.*'

'Over my dead body! What shall we do – duke it out?'

'I'd win.'

She gave him a scornful look. 'Don't bet on it.'

'Frankie, I'm not going to fight you for the paper. I wanted to buy it to make you believe that I'm not lying about staying in Sweet Meadow, and I was hoping to persuade you to stay, too. I thought that if you had your very own paper, where you could write what you want…'

Frankie was thunderstruck. '*That* was your reason?'

He nodded. 'You can have the paper. Neil is right, I know zilch about the publishing business. I would have liked to work alongside you, to help Sweet Meadow's paper flourish, but you'll do that all by yourself. You don't need me. I love you, Frankie, and I don't want to throw away what we've got. It's too special.'

Frankie studied his face, the honesty and pleading in his eyes, the tension in his jaw, the hunched set of his shoulders, and she suddenly understood that he might need *The Observer* as much as *she* did. She also understood that he was telling the truth – he was staying in this quiet little town where nothing ever happened. Just as she was.

'I love you, too' she said simply.

There were tears in his eyes as he told her, 'I love you with all my heart, and I don't want to lose you, Frankie. I *can't* lose you. I've had a taste of life without you in it, and I didn't like it.'

Frankie didn't speak. She couldn't. The love she felt for the man standing before her was too deep to put into words.

So she kissed him instead, and that kiss said everything she couldn't. And afterwards, when she lay in his arms, she knew there was nowhere else in the world she wanted to be.

CHAPTER 23

Frankie didn't want to get out of bed. She was far too warm and cosy to move, but Julian was itching to get up.

'No…' she murmured, tightening her grip on him. 'Five more minutes.'

'I can't. You know what day it is.' He squirmed free.

'It's only seven o'clock,' she protested, reaching for him.

'I have to be in the park by seven-thirty, and I need breakfast first and a shower.'

Frankie squinted as he switched on the bedside lamp, 'A shower sounds good.'

'Oh no, you don't, lady. I'm taking this shower on my own.'

'Think of the water and electricity we could save by showering together?'

He gave her a well-deserved sceptical look, and she shrugged. 'You can't blame a girl for trying. I'll go make some coffee.' Reluctantly, she pushed the bedclothes aside and swung her feet to the floor, watching Julian pad out of the room wearing nothing but a smile.

Dragging on a pair of sweatpants and one of Julian's hoodies, she trotted downstairs to make breakfast.

It was still dark, stars twinkling out of a clear inky sky, with streaks of apricot and salmon to the east. The day promised to be fine and cold, perfect for Sweet Meadow Park's Festive Fayre.

Vendors would be arriving from eight o'clock to set up the stalls, with the official opening at ten, and Frankie was looking forward to it. Yesterday had been a blur of activity, with the rest of the stalls being built, and the shed that Liam's dad didn't want, reconstructed. Frankie could truthfully say that if she never saw another sheet of tarpaulin in her life, she would be happy.

Her hands were sore from gripping the staple gun, her arms and shoulders ached, and her back was in bits. Julian hadn't fared much better, and they'd clambered into bed last night like a pair of arthritic pensioners – and that was after a hot soak in the bath. Though since the hot soak had been taken together, it hadn't been as relaxing as it could have been, and Frankie had done her floor-mop-shuffle afterwards because so much water had ended up on the floor. The memory warmed her just as much as the hot coffee she was drinking.

'Would you like me to make you some toast?' she offered, when Julian appeared in the kitchen fully dressed and ready to start the day.

'Why don't you move in?'

The suggestion took her by surprise, and she was speechless for a second or two.

He added, 'It makes financial sense.'

'It does, does it?' She shoved two slices of bread in the toaster.

'Absolutely!'

'Is that the only reason?'

'Course not. I need someone to make me breakfast every morning.'

She scowled at him. 'Is that right? What about dinner?'

'Dinner would be nice, and maybe you could do the laundry and some housework?' he teased. 'Seriously, you're not going to be spending much time at your place, are you?'

Probably not, she thought. She'd be sad to give up her flat though. It was her first proper home since she'd moved out of her parents' house after she'd landed her job at *The Observer*.

Thinking of the newspaper reminded her that she and Julian would shortly be business partners, as soon

Liz Davies

as all the legal stuff was sorted out. It had seemed silly for her to take someone else on, so she'd agreed that they should have equal shares in the business.

They would be life partners too, if she moved in. It was a big decision…

'No pressure,' he said, wrapping his arms around her, his chest pressed against her back as he kissed her neck. 'If you're not ready, that's fine. It was just a thought.'

Frankie realised that she *was* ready. Hadn't she told him that she was an all-or-nothing girl? She would love to wake up next to him every morning and fall asleep in his arms every night.

When you know, you know. And Frankie *knew*.

***

Ha! Frankie had found something that Julian wasn't good at – ice skating! Mind you, neither was she, she discovered as the pair of them wobbled around the rink in precariously unbalanced circles, holding onto each other for dear life. She hadn't laughed so hard in ages. The terror on Julian's face was hysterical.

She caught sight of a figure waving frantically at her from the side, and she glanced in their direction at the very same moment that she lost her balance. Arms pin-

330

wheeling, she remained upright for a split second, before going down and taking Julian with her.

Lying there winded, she looked up and saw Vince grinning at her and pointing to his camera.

Frankie scowled, but it was a good-natured one. She hoped he'd taken a decent action shot.

'Can we stop now?' Julian groaned. 'My tailbone hurts.'

Hers did as well, and after a struggle to get to their feet, they inched their way off the rink.

'I'll stick to skiing,' he said, rubbing his backside.

'I'm dying for a hot chocolate. Shall we go sit down?'

'I don't think I'll be able to,' he said. 'I'll have to drink mine standing up. We both will.' He pointed to the busy cafe. 'It's heaving in there.'

Frankie was delighted to see the cafe doing such a roaring trade. The rest of the park was busy too, with children queuing to see Santa, or waiting for a skating session, and loads of people flocking to the stalls. Harper had rigged up some outdoor speakers, so Christmas tunes filled the air, along with laughter and chatter.

Sipping marshmallow-topped hot chocolates, Frankie and Julian stood outside the cafe and people-watched, absorbing the atmosphere.

He draped an arm around her shoulders. 'I'm so glad it's a success, after everyone's hard work.'

'Molly's thrilled,' Frankie said. 'She's already making noises about the Festive Fayre becoming an annual event.'

'We'll make it even bigger and better next year,' he vowed, and she sighed with happiness as she thought of the future stretching out before them.

It would be hard work to turn the newspaper around, but they had each other, and in her own way Frankie could be as determined and dedicated as Molly.

As she gazed around Sweet Meadow Park's first (but not the last) Festive Fayre, Frankie saw her parents, arm-in-arm, threading their way through the crowd, laughter on their faces. And there was Neil, looking more relaxed than she'd ever seen him, his wife by his side.

Harper and Gavin were watching the skaters, and Frankie could tell by the way Harper was nudging him and pointing, that she was trying to persuade him to have a go, and when he put an arm around her waist, Frankie guessed they didn't need her to matchmake after all.

Liam and Connor waved to her as they trotted past, a gang of teenagers in their wake, and she noted with satisfaction that when one of the youngsters dropped a wrapper on the floor, Liam was quick to pick it up and put it in the bin, scolding the girl as he did so.

It was wonderful to see people take ownership of the park, to see it filled with revellers enjoying themselves. The community had come together to make this a success, and the individuals in it deserved to have their stories told, their wins celebrated, and their losses acknowledged.

Molly and the park had brought people together and had shown them what could be achieved. She'd certainly shown Frankie, and Frankie was honoured that the little newspaper that she and Julian had rescued from near extinction would continue to give the people of Sweet Meadow a voice.

Grabbing Julian's hand and brandishing her camera, Frankie cried, 'We can't stand here all day enjoying ourselves, we've got work to do!'

The special festive edition of The Sweet Meadow Observer wasn't going to write itself!

***

'What on earth have you got there?' Arnie exclaimed, as Julian staggered inside with the wrapped Christmas hamper, Frankie dancing into her parents' house ahead of him.

'Merry Christmas, Dad!' she cried, giving her father a hug and a kiss. 'Where's Mum?'

'In the kitchen. Need a hand?' he asked Julian.

'I've got it, thanks,' Julian puffed. If he'd realised the hamper was going to be this heavy, he'd have insisted that they drive to Frankie's parents for Christmas lunch. He could have left the car here and walked back later. But oh, no, Frankie had wanted to stroll through the park to "work up an appetite". And what Frankie wanted, Julian would move heaven and earth to give her.

'Put it under the tree,' Arnie instructed, and Julian set it down carefully. 'I expect you could do with a drink. How about a sherry? It's a bit kitsch, but Yvonne insists that Christmas wouldn't be Christmas without a sherry before lunch. Mind you, she says that about eggnog, and Baileys Irish Cream.'

Frankie came bounding into the living room, her mother following more sedately behind her.

'Presents!' Frankie squealed. 'Can we open them now?'

Her mum said, 'You know the rules – not until Nan and Pop arrive. They should be here any minute. Actually, I think we should leave the present opening until after lunch. Arnie, where are your manners? Get Julian a drink.'

'I was about to,' Arnie tutted and rolled his eyes. 'She's been like a cat on a hot tin roof all morning.'

'Christmas dinner takes time and effort,' she said.

'I *know*, I'm the one cooking it!'

'Not on your own,' she pointed out. 'I'm helping.'

'I call it *interfering*. She doesn't trust me to do a good job. What were you doing in the kitchen while I was answering the door?'

'Nothing.' Yvonne's face was the epitome of innocence.

'Frankie, what was she doing? If she's been fiddling with my parsnips, I'll…' Arnie muttered, hurrying into the kitchen.

Frankie burst out laughing. 'Why is Dad cooking Christmas dinner?'

'I lost a bet,' her mother said. Her gaze flicked to Julian. 'Ooh, matching Christmas jumpers. Nice!' He'd taken his coat off and was holding it uncertainly. 'Frankie, hang Julian's coat up, while I get him a sherry. You'll have a sherry, won't you, Julian? It's tradition.'

He exchanged his coat for a glass of sherry, trying not to laugh as he heard cross mumbling coming from the kitchen.

'It's all right,' Yvonne whispered in a conspiratorial tone. 'I'm checking that he's not making a pig's ear of it. Or should I say, a pig's blanket?' She giggled, and Julian wondered how many sherries she'd had already.

Frankie sat on the sofa, patting the cushion beside her. 'Come sit next to me,' she said to him. 'What was the bet, Mum?'

'Oh, er, you don't want to know.'

Frankie's eyes widened and Julian couldn't hold back the laughter any longer, especially when Yvonne's cheeks flamed.

'Did Frankie have you up at the crack of dawn, Julian?' Yvonne said, deliberately changing the subject. 'One year she got her dad and me up at four in the morning to open her presents.'

It was Julian's turn to blush as he recalled what he and Frankie had been doing. She'd woken him early, all right, but it hadn't been to open presents.

He was saved from embarrassment by the arrival of Frankie's grandparents. Nan and Pop (that was what they were introduced to him as) were in their eighties and wore matching jumpers and big smiles.

'You'll never guess what Pop bought me,' Nan cried excitedly. 'A flying lesson! I'm going to learn to fly!'

'That's nice,' Yvonne said faintly. 'What did you get him?'

'Golf clubs.'

'He doesn't play golf.' That was from Arnie, who'd poked his head out of the kitchen. His cheeks were pink, and he looked a little flustered. A vague smell of burning drifted in the air.

'He does now,' Nan said. 'It'll get him out of the house and give me a bit of peace. I can't be doing with him under my feet all day. Take it from me, Yvonne, if a man doesn't have something to occupy him, he becomes a nuisance. Get Arnie started on a hobby before he retires. Two or three, if you can. They're like kids – they get whiney if they're bored. Can I smell burning?'

Arnie blanched. 'The parsnips! Bugger.' He shot back into the kitchen and Yvonne hurried after him, muttering under her breath.

Frankie hadn't been exaggerating when she'd told him that Christmas lunch at her parents' house would be entertaining. Julian had only been here five minutes, and he was already struggling to keep a straight face.

Frankie didn't bother. She was openly laughing, and her joy was so infectious, that Julian found himself laughing along with her.

'Flying lessons?' she murmured. 'Now *that's* what I call love.' And when he gave her a questioning look, she explained, 'Pop hates the thought of flying. He's terrified of it. They've never been on a plane, but he knew it was something Nan always wanted to do.' She slipped her hand in his. 'Do you want to open your present now?'

'I thought we were doing that after lunch?' He'd expected him and Frankie to exchange gifts this morning before they ventured out, but Frankie had insisted on waiting until they were at her parents' house. It was another one of her traditions.

'I want you to have it now,' she insisted, reaching into her jean pocket and handing him an envelope.

Julian opened it and was instantly confused. 'Skiing lessons?'

'They're for me,' she said. 'I want to learn, so we can go skiing together. You'll never have to go on your own again, if you don't want to.'

Julian felt like crying. What an incredibly lovely, thoughtful thing to do. 'You'd better open mine,' he said, his voice thick with emotion.

She took the envelope he held out to her, her expression quizzical. 'Don't tell me you had the same idea?'

'Not quite.'

She peered inside and withdrew a piece of paper.

When she read it, her eyes were huge. 'Two weeks in *Bali?*'

Nervous, he nodded. He couldn't tell whether she was pleased or not.

'When are we going to fit it all in?' she asked. 'Skiing, exotic holidays, the *newspaper?*'

'You heard Nan, you've got to keep men busy, otherwise they'll become a nuisance.'

'But not *too* busy,' she warned, and he could hear the anxiety in her voice.

'This isn't busy: this is fun, and I'll be doing it with the woman I love.'

'Aww…' Frankie wrapped her arms around his neck and kissed him.

For a delicious second, he forgot where he was, until a cross voice said, 'For goodness' sake, put him down, Frankie, and help me find the channel *The Sound of Music* is on.' Nan scowled at them. 'And I don't want you giving Pop ideas.'

Pop said to them, 'I don't need anyone to give me ideas. I've got enough of my own. I've had ideas since the first day I saw your grandmother, Frankie. Seventeen, she was, and as pretty as a picture, messing about on the swings. If I hadn't been cutting through the park because I was late for tea, I never would have seen her. I found the love of my life that day.'

Nan smiled at her husband, and her face was filled with so much love that it made Julian's heart ache to see it.

With his arms around her, he whispered in Frankie's ear, 'He's not the only one. I found the love of *my* life in Sweet Meadow Park, too.'

'And have you got ideas?' she whispered back.

'Loads of them.'

'Good, you can share them with me later.'

339

She kissed him again, and as she did, Julian had another idea: he would ask her to marry him. Not today, probably not tomorrow, but soon. And it would be the best idea he'd ever had!

Other books in the series

ABOUT THE AUTHOR

Liz Davies writes feel-good, light-hearted stories with a hefty dose of romance, a smattering of humour, and a great deal of love.

She's married to her best friend, has one grown-up daughter, and when she isn't scribbling away in the notepad she carries with her everywhere (just in case inspiration strikes), you'll find her searching for that perfect pair of shoes. She loves to cook but isn't very good at it, and loves to eat - she's much better at that! Liz also enjoys walking (preferably on the flat), cycling (also on the flat), and lots of sitting around in the garden on warm, sunny days.

She currently lives with her family in Wales, but would ideally love to buy a camper van and travel the world in it.

9 781915 940360